CW00872104

THE PHOENIX CHRONICLES

VAMPIRE'S
BLOOD

Phoenix Chronicles, Book 1: Vampire's Blood

THE PHOENIX CHRONICLES

VAMPIRE'S BLOOD

AMANDA COLEMAN

This book is dedicated in loving memory to Wanda Mae Darlington, a wonderfully talented story teller that never received any recognition on earth.

Granny
May 30, 1938 to October 24, 2008

TABLE OF CONTENTS

TABLE OF CONTENTS

Part 02: Eve of Blood

PREFACE

NOTES
(BEHIND THE PHOENIX CHRONICLES)

More than a decade ago, I sat down in the computer room of my parents house writing scenarios as I talked them over with my little sister Samantha. It was in between my sophomore and junior year of high school in the summer of 2003. Afterwards, I emailed my best friend Joshua and told him of the crazy idea running through my head.

At the time, the Phoenix Chronicles didn't exist as they do now. There was less substance and a lot more shenanigans. I only planned one book and it was all about a group of teenagers that didn't fit in. The teens made friends of each other and then pulled random pranks that they almost never got caught for.

The series actually started as a book and then went to a graphic novel. The original birth of the series was to be called the Pranksters.

Samantha got to work right away drawing rough sketches of the characters. To make matters more interesting, I shared the idea with my science instructor. Mr. Bardin was and is a very talented artist when he isn't teaching. He contributed a masterful piece depicting Dr. Saffron, the dragon instructor. Unfortunately, none of the original pieces are still around.

Pranksters never had a chance as a series though because there was no plot to the book. I toyed with several different ideas for the book including one where the characters were victims of a terrible tragedy caused by the destruction of Earth. Having survived the tragedy, the characters discovered special mutant-like powers that helped them carry out pranks and get revenge for what happened to them. Too similar to certain other popular literature, I scrapped the idea before it got out of the gate.

By the time I graduated, I had a handful of chapters involving the characters meeting or certain events that shaped the characters' lives. None of the chapters were completed and most didn't even go to the same book! At that point, I was planning for six books total: Dawn of Flame, Dusk of Flame, Morn of Blood, Eve of Blood, Rise of War, Set of War.

Sound familiar? They should, I loved the original titles and decided to keep using them for the individual books when the story took another turn.

A year out of school, I was working and piddling with the story when I had time. Bits and pieces came to me in spurts. I would write what I saw happening in the series and then leave the snippets alone. That was until the unthinkable happened: my computer crashed, taking most of my notes and all of the scanned artwork with it.

It was time to take a break from the series to focus more on life. In 2008, I married a childhood boyfriend that I reconnected with. Then I went on to have children: a daughter in 2009 and son in 2011.

I didn't pick up my pen again until 2012 when I found a folder with old notes about the series. It was just notes because I never printed anything out; however, I was no longer in contact with Joshua who had been my sounding board for ideas for this series. So, I still didn't write.

In 2013, my friends Analee and Marina told me about National Novel Writing Month or NaNoWriMo for short. I figured if I was ever going to write any books, this would be the perfect opportunity.

It wasn't exactly the best timing though! My husband and I were in the middle of moving with two toddlers in tow. I had to write and pack at the same time. I'm not exactly proud of how much I flip flopped back and forth with the first draft but I did finish that draft by the end of November.

It took more than a year to get anyone to read the draft and give me feedback. By that time, the draft changed in two important ways: the title changed to Vampire's Blood and the plot in the first book was altered in a way that lined it up for a sequel and made the series real.

ACKNOWLEDGMENTS

THANKS
(TO MY FRIENDS AND FAMILY)

I would just like to acknowledge and offer my gratitude to my good friend Analee Harriman and my sister Melissa Welch. I emailed, texted, messaged, and spoke to in person and over the phone with so many people just trying to get someone to read this book. In the end, the only people that bothered were Analee and Melissa. Without their encouragement, this book may never have been published.

Furthermore, everyone has their own beliefs and principles just like myself. To me, the entire inspiration for this book came from God. From the dreams (night or day), the random spurts that often popped into my head at random times. If not for His guidance, this book would still be in a half-finished state with no immediate plans for publishing. I dare say I might have given up entirely if not for His guiding hand.

Also, I'd like to acknowledge that if not for the love and support of my husband, James, who has worked full time to allow me the time and opportunity to write, this book wouldn't have been possible.

PROLOGUE

KEY
(THE COUNCIL CONVENES)

Waylon Radcliffe was head of the Council of Seven or so the leaders of the allied non-humans were called. In reality, the council was much larger than seven people which confused outsiders. The 'seven' part of their name actually referenced the seven different types of non-humans in existence on the planet.

The Council of Seven was founded nine years after the Phoenix Wars drew to a close. Most of the phoenixes had been massacred by then but the Council wished to protect the survivors and the other non-humans from future power struggles with the humans. Humans were forbidden from attending, joining, and knowing about the council by the council founders. Nearly two hundred years later, the original laws regarding the humans and the descendants of the surviving phoenix people held firm.

The non-human groups sent their best, their strongest, their brightest, and in some cases, their most charismatic to serve on the council that would decide on how they should govern their lives. Currently, the council consisted of three mages, two dragons, one demon, two shape-shifters, three faeries, one vampire, and no phoenixes.

As mismatched as that might have seemed, the council members were held to such high standards that only those on the council managed to pass the rigorous requirements and tests. Only someone who had the best interests of the seven were allowed to govern them.

After the wars, the last of the phoenixes were nowhere to be found. The other non-humans assumed the majestic race had gone into hiding because so few remained of the magical beings. The survivors left behind just enough clues to support that theory. So if they knew of the Council, they did not care to join or even deal with non-phoenix beings ever again.

Waylon, a mage, had been on many journeys and explorations to search for the phoenix people with little success. The only thing he managed to find were documents from research conducted on the phoenix people, petrified ashes, and eventually a hidden city where the ancient phoenix people once resided. The city records told of how they were hunted to near extinction and when only a few remained, they scattered. The last record listed only one living phoenix as the rest had been captured or killed.

That was fifty years past and the phoenix people were believed to be completely extinct now. So when the faeries called for an emergency council meeting with a claim of a living phoenix, it came as a great shock. The council members scrambled as fast as they could to Demont where the faeries insisted the meeting must take place.

"What's going on?" demanded the often furious Lucien, the demon among the council. The demon's wings were fully extended as he stormed into the meeting room but he quickly folded them neatly back in place where they resembled a cloak thrown across his shoulders.

Debora, the female shape-shifter, was practically bouncing on her feet as she answered him, "The faeries have found a living phoenix! At last!"

"After all those years of searching, to think the phoenix was hidden away in this forsaken city!" piped up Howard, a faerie that also happened to be the youngest member of the Council of Seven. He'd been on the council for the better part of eight years now.

Lucien glared at the two, clearly not pleased with the information. "And what do you plan on doing with it?"

"That is what this council has been called to decide. The fate of the hatchling phoenix is ours to decide," Waylon responded quickly.

"I've got a cage that will just fit that bird," volunteered Sephone, the brighter colored dragon of the two. Her scales glistened a blue green telling of her heritage as a water dragon.

"You can't be serious!" exclaimed Felton, the other dragon. His scales were a dull red to reflect his home near the volcanic mountains of Furiete where the other mountain dragons lived. "The phoenix is not a pet and you cannot lock it in a cage!"

"It's just a magical bird!" retorted Lucien, the demon. He'd grabbed onto the back of a seat away from the other council members but had yet to sit down. Instead, the elder demon was dusting himself off like the matter was of little concern.

Clarane, a faerie, clutched a brilliant fire-colored bird close to herself. "She is a living being just as you and I are!" the lone female faerie in the group growled at the demon. Her small iridescent wings fluttered in agitation behind her.

"Living or no, the life of a phoenix will cause strife if the humans find out about it," the cold voice of Zelos resonated around the room.

"I'd just as soon as see it dead before the humans find out about it," Lucien responded, his voice dripping in disgust.

Clarane clutched the sleeping phoenix closer before the magical bird began to glow brightly like a raging fire starting to burn out of control. The bird elongated and took on a human form. In the faerie's arms lay a sleeping child of no more than eight.

Lucien took a step back, his expression radiated shock. Many others in the room too uttered exclamations of surprise. The only group that didn't seem surprised by the turn of events was the faeries who had been prepared beforehand.

Howard, his blond hair shining, tucked a blanket around the sleeping child in Clarane's arms. "A child can grow and be guided to help and to prosper. She is meant to be protected at all costs." His expression was neutral but still a great power seemed to radiate out from his words. The faeries saw something in the future of the hatchling phoenix. Even the often angry Zelos seemed subdued now.

"What? What have you seen?" demanded Leland, an impatient mage still too young to understand the nature of faeries. They -the faeries- only revealed what they wanted and even that was never enough.

"A guard should be formed. This child will need guidance from someone not afraid of the gifts she will display. Someone we can trust not to lead her astray," Clarane dictated.

Waylon nodded in agreement, his mind searching for the perfect person for that job. It took but a moment for the answer to come to him, "I know just the person – a nomadic mage. Surely, keeping the child moving from place to place will safeguard her from the humans?" He looked to the faeries for confirmation.

"Wait one minute now, Waylon! Just because you are chief among us does not give you the right to decide who will guard that creature," Lucien declared, his temper flaring. "We should all have a say!"

"Ah, but anyone you would bring forth would undoubtedly be corrupt and just kill the child without a second thought," the ancient vampire in their midst finally spoke. A veil hung over her face lending a shroud of mystery to her. Her hair hung loose about her body with a cloak about her shoulders. Having survived centuries, Bettye Rosiopolis had no intention of sacrificing her life to the sun's light. "I seem to recall that humans weren't the only ones during the phoenix wars to have hunted that majestic creature to death. Did you know that a demon family quite prominent among this nation was one of the most aggressive and deadly against them?"

Lucien narrowed his eyes at the vampire, "A person cannot be held responsible for the actions of their ancestors."

"Ah, but as his direct descendant, you share his very blood," Bettye smiled sadistically, "and his murderous nature."

The demon's expression lightened as if to prove his point, "Very distant descendant, at least ten generations separate us." Lucien only threw the number out there as a way of distancing himself from his great grandfather's cruelty during the war. In truth, thanks to the longevity of the demon species, Lucien was only in the fourth generation since the Phoenix war. "Horatio's blood is so diluted over the many generations, I would dare say we might not even come up as related at all." He tried to look unconcerned, like the information he threw to the rest of the council wasn't a big deal.

As the oldest living being at the meeting, Bettye started to shake her head and contradict him but was interrupted by Waylon. "We are not hear to discuss the past transgressions of family members that are no longer among the living and have not been for at least a century if not longer." The mage was rolling his eyes. Truly, the demon and vampire were not known for getting along. If one never spoke up during a meeting, Waylon counted it a blessing because it meant the other would keep quiet as well. "We came together to discuss what to do about this being." Waylon gestured at the sleeping child-phoenix in emphasis.

"It shall be as you suggested," Jeron the male shape-shifter finally responded. "The child will need guidance but I am not so sure it should be a mage. They can be turned just as easily as humans." Jeron was shaking his head the entire time. Of course, he would wish for a shape-shifter to guard the phoenix-child.

"As can shape-shifters," said Sephone, glaring at Jeron. "Maybe we should appoint a dragon. Our brethren have always been honorable." The dragon had puffed out her chest just a bit trying to look proud and majestic from her place next to her fellow dragon.

"And she shall stick out like a sore thumb among the humans!" Leland argued, shaking his head. "Honestly! What are you people thinking, she can't be raised by anyone but a mage."

"Why is that, young one? What is so special about mages?" Bettye asked.

The young mage gulped audibly at the vampire's attention. "I'm not saying the other six cannot protect her! I'm not. It's just, she'll be too exposed with the other six," Leland started.

"Explain," Lucien ordered.

"It's like this: any of the six with special appendages and noticeable differences will draw attention to her. If the dragons raised her, they would question where she came from and eventually find out. If the demons raise her then she'll have to deal with the prejudices and possibly murdered just because she associates with them. Vampires can't go out in the day and that is no way for a creature of magic and light to live. A phoenix isn't meant to be constrained by day or night but free. The child would grow to resent her caregivers for being forced out of the light that she so desperately needs."

Debora was glaring, daring the young mage to speak out against the shape-shifters, "But what of us shape-shifters, then? We are most like the humans and can hide in plain site."

"Exactly!" exclaimed Jeron, clearly, not seeing the issue.

Zelos nodded, "So you see yourself why the shape-shifters can not take the child. You are too similar to humans and thus too ready to switch your natures. Shape-shifters could turn and do more harm than good."

"How dare you accuse.." Debora started to yell.

"Wait! That isn't the problem!" Leland interrupted trying to prevent the fight. "Shape-shifters have no real powers other than being able to shift forms as they please; however, sometimes they are outed by the humans and thrown to the wolves so to speak. The humans hate the shape-shifters more than they do the demons. Should we really allow the child-phoenix to live with someone that must live in fear of their secret coming out?"

The female shape-shifter growled but was forced to acquiesce, "Point taken."

"And faeries? We see the future and could get her out of trouble before it happens. Why then cannot we care for the child-phoenix?" Clarane asked, still staring at the sleeping child in her arms. She already knew the answer. This argument had already been made in her visions but it had to play out completely.

"That's all well and good but faeries have no defenses

against the humans. Your wings give you away and faeries are non-violent by nature. If it came down to a fight, you'd be powerless to stop whomever from taking her and doing what they will," the young mage sounded upset at the explanation. "I propose we have a team of people with the primary guardian being a mage. Not a large team but enough to protect and watch out for the child in every environment should the child need it."

Bettye nodded, "No one person should know the number or the people protecting her. She should be safest that way."

"How will we know who to get in touch with about her then?" asked Lucien. "How do we keep tabs on this phoenix-child and the influences that will guide her?"

"I will be responsible for her primary caretaker," Waylon responded. "He or she will be required to send a courier with updates regarding the child. Each group of the other six shall decide more guardians that shall be stationed in different cities across Jodacai should the nomadic mage travel to that city with the child."

Most of the council members nodded in agreement: the plan was sound. "I have but one more question." Regina stated. "What did you see?" she asked of the faerie group.

Clarane never lifted her head and Howard stepped back deferring to his superiors. Zelos simply stared, pondering how to answer before stating, "She is the key." And the faeries would say no more.

When the meeting ended, guardians had been chosen from all across Jodacai; however the knowledge of the guardians was limited to the Council of Seven. Only the council would know how many and who. The guardians would be kept in the dark about other guardians so they would remain focused to protect the last phoenix.

As the council dispersed, Regina suddenly put a hand on Waylon's arm, stopping him in his tracks. "Don't you feel it, Waylon? Ancient magic," Regina was staring incredulously at the sleeping child. "That phoenix is tied to this place!" she gestured all around her. "The magic has placed a restriction on her."

Waylon stared at his fellow mage, perplexed by the facts she presented. When he snapped out of his stupor, he realized that Regina was still looking to him for a response. "You know I can't quite feel magic as you do, dear girl," he soothed, patting her hand as if she were a child instead of the nearly two hundred year old mage that she was. Waylon was nearly twice her age and the second oldest member of the council. Everyone was 'dear girl' or 'my boy' to him.

Regina didn't seem troubled by his comment and only nodded in quiet understanding. This was not the first time the mage had spotted ancient magic at work. It was one of the reasons she was given a seat on the council. "She cannot leave this place."

"You're sure of this, Regina?" he asked his fellow mage.

Regina nodded, "The magic is so strong. She cannot leave for long before the magic will pull her back."

"Do not speak of this to anyone," Waylon ordered her.

"What about the council?" she asked concerned.

Waylon shook his head, "Especially not the council."

The only female mage on the council nodded in understanding before she turned to walk away. The phoenix-child was in the hands of Waylon until his chosen primary guardian would arrive. Now all Waylon had to do was convince, his nomadic mage to settle down in this abysmal town so littered with prejudices that other non-humans steered clear of it.

MORN
OF
BLOOD

CHAPTER 1

RETURNING
(REUNITING OLD ACQUAINTANCES)

Many years ago, a fourth of the buildings and grounds of the ancient city Demont was destroyed in a great blaze that killed a third of the population and forced many others to move away or rebuild. The Daemione family's ancestral home was destroyed beyond repair and the family was left homeless. Instead of rebuilding, the family left Demont for nearly a decade. Now the family was returning to the place they once called home to start over again and reclaim the place left them by their ancestors.

The Daemione family wasn't a normal human family by any standard. Classified as demons, they had a slight control of fire and heat coupled with wings that enabled them to fly. However, when not in use, their wings folded about their shoulders and back in such a way that they only appeared to be wearing cloaks or jackets which helped to keep their secret from the rest of the world. Some of the other non-human inhabitants of the world had been readily accepted; demons were not. Humans associated them with the devil of biblical times on Earth; however, the capacity to be evil lay with each individual demon or human. The planet Gaeshar was learning that lesson slowly.

While Demont had never been far from Lucien and Anne Daemione's minds, their teen-aged son and young daughter could have gone the rest of their lives without returning to the accursed town. Their teen-aged son Lucas was eight when the fire destroyed their home and his sister was only two. They'd been home alone just after Lucien and Anne were called away on urgent business. In their absence, their home was set ablaze with Lucas and his little sister Julie trapped inside. When their parents returned, Lucas told a fantastical tale of attempted murder, arson, and a faerie savior but his parents refused to believe him.

Eight years was a long time and Lucas never forgot. He resented his parents for not believing him but resented them more for bringing him back to Demont. He wanted little help from them and wasn't afraid to voice his opinions with animosity mostly directed at his father. Lucas argued with his parents about everything from when he chose to go flying to matters concerning his education. "I'm old enough to finish enrolling myself in school," Lucas angrily told his parents.

"But what if they ask for..." his mother, Anne, began to protest.

"I'll be fine!" he responded, aggravated.

His father, Lucien, glared at him. "You won't be rude to your mother, boy!" he told his son in a deadly calm voice before whacking the back of his son's head with his hand. Then Lucien glanced at the sky before he turned to address his wife, "It looks like the weather's turning and I'd like to get on our way before the rain starts. Let the boy alone since he thinks he can do everything by himself." His tone wasn't pleasant and his demeanor showed anger and annoyance. To his son, he merely said, "I'll deal with your attitude when you get home." With one last glare, Lucien turned back to continue checking the ropes on their carriage.

Anne looked torn between her son and husband, "Well, okay," she caved. "We'll be in town for a little while longer dear in case you need us. Just let us know and we'll get it all settled." She smiled sadly at her son. "Try to make some friends," Anne added quietly, only for him to hear. His mother was overprotective of him and feared he'd grow up alone like she'd mostly done before meeting his father.

"I'll try," he whispered into the air as he walked away down the road. Lucas knew the school was only a few streets over from the large town square directly in front of city hall. Turning left onto Saxon Avenue, he continued walking for two blocks before turning right onto Foster Boulevard. The school was right in front of him now but he'd have to walk a combined two blocks before he got to the front door.

Five minutes later, Lucas was walking through the front doors of the school and straight into the office to enroll and register for classes. Spotting a short, dumpy woman sitting behind a desk, he called out to her, "Excuse me, ma'am!" He'd interrupted her work, "My name is Lucas Daemione. My parents spoke with someone a few days ago about my transfer. I'm here to register for classes."

The secretary glanced up and pointed to a stack of papers, "Ah, Mr. Daemione, we've been expecting you. You'll need to fill out those forms." She pointed to a stack of forms clipped together in the corner of the large counter, "Then I will need you to bring them back so I can get you sorted into the proper classes." The secretary suddenly stood and walked into an adjacent room.

Lucas reached for the papers and glanced through them before sitting in the chair placed directly against the wall. Really, he didn't have much to fill out as the forms were mostly already filled in. More than likely, the forms had been filled out when his parents spoke to the school about his transfer. The forms only lacked little nuances of information that his parents must have neglected till they were there to do so in person.

Lucas jumped when a large bell sounded signaling the end of the period. The hallway, which had been quiet only moments before, suddenly grew louder with the passing of students to and from their lockers and next classes.

Just down the hall, Lily Nightshade and Jonah Williams were bantering back and forth about a book when suddenly, Lily grabbed the book from Jonah and sprinted away. She dodged around other students, being careful not to run into anyone and Jonah gave chase.

"Lily!" he shouted as he knocked a student back into the lockers. He pushed past an instructor causing the poor man to fall into a group of students, "Oops! Sorry, Dr.

Rawlings!" However, Jonah only continued chasing after the fiery-headed teenager.

Smiling brightly, Lily ran full out, only stopping to deposit a book behind a potted tree just outside the front office. Deed complete, she quickly slipped into the office to hide.

Lucas looked up from his forms startled to see the lithe form of a redhead with bright brown eyes. Her eyes sparkled in merriment and he was taken with the ethereal magical aura surrounding her. Lily in turn took a single look over her shoulder before jumping behind Lucas. His attention jerked back to the door where it suddenly flew open. He stood quickly, standing at her defense. Lucas wasn't sure what had come over him as he didn't even know this girl.

Lily's eyes danced, the amusement playing clearly through them, as she hid behind the new boy. Though he was much taller than her, she could still see over his shoulder at the enraged Jonah.

Stunned at Lucas's defense of Lily, Jonah started to open his mouth in protestation before his eyes met the brilliant dark gray eyes of her defender. A memory flashed forth in his mind of a similar situation only Lucas had been defending a seemingly helpless bird. Jonah growled, disgusted, "What are you doing here?"

"What am I doing here?" Lucas responded. "What are you doing at my new school?" he suddenly demanded. Lucas thought he was forever rid of the other boy years ago when he left the faerie encampment to return to the charred remains of his family's home.

"Your new school?" Jonah practically howled with laughter. "I'll have you know that this is my school. I've been in Demont since I was in diapers. And I won't have you stinking up the place with your..." he started before he was interrupted by the musical voice from behind Lucas.

"Get over yourself, Jonah. The school is big enough for the both of you." Lily waved her arms about in a grand gesture at the large school.

Lucas turned to eye the enchanting imp behind him. "Umm, I should probably introduce myself." He smiled shyly,

"The name's Lucas. Lucas Daemione." He stuck his hand forward to shake with the girl.

Lily smiled brightly as she latched onto his hand and shook fiercely. "I'm Lily Nightshade. Welcome to Demont Secondary."

"This is all your fault!" Jonah glared at Lily.

Lily stepped back, frowning at her friend, "What do you mean?"

Jonah's eyes narrowed to slits, "Don't play innocent with me. This has your name written all over it." Lily merely shook her head in disagreement until Jonah growled at her. "One of these days, you'll wake up in a cage or something." He stormed from the office only to return a moment later to grab his book from inside the potted tree.

"Hmm," Lily pondered, "I wonder if I should tell him that he has the wrong book?" She pulled a book from behind her back, a blank expression on her face.

Disgruntled, Lucas glanced at her, "After that cage remark, I don't see why you should even associate with him."

Lily shrugged in indifference. "He doesn't mean anything by his off the wall comments like that." She frowned before adding, "He's really a pushover but don't tell him I said that. Jonah would deny it till he's blue in the face, the big softy."

Conveniently, the secretary chose that moment to return from the next room, her expression a mask of pure contempt toward Lucas. Apparently, she'd heard all the commotion and was not pleased.

Lucas gave a weak smile before holding up his forms, "All finished. When do I get my class schedule?"

Her frown disappeared, replaced by a serious expression, "Let me add you to the rosters first, young man. Everything takes time."

"Ms. Juniper, may I show Lucas around the school while he's waiting?" she inquired of the secretary. Lily had a sweet innocent smile plastered on her face and she oozed waves of calmness.

"That would be fine, dear. Thank you." The secretary beamed at her and moved to start processing the paperwork.

Before the pair could get out of the office, she called back to them, "Ahh, just a second dear! It looks like your class schedule won't be ready till tomorrow. You might as well go on home and Miss Nightshade can show you around tomorrow."

Lucas nodded at her and turned to leave, Lily trailing behind him. Just outside Demont Secondary, Lily spoke again, "You know, I could still give you the tour, if you'd like."

Her offer took him by surprise and he looked up sharply, noticing that she had a genuine smile on her face. His expression softened immediately; there was something about her that he couldn't explain. It was something that he couldn't help but like. Lucas had only just met her that day but already he felt like he'd met her somewhere before. "You won't get in trouble for not being in class?" he asked quickly.

"Free period. I usually spend it helping in the library but this is better," Lily smiled shyly.

"So, what do I need to know about this place?" he replied, a quick grin spreading across his face.

"That depends on what you like to do." Leading him back inside, Lily pointed to a set of large ornate double doors. "That's the library. It's a reader's dream," she sighed. "It's even bigger than the public library and has a better selection of books!"

He laughed. "How about if I like music?" he asked. "Or experimenting?" he added as an afterthought.

"Ah, then follow me if you dare," she chanted, "to the Music Wing." She moved through the less ornate double doors into a long hallway with a few passages littered throughout. He squinted and could just barely make out tables in a large room at the very end of the hall.

She stopped when they came to a set of lockers on the right side. Just beyond the lockers was a passage with four doors, two on either side. "This is the Music Wing. There are four classrooms and each is for a different type of music: choir, orchestra, specialized tutelage, and dance."

One by one she took him down each hall showing where each class was. Lily described the classes and they discussed which classes he'd probably be in. They even talked of possible classes for the next semester and year. "And this is where the student body gathers to have their midday meal. You can eat inside or out. A couple years back, the school added tables to the quad outside."

Lucas nodded before Lily held up a small skeleton key, a sly, mischievous smile adorning her face. He laughed uneasily as he wasn't sure what she was up to. Glancing about to make sure no one was around to see them, Lily led Lucas outside into the quad – a pebbled rectangular area with a small handful of round stone tables. At the other end of the quad was a decrepit building. He couldn't see the door from this side but he was being led around to it and would see it any second now.

Lily pulled up to the front of the building, glancing about again to make sure no one saw and pulled Lucas down the stairs to the locked door way. It was the only way in and no one had a key except the mischievous Lily.

When the city officials wanted to tear the old building down, a large number of families had stepped up and protested. They wanted the small building to remain in memory of the great fire. It was the only building left of the original school. A small historical sign stood outside of it now telling what the building was and why it was still standing.

She carefully unlocked the door, slipping inside. When Lucas didn't immediately come in, her hand snaked back outside and pulled him in.

"Ack!" he cried as he nearly fell.

"Oops, sorry," she apologized, sheepishly. "It's just that I haven't had anyone to show this place to in ages. It's my little hide away from the rest of the school." She moved around behind a divider that blocked the rest of the room from view.

He moved to follow, eyeing the place carefully as he went. "What is this place?"

Lily was sitting on a desk when he came into the main room. A patch of light from a sole window briefly illuminated her before a cloud must have passed over the sun and she was cast back into darkness. "You know about the great fire, right?" she asked and then continued when he nodded. "Well, this is the last remaining part of the old school.

The rest of it burnt down."

"It looks like it's falling apart on the outside. What magic keeps it in place?" he asked, not thinking of who he was talking to. For all he knew Lily was normal; although, he doubted that. When her eyes flashed, he knew he was right. Lucas just didn't know what she was. So, it was best to play it safe, he'd not reveal his true form yet.

"The building itself is under a powerful magic preservation spell. While the outside looks as it has for the last eight years, the inside has been preserved and made so that it will not fall apart due to age or other means," she answered.

He thought it odd that she'd know the exact nature of the spells and wondered if she were a mage before brushing it from his mind. Mages had a distinct air and smell about them. If you knew what to look for, you could spot a mage from a mile away without them ever seeing you and Lily couldn't possibly be one. Instead of addressing what she was, he opted for a less personal question, "How did you end up with a key, anyhow?"

She laughed nervously, "Would you believe that I just stumbled across it one day?"
Lucas eyed her skeptically.

Lily hung her head and sighed. "I really did just find it one day," she tried. "Granted, it was hanging on a hook in the principal's office and I knew what it went to before I took it. I like keys," she responded by way of explanation. "Besides, no one is allowed in here, so I figured no one would miss it. I've had it since my first year at Demont Secondary. I cleared out all the trash and old desks myself," she admitted.

He wanted to ask why of all people she'd share the place with him but couldn't work up the courage. Instead he just nodded in understanding, "Your secret is safe with me."

CHAPTER 2

CLUES
(TALKING STAFF IN SCIENCE CLASS)

"Welcome back," Lily greeted warmly. She was waiting just outside the office for him, a slip of paper in her hand.

"Hey!" Lucas smiled at her and reached for the slip of paper as Lily thrust it forward to him. Lucas examined what turned out to be his class schedule, muttering a quick thank you in return.

She smiled, "I guess we ought to get to our first class. We have Dr. Saffron first thing this morning. You'll really like him."

He started to nod before he caught what she'd said, "Wait a minute! We're in the same class?"

Lily laughed, "Well, yeah! I'm a fifth year just like you."

He smiled and the pair made their way to the Science Wing. Lucas's first class was a science class in a classroom decorated like the night sky complete with stars, planets, and moons. Lily told him the classroom itself was just as eccentric as the instructor, Dr. Saffron. But his mischievous new friend refused to tell him anything else. Lily's excuse was that she wanted Lucas to learn for himself. So Lucas sat patiently next to Lily watching for the instructor. Fortunately, he didn't have to wait long for the eccentric Dr. Saffron.

Imagine Lucas's surprise, when in walked a dragon using a walking staff as if to hold himself upright. The staff was surely magical to be able to hold the weight of the dragon.

"Settle down, class!" Dr. Saffron called as he settled at a desk in the front of the room.

The staff itself was muttering so quietly at first that Lucas could not hear anything but a slight buzzing in his head.

"I see we've got a new student. Why don't you introduce yourself," Dr. Saffron motioned for Lucas to stand.

"Another insufferable brat!" the staff chirped hatefully.

Lucas thought he'd misheard. Surely, the staff hadn't just insulted him? Standing, he started to speak when suddenly the instructor shouted at his own staff to shut up. Lucas stood surprised and looked down at Lily for an explanation. She was smiling innocently again but her eyes were dancing with laughter.

"Go ahead," Dr. Saffron instructed at Lucas before glaring at his staff again.

"I'm Lucas Daemione. My family and I just moved back to Demont from Nyaite." It wasn't a lie, Lucas told himself. His family stayed in Nyaite for a few months in between Troale and Demont. In the young demon's mind, Troale would always be his home.

"Bunch of pansies!" the staff hollered.

Now Lucas was sure the staff had insulted him. It was quite rude.

"I told you to be silent!" Dr. Saffron said angrily at the staff.

Lucas sat back down and whispered to Lily, "Does it always do that?" He was eyeing the rude staff that was now arguing back and forth with the instructor.

Lily was trying not to laugh at the arguing and then at Lucas's facial expression. "Usually, that staff is rude to everyone but is usually worse with Dr. Saffron," she answered in a whisper. "It's quite disruptive," Lily continued conspiratorially, "but it makes for an interesting class. One of my favorites!"

Dr. Saffron was threatening to douse the staff in a particularly nasty chemical before throwing it into a lake when Lucas tuned back in. Surprisingly the staff shut up. "Now class, today's lesson is on the reactions of certain chemicals to water."

He pulled a small bag out of his desk drawer and stood from his desk. Dr. Saffron moved to a lab table across the room from his desk and far enough away from any students to be considered safe. "Now watch what happens to this chemical."

Dr. Saffron put an odd looking hat on then pulled a cover down in front of his eyes and snout. He reached into the bag with a pair of tweezers and brought out a small solid block. He moved the tweezers over a beaker of water before loosening his hold on the small block.

The block plunged into the water and Dr. Saffron took a couple steps backwards. Suddenly, the chemical reaction in the beaker caused an explosion that sent water splattering into the air and around the room.

The instructor's staff was coated in the chemical laced water and seemed to sputter angrily at Dr. Saffron but didn't speak another word.

Dr. Saffron pulled the facial cover back up off his face, an evil smirk playing across his snout as he eyed his staff. The smirk didn't leave his face as he turned to address his students, "Now, your assignment for today is to research what this chemical was based on its reaction to water and the information given on the board."

He pointed toward the board which the class noticed was full of information regarding different chemicals. "You'll need to read chapter three to gain some clarity in your research."

The dragon instructor moved back to his desk where he sat back down and argued with his staff the rest of the class period.

Lily and Lucas carefully related in notes what they'd seen of the chemical and later its reaction before transcribing the text on the board and reading quietly in their book. By the end of class, both had identified the chemical as an alkali metal most probably potassium or sodium.

The bell sounded and both put their books and notes

away in their bags quickly. "Do you think you can find the next class on your own or do you need help?"

"I can manage. Thanks, Lil," he smiled at her.

Startled by the nickname, she blushed lightly before muttering, "You're welcome. I'll see you later in Theater." Lily slung her bag over her shoulder and bolted for her next class.

Lucas made sure the class was empty save himself and the instructor before grabbing his own bag. He walked up to speak to the dragon. "Dr. Saffron, may I have a word?"

"Ah, Lucas, I'll bet you'd like to ask about my staff?" the dragon asked. When Lucas did nothing but blink in surprise, Dr. Saffron laughed, "You aren't the first student that has asked and you won't be the last, I'd wager."

Lucas cleared his throat nervously, "I just wondered how it worked?"

The staff growled, "I'm right here, you know! Imbecilic students thinking they're above talking to me!"

Lucas growled at it. "One more word and I'll light you on fire!" Already it seemed, the staff was getting on his nerves.

The dragon instructor laughed at him, "Ah, a demon. I haven't seen such a bold one of those in Demont in nearly a decade."

Lucas jumped in surprise and backed up suddenly. "How did you know?" he asked quietly. The teen demon was glancing around as if afraid someone would pop out with a torch or flaming arrow.

"Only a demon would threaten my rather rude staff with fire. The other non-humans all have their own threats unique to their abilities. At least the ones that threaten it," he finished with a frown.

Curious, Lucas asked suddenly, "Is it rude to everyone?"

"Mostly, but only non-humans can hear it because normal humans don't have the required magic in their blood."

"So, she is special!" Lucas muttered triumphantly.

Dr. Saffron eyed Lucas wearily, "She's more special than you could ever know."

Before Lucas could ponder that, the bell sounded telling Lucas he was late for his next class. Without responding, he raced from the room and down the hall to his next class - a specialized music lesson.

The rest of the day continued on in much the same fashion, with never a dull moment. Lucas enjoyed his classes with Lily as the two shared three of their seven classes and their midday meal. He counted himself lucky that he only had to share one class with Jonah. So far, it seemed his favorite class would be the private music lessons he had with his old friend Daniel Brooks.

Lucas and Daniel had been childhood best friends before the fire. While the two had kept in touch over the years, they weren't nearly as close as they used to be. The distance had truly taken its toll and so the two were left to rekindle their friendship. Like Lucas and Lily, Daniel and Lucas shared three classes but not the same ones that Lucas shared with Lily.

That night, Lucas told his mother all about his classes, Jonah, and Daniel. Knowing his mother as he did, Lucas didn't tell her about Lily. He figured that was a discussion for another day. When Lucas laid his head down to sleep that night, he dreamed of flying as he'd not been able to truly do in forever.

Lucas opened the back door and stepped out onto the patio. Darkness had fallen and the first stars were beginning to show themselves. It was cold, as Lucas had known it would be, but he didn't have his cloak on.

Lucas walked to the very edge of the patio against the house where he felt around on the wall until he felt a brick protruding out no more than a few inches. Lifting his right leg, Lucas put his foot on the brick, then pressed himself close to the wall before pushing himself up to the next brick. All up the back wall of the manor, these bricks formed a type of ladder all the way up to the roof. As he reached the last brick, he pushed himself up and onto the roof. Lucas looked up at the stars and marveled. Even at such a young age, he had always had a great appreciation for the beauty of the night sky.

He looked around to make sure there were no townsfolk around to see him. Seeing no one around, Lucas crouched down, sprung from the roof, and spread his wings in flight.

Lucas glided for a few moments before pulling up, flapping his wings a few more times and rising above the sparse clouds. He soared over the countryside and all of his cares seemed to disappear. Lucas loved using his wings, but due to the fear of society, he was forbidden to fly during the day. He was only allowed to fly sparingly, mostly at night.

Lucas didn't think that the thought would ever cross his father's mind that if he flew high enough, then no one would see him anyway. The young demon never mentioned this to his father since Lucien tended to react with a harsh temper when opposed. Sometimes, you had to choose your battles and Lucas had more important concerns.

As he flew, pleasant warmth spread throughout his body, starting in his back and working its way all over his body. Lucas continued flying, feeling completely at peace. He decided to chance a dip below the clouds. If anyone saw Lucas from this height, they would just assume he was a large bird. As he dipped, he examined the countryside below him. Cattle were grazing near a forested area, probably Flamewood Forest. No one was around so Lucas decided to land but as his feet touched the grass he was startled awake by the sound of smashing pottery.

Lucas woke up to hear loud arguing from downstairs. His parents must have been fighting again. He thought about going downstairs and just letting his father see him. It would end the argument as Lucien would be railing at him instead.

Another plate crashed into the wall or floor and then someone came running up the stairs and straight into the library. Lucas heard the soft sobbing and knew the fight was over.

Briefly, he entertained the thought of going to find out what this one had been about but that passed shortly. The teenage demon noticed that someone had covered him with a blanket while he dreamed before Lucas fell right back to sleep.

Meanwhile, across the city, an older man wearing a tailored maroon suit sat behind a desk listening as his chief research investigator revealed the results of years of testing.

"Master, the evidence concludes that the fire was set

intentionally by the townsfolk killed in Flamewood Forest that night. The fire started at the old Daemione Manor," the investigator stated. "However, we've found signs that the original fire was joined by a magical fire in the forest that night. The magical fire is what kept the townsfolk from being able to put the fire out faster. It also caused the death of all those people just inside the forest."

"I already knew all that," he responded, rolling his eyes. "I hired you and your team to tell me what started the magical fire!" he ground out annoyed.

The investigator looked flustered for a second before he shook his head. "Right sir! Sorry! We've determined the townsfolk were killed by a magical fire caused by the burning of a phoenix. The original investigators didn't know what they had when they collected some of the ashes." Smiling proudly, the investigator pulled a glass jar containing ash from inside his robe pocket. "We've tested the various samples and it appears, after setting the fire, a phoenix burned before disappearing. Further testing indicate that the phoenix is still in Demont but it is unknown at this time who or where that phoenix is."

The old man smiled, an evil glint flashing in his eyes. His expression suddenly changed to one of suspicion and he eyed the investigator. "Who else knows about this?"

The investigator looked nervous again. Swallowing the lump in his throat, his voice cracked just a fraction when he answered, "Just my team. Investigations are confidential unless the client chooses to divulge information to the public as our policy dictates."

"Splendid!" the old man responded. "I'll be meeting with you and your team tomorrow. You're dismissed!"

The investigator didn't waste time as he rushed from the room, closing the door swiftly behind him.

The old man pulled a large map from inside the drawer of his desk, "Come out, come out wherever you are, little phoenix! Soon, you'll be just another of my experiments." His cold, dark laughter reverberated across the room and throughout his home.

The investigator nearly ran from the house that

night, suddenly very scared for his own life. David Hatchett thought about fleeing from Demont. He thought about warning his team so that they could escape as well. In the end, David knew that there would be no saving any of them. He and his team were doomed the moment they agreed to research the Great Fire. It didn't matter if they tried to run, the old man known only as 'Master' would find them and he would do what it took to keep his secrets.

There was only one thing he could do so that the old man would not win: David scribbled out a quick but informative letter to an old military friend. Sending a letter by courier was the only safe way to deliver this letter and the only way the old man wouldn't intercept it. David's letter detailed the investigation and their findings. He wrote that he feared for his very life and the lives of his team. Included in the letter were short messages to his parents and instructions for his funeral and belongings.

After sending off his letter with the courier, David met with his team to warn them of his suspicions. He wanted to give them a fighting chance or at least be able to say goodbye to their loved ones. By morning, all five members of his team were dead including David: someone had poisoned their drinks when they'd met up for David to warn them. Only David managed to get any kind of letter out.

CHAPTER 3

POTIONS
(A DRAGON'S SUSPICIONS)

Mrs. Quaid agreed to come to Demont Secondary only because a rather wealthy benefactor offered her a rather large amount of money that she couldn't refuse. All she had to do was teach a bunch of teenagers and discover the identity of a special child. Easier said than done: thanks largely to the students at the school, she was very quickly being driven mad. Some classes were better than others but most were still terrible.

Mrs. Quaid had been teaching for more than a decade but had never encountered such a rude and disrespectful class of students. From the moment she started teaching at Demont, the students refused to be anything resembling decent. Many students only came to class long enough for the attendance check before getting up and walking out. When Mrs. Quaid went to the principal about all of the disruptive behavior, she was told that the students would only respect her if she could handle the issues herself.

Students stole her answer keys for tests so they could cheat. Several of them picked fights so frequently that the school didn't have time to fix the damaged desks, chairs, or whatever was broken before the students broke something else. Occasionally they stole her lesson journals where she kept all her notes about past and upcoming lessons. She kept a secondary journal for infractions against her or the school where she detailed the wrong doing and then recorded who she felt was responsible. She never caught the students in the act.

If that had been all, she might have been able to handle it but it had gotten much worse. She could never catch a student in the act of destroying school property or disrupting her lessons. Whoever was doing so was always one step ahead of her and since she couldn't catch the student in the act, she could not punish the student. Oh, she had tried but the principal often overruled her on every matter.

The principal told her that if she wanted her classes to respect her, she had to show some form of appropriate discipline. All that meant was that if she didn't catch the student, she couldn't punish them. If she tried to send the suspect to the office, the principal would just send the student back to class and the cycle would repeat itself. Truthfully, the principal did not believe her because she was the only instructor having that type of trouble.

Afterward, the students started knocking holes in her classroom walls while her back was turned. When no student would own up to the damage, she bought a mirror to place at the front of the room. After it was installed, the students started turning the lights out and hollering "Use your mirror!" More holes littered the wall when the lights were turned back on. It was disparaging to say the least but the shenanigans and delinquent behavior would not end.

Mrs. Quaid barely had time to search for the special student for all the chaos in her classes. She knew she had to do something though because her benefactor was getting impatient. Under normal circumstances the instructor would never even consider meeting with a shady salesman that was selling highly illegal potions but these weren't normal circumstances.

"What exactly does it do?" she questioned the salesman.

The scruffy looking salesman sneered at her, "Exactly what the potion says. It reveals." He held up five jars full of the potion. "You just get the person to touch it and within seconds their skin turns all red."

"For how long? No one can know what I've done,"

Mrs. Quaid was fidgeting now, worried she was going to get caught. The master was getting impatient; she had no choice. She just kept repeating that to herself over again to reassure herself.

Rolling his eyes, the salesman huffed in exasperation. "Whomever you use this on will not be able to see it at all. For argument sake, the effects last but an hour and not longer." He was getting impatient too. "Do you want the stuff or not?"

"Of course! But I need to know how it works first." Mrs. Quaid held out silver coins. "I'm not going into this thing blind!" she growled out. "This just works on non-humans, right?"

"Yes, no effect whatsoever on humans," he shrugged.

Mrs. Quaid nodded but she did not trust the shady salesman; however, if the potion worked, her search would not take as long. "And what do I do with it again?" she asked double checking what she'd read about the potion.

"Just add a tablespoon of the Revealer Potion to each liter of water. You can use it like a cleaner and wipe the surface of objects for best results. You know, where ever you intend on using it. Now is that all lady? I've got other places I need to be and other customers I have to see." He took her money and handed over the potion jars.

"If this stuff works like you say, I'll be back for more." That said, Mrs. Quaid turned and walked away. There was work to be done but first she had to ensure the potion was what she was told it was. For that, she needed the cooperation of a potions expert.

The next day found Mrs. Quaid rushing off to the resident non-human science instructor. She had waited the entire day so she could pretend a student or maybe another adult had dropped the potion in her class. She didn't want anyone contradicting her story and she didn't want the dragon to suspect herself.

Surely, the dragon would be able to tell her the potion would work. She just had to play the right part. "Dr. Saffron, I'm so glad I caught you before you left! I found something that I think you should take a look at." She pulled a smaller vial of the Revealer Potion from her pocket. All Mrs. Quaid needed was to confirm the ingredients in the vial to know her potions were authentic. "I found this in my classroom floor. One of my students must have dropped it."

"Why didn't you just take it to the office?" the dragon questioned confused. Classes were over for the day and the students had cleared out some time before since he didn't have a class the last hour of the day.

Mrs. Quaid paused but a moment to think about her answer, "I don't know who dropped it and I didn't know if it was merely medicine or something else. I thought it best to find out what the potion is before I turned it in." Of course, she had no intention of turning in her own potion but the lies were believable enough. "It might not even belong to a student for all I know. No, it's best to find out what it is first or at least what's in it."

The dragon shrugged at her explanation. "Is that why you've brought it to me?"

The sinister woman smiled, "Yes actually! I've heard so much about you from my students that I just knew you would be able to find out for me!"

If dragons could blush, Dr. Saffron would be bright red. "I'm sure the students exaggerated a little bit."

"Are you saying you can't figure it out?" she asked, attempting to look aghast at the insinuation. "Nonsense! I believe what my students had to say on this matter. You're an excellent instructor."

"I can tell you what's in here. I'll let you know first thing tomorrow. Does that sound all right to you?" he asked her.

She nodded, "Thank you, Dr. Saffron." She stayed and talked to him a few minutes more before looking at the time and making a big production about not realizing how late it was. She excused herself by claiming she was late for an appointment.

Dr. Saffron poured out half the potion and stored the rest for later. He didn't need the entire amount to learn what was in it. Carefully, he began the process, identifying each ingredient as he went. It took him about an hour and when the last ingredient was identified, he sucked in a breath. He knew what this potion was now and it sent warning bells blaring in his mind.

Dr. Saffron had to let them know. He hurriedly cleaned the lab table and threw out the used up potion before rushing with the other half to the other guardian and her shop across town. Fortunately, she hadn't closed up shop for the night yet. "I'm telling you, Christine! Someone knows and they're searching as we speak," warned Dr. Saffron.

The mage shook her head, "What makes you so sure?"

Taking a vial of potion from his jacket pocket, the dragon held the potion up to the light. "Another instructor brought this to me. Quaid is human but she knows that you don't tamper with unmarked potions. Fortunately, this potion isn't lethal but it's still illegal, Christine."

"May I?" Christine held her hand out for the potion and was met with a weary look but Dr. Saffron still handed over the potion. She turned away from her companion and went to her lab. The potion was murky but otherwise clear and smelled of oranges.

Christine set out five separate small containers before removing one. Unstoppering the vial, she held it above the containers. Christine commanded, "Pesot," of the vial. Suddenly the potion seemed to coagulate in midair and separated itself into the small containers.

Dr. Saffron blinked. "I don't think I'll ever get used to that," he uttered in astonishment.

Christine smiled, "I don't use that spell too often. Some ingredients don't separate well." She shrugged and continued her work. "This would be the citrus to disguise the potion and this one the vinegar." Christine was shaking her head but slid the two containers away. "This one is interesting though - faerie's plume. Used to conceal from the victim the purpose of the potion." She put the vinegar and citrus back into the original vial before adding the faerie's plume back. "This last ingredient though..." Christine raised the container to eye level to get a closer look, "I'm not entirely sure what this is. Illegal, you said?"

The mage did not wait for his answer before going to a book carefully tucked away from any harm that might become it in the lab. She carefully set the ingredient down before she took the book from its hiding place. "Illegal potions aren't very fun. They almost always require ingredients that require murder to get them. Granted the humans would be all too happy murdering us non-humans," she rambled. "Thanks to the Council, we're able to live more freely and the humans can't just do what they want. I swear they're the only reason these potions were even banned." Christine was rapidly flipping through pages as she talked.

"It's not as bad as some of the others but it precedes more deadly potions. It's only the beginning, my friend," Dr. Saffron warned.

Christine suddenly slowed down, eliminating potions and ingredients that pertained to this particular one. "Ah ha! Here it is," she was reading the list of ingredients now. Her hand flew to her mouth, "Oh no, powdered vampire fang. I was afraid of this: You have to pull the fangs out while the vampire is still alive. They're no good if the vampire is dead already." She sighed, closing her eyes.

"Hence why it is illegal," the dragon responded. "The potion is mostly harmless unless ingested but I'm sure who ever had it did not intend for someone to drink it."

"No, they intended to reveal non-humans amongst the humans. You're right, old friend. The secret is out."

"What secret?" asked Lucas as he and Lily came through the outer door.

"Nothing for you to worry about, kiddo. What are you doing here?" asked Dr. Saffron stepping to block the teenagers' view of the lab and Christine.

Christine added the powdered vampire fang back to the rest of the potion and stoppered it before slipping it into a secret drawer that only she knew about. She would have to label the potion later or else separate the ingredients to be used for other potions.

"Came to hang out with Lily and Danah," Lucas shrugged, seating himself on the closest piece of furniture.

Lily and Christine shared a look before Lily left the front room in the shop to find her sister. The visit would have to be cut short and she knew just the way to do it. Lily went to a back room and found her sister doodling on some plain paper. "I'm telling Lucas you're not feeling well. Cissy wants to talk," she rolled her eyes.

For her part, Danah just nodded her head and kept doodling. "Just let me know when he's gone so I can come out."

A minute later, Lily was back in the front room to make excuses, "She's not feeling well, Lucas. You better get home. It might be contagious."

Lucas stood, "Oh? Okay. Will you be at school tomorrow?"

Lily glanced at Christine who nodded but didn't say a word, "Yes, nothing could keep me away." She smiled at her friend. "Meet you in the quad?"

The demon boy nodded and started to leave.

"Oh, Jonah was supposed to come by. If you see him, can you let him know?" Lily asked. She was moving things about the room, something she did quite often. Lily could not stand for things being in the same place for very long. Christine didn't mind too much as moving things around in her shop increased sales.

Lucas rolled his eyes. "Sure, I'll let the canary know," he replied earning a frown from his best friend. He left the shop, not really expecting to see the faerie so was surprised when he ran into him literally two streets over from the shop. Both boys fell to the ground.

"Hey! Watch where you're going you dummy!" shouted Jonah standing back up.

The dummy in question jumped to his feet, anger coursing through him. "Who are you calling names?" he growled.

"The dummy that ran into me and knocked me over," the faerie replied snidely.

Lucas started to respond before it dawned on him that he had done exactly that. "Oh, sorry. Don't be calling me names!" He hesitated before continuing, knowing he needed to let the faerie know about Danah. "Look, Lily asked me to tell you that Danah is sick and that it might be contagious. No visitors."

"Did she actually say 'No visitors'?" Surprisingly to

Lucas, the faerie looked concerned.

"Well, no but Lily did say it might be contagious," Lucas responded.

"Then I might as well go see how Danah is feeling." Jonah ran off toward the shop, leaving Lucas in his dust.

Lucas stared off at the irksome faerie before continuing home to Daemione Manor. Maybe Jonah would get sick and Lucas wouldn't have to deal with him for a few days, he thought. A demon could dream.

CHAPTER 4

NIGHTMARES
(CAVERN UNDER THE LAKE)

Theater class was well underway in practice for the performance this semester. Unfortunately for Lily, she'd been cast as an understudy yet again. The lead roles were given to the more popular students. Lily was beyond frustrated because every year it was the same old thing in this class.

The school couldn't keep an instructor in the subject and each new instructor would cast based on popularity. The instructor's logic was that more money could be raised in final production dinner parties if it were well-known and well-liked students.

Unfortunately, that meant that the students that could act were usually cast as understudies and never got their day on stage. A few times, an understudy was thrust in at the last minute and was able to show how well they could act.

Mostly, the class lost money in the dinner parties because people stopped paying to come see them after the first production since the majority of the popular students couldn't act the parts to save their lives. The actors couldn't remember their lines, they flunked out of their classes, sometimes they deadpanned the entire performance with absolutely no emotion whatsoever.

The performances were terrible but until the new instructors either listened to the students that could act or the school was able to keep an instructor for more than a year,

Lily and students like her would continue to be cast as understudies and the plays would continue to do poorly.

This season, Jonah was the fortunate one or their group as the lead actor flunked out of two of his classes. So Jonah was allowed to step in and play the lead role. This play was about the age old stereotypical vampires that sucked your blood till you died and left your body behind for someone else to find. Only Jonah was playing an age old vampire whose mother, also a vampire, wanted him to settle down and have children. So the play was more about Nosferatu finding love, than anything else.

Lily spent her time in class helping to make props and costumes. Outside of class, she helped Jonah learn his lines or spent time with Lucas. As for Lucas, he was assigned a position on the light and sound crew ensuring the performance went off without a hitch. He managed to be appointed assistant light and sound manager. So between the three of them, they had the entire performance worked out.

Lucas, Lily, and Jonah had taken to meeting outside a cave in the eastern woods known as Flamewood Forest. A somewhat tricky path through the cave full of multiple twists, turns, and divided pathways led to a hidden doorway in a far off cave wall.

Lily and Jonah started meeting there many years before when Lily's sister Christine made the cave accessible for them. The hidden doorway actually led into a large network of caverns occupied by Lily and her sisters, Christine and Danah.

Unfortunately for Lucas, he had to put up with Jonah in order to hang out with Lily. He and Jonah made it a game of sorts now: They insulted each other frequently, trying for the best insults. When they pulled off a truly original insult, they gave points. Currently, Jonah was in the lead.

It wasn't long before Lucas's little sister, Julie, joined the group. Mostly, she came and Christine had books or toys for her. For someone that never wanted children of her own, Christine was great with them. When Julie mentioned having nightmares, Christine paid a visit to Lucas and Julie's parents. At least, Christine tried to pay the pair a visit -

Lucien was always away on business.

Eight years ago, his sister had only been a couple years old and her fire immunities not yet developed; Lucas's immunities were only partially developed at the time. Still, he managed to escape the flames with Julie in tow. The aftermath was largely a blur that his parents never believed.

Sometimes, Lucas wondered if his 'wild' tale from that night was true or just the product of an overactive imagination. True or not, the ordeal was real enough to give Julie nightmares but maybe not real enough for the fantastical things to have happened as they did.

Julie woke up screaming with nightmares for years after the family left Demont behind. When the family of four came back, the nightmares returned acting as a lasting scar from the Great Fire.

Unable to watch a child suffer, Christine proceeded to create a potion to stop Julie's nightmares on their own without hurting her or creating a dependency on the potion. Lucas's mother Anne was thrilled but his father was not as pleased.

Lucien was not fond of outside interference in his family and was beyond angry when he learned of the mage's offered help. The family patriarch mistrusted everyone especially anyone that Lucas came across and introduced to the family.

For her part, Christine did a lot to ease Lucien and Anne's fears and distrust. She wasn't an expert in her field for no reason. Some of Christine's invented potions were known the nation over for their effectiveness.

Lucas was privy to one of the conversations between Christine and his parents. Unfortunately, the mage came alone and Lucas was forced to sit through what he deemed a boring discussion on the Nightmare Relieving Potion and why it would work versus the previous types of remedies that weren't working. The only good that came of that discussion was Lucas learning that Christine was a mage that specialized in medicinal potion making.

The small group of friends had been meeting for some time outside the cave when Lily announced that her sister was working on a more convenient entrance that didn't take half an hour just to navigate around. She refused to say more about it but promised to let them both know when it was ready.

A few weeks later, Lily spoke with both Lucas and Jonah separately, asking them to meet her at the lake on the weekend for a surprise. Even after knowing each other for a few months and being shoved together at all junctures, Lucas and Jonah still fought like a stray cat and dog. So Lily knew, she had no other choice in the matter but to deceive them into meeting her at the same place and time.

When the weekend dawned, Lucas found himself leaping happily from branch to branch as he sped through the forest. Lily wanted him at the lake today at noon and he was, as usual, running late. He reached the end of the forest abruptly and nearly jumped into thin air. His wings would have carried him safely to the ground had they not been folded securely across his shoulders and back.

Recovering from nearly falling, Lucas noticed his arch nemesis Jonah standing in front of him just before the lake. Surely, Lily wouldn't have invited them both here. She knew how the two detested each other.

Lucas stared down at the ground from the large branch he was hanging on. Frowning down at Lily, who was sitting directly beneath the tree, he accused, "You didn't say that he was coming too."

"And you didn't tell me that he would be here either," Jonah glared over his shoulder suddenly.

"Oh, just hush! I didn't tell either of you because I know how childish you both are," Lily growled at the pair. "However, that is neither here nor there. I've asked you both here to show you something!" She stood, her eyes bright with excitement. "It's ready!" she announced, rubbing her hands together as if she were up to no good.

Lucas rolled over, allowing himself to hang upside down as he held onto the large branch with only his legs. "Really? And what is that?" he queried as his wings started to unfold of their own accord a tiny bit before he flipped down toward the ground.

He knew that he could hang from the branch safely

but a second longer, his wings would have fully distended and revealed his demon ancestry to whomever might be watching. Lucas was not yet ready to share that secret with Lily, even if the dreaded Jonah knew all about it.

Lily shouted as he nearly flipped right on top of her. "Hey!" She clambered out of the way just in time to avoid him.

Jonah snorted with disgust, "Blasted monkey! So clumsy that you'd hurt a fly even if it were no where near you." The jibe was a clue to an even bigger secret than Lucas's own but Jonah knew enough to make it sound as nothing more than an insult to the demon that he loved to hate.

"Flightless bird!" Lucas responded angrily.

Lily growled at them both, "As amusing as the two of you fighting is, there are more important matters to discuss."

"Why did you ask us here for?" Lucas asked.

She rolled her eyes, "I just told you. The second entrance to the cavern is finally ready! Christine, Danah, and I have been working day and night so that it would get done quicker and for some unfathomable reason, I wanted to show you two clowns," Lily stated rather matter-of-factually. She calmly stepped onto the water in front of them and continued walking across the water as if it was the easiest thing in the world.

Lucas and Jonah looked at her surprised before turning wide eyes on each other. "You go first!" Jonah said.

"Chicken!" Lucas growled before taking a step closer to the water. "Umm, Lily? How are you doing that?"

Lily's musical laugh caught them both off guard, "There's an invisible path. Just follow me." She was almost to the small island twenty meters from the shore of the lake.

Lucas took off at a sprint to catch up with Lily but Jonah waited till she was already fully across before he would even give the pathway a try. By the time Lucas made it across, Jonah was halfway to the small island, if you could call it that. Before he could finish crossing, something flew out of the trees and knocked him clear across the pathway and into the water.

Lucas burst into laughter while Jonah swam over to the island. By the time he'd made it, Lucas had fallen to the ground, he was laughing so hard. Or he was until Jonah splashed him getting out of the lake. Lucas growled and started to retaliate before Lily stepped in and made them both behave.

"What was that?" Jonah asked, concerned.

Lily laughed nervously, "Cissy put some safety measures in place. You know, to keep people from following us across." She was frowning slightly, thinking of what must have set the safety precautions off. "Lucas must have triggered them when he ran across. Odd, I'll have to talk to Cissy about this."

The attention back on Lucas, he laughed. "I don't think I could have done that better if I'd planned it! I'll have to thank your sister."

"Why you!" Jonah yelled and lunged at the demon. Lucas was only standing for a moment before Jonah completely knocked him to the ground.

Thinking better of yelling to break them up, Lily just grabbed on to one of Jonah's wings and the faerie immediately jumped back to his feet and off of Lucas. She was shaking her head angrily at her two friends. "You would think you were five instead of sixteen," she stated. "We don't have time for this. Let's go!" Lily demanded and walked into a dense set of trees and bushes on the small island. Really, the island only had room for the small grove and nothing more.

In the brush was a cleverly hidden trap door that went down into the ground. The tunnel went for a ways before they were able to step down onto solid ground.

The three walked along a corridor into a large spacious room. "Wow," whispered Lucas and Jonah at the same time much to each others disgust.

After looking around the spacious cavern, Jonah went home to change into dry clothes, leaving Lily and Lucas alone. "So what do you think?" Lily asked him.

He didn't look at her in case he lost the courage he'd mustered, "I think it's brilliant. It'll be great to meet up here and plan pranks or just meet up to do homework." Lucas turned to Lily, "You want to come over for dinner?" When she didn't immediately answer, he started rambling, "Umm, I didn't have a lot of friends at my last school. Especially none I

could trust with my secret." Lucas suddenly unfolded his
wings. When Lily still didn't respond, Lucas thought he might
have made a mistake in trusting Lily. As he started to fold his
wings back around his shoulders, he mumbled, "It's just my
mom worries about me."

Reaching out to stop him, Lily smiled sadly. "Stop
talking," she commanded evenly. "I'll come."

"You will?" he asked, somewhat hopeful.
She laughed, "Yeah."

The two talked a little longer about his parents and
what to expect. After he'd given her directions, the two parted
ways: Lucas to tell his parents that she was coming for dinner
and Lily to get ready.

Anne Daemione was still cooking when Lucas finally
came home with the news that a friend was coming for dinner.
Anne was happy for her son because she knew how hard it
was for Lucas to make friends. However, she was nervous at
the same time because he'd never had a friend over before.
The family had reason to be wary of someone in their home
when they were pretending to be normal humans but really
weren't. "Darling, does your friend know about us?" she asked
tentatively.

Lucien looked up from reading his paper and glared
over at his son, awaiting the answer.

For the most part, Lucas didn't look intimidated. He
knew that the right answer would be to tell his parents that
Lily didn't know but he didn't want his friendship with Lily
tainted with such a lie. Lucas took a deep breath before
answering, bracing for the fall out, "Yes, she knows."

Lucien stood, ready to blow his fuse before his mom
registered what he said. "Wait, 'she'? Your friend is a girl?"
Anne asked quickly.

Lucas nodded, unperturbed by the question. He
thought he'd told them about Lily but he must have forgotten.
His father seemed to calm down suddenly, taken completely
by surprise. Instead of tearing into his son, Lucien left the
room.

"Is she like us?" his mother pestered for more
information as she took the last pot from the stove top.

Lucas smiled, his mother was always curious. He supposed that was where he got his own curiosity from. "Yes and no," he answered. "She's not a demon but she isn't a normal human," he added by way of explanation. "I know she isn't a mage like her 'sister' but I can't quite figure out what she is. There's something about her..." he trailed off.

Lost in thought, Lucas was startled when he heard his mother laugh, "Oh dear! You like her, don't you?"

He blushed scarlet at her words and grumbled slightly which only caused his mother to laugh harder.

Suddenly, there was a knock at the door. "I'll get it," he said quickly and raced from the room. In the doorway, Lucas was surprised to see his father in the entrance hall, answering the door. A smile was plastered to his father's face so Lucas knew he was in presentation mode.

"Welcome to our home, Ms..." his father trailed off.

Lily smiled at him, curtsying. "Nightshade. Please, call me Lily," she told Lucien.

Lucas watched the exchange from the safety of the shadows. He had steeled himself to interfere until he'd seen the dress Lily wore. It wasn't revealing or anything. In fact, the dress was just a plain black dress that went to just below her knees with long sleeves. He thought the material looked soft and suddenly, anything Lucas was about to say was lost. In the three months he'd known her, Lucas had never seen her in a dress.

Lily caught something from the corner of her eye and glanced around the man who'd introduced himself as Mr. Daemione. Lucas was standing in what looked to be a hall. She smiled at him

Snapping out of his stupor, Lucas came forward to 'rescue' her from his father. He didn't trust the man and he wasn't about to leave Lily alone with him. He took Lily to introduce her to his mother and then Lily volunteered to help set the table. While they were setting the table, Lucas's little sister Julie came down from her room.

"Who are you?" the little girl asked bluntly.

Lucas glared at his sister until Lily giggled, "I'm a friend of your brothers. My name's Lily, what's yours?"

The girl smiled somewhat, "My name's Julie! Do you want to play tea party with me?"

"That sounds lovely," Lily answered. "When do you want to have it?"

Julie looked thoughtful for a moment thinking of when the best time for a tea party would be. However, she never got a chance to answer because Anne announced that dinner was ready.

After dinner, Lily played a game of cards with Lucas, Julie, and Anne. Whether or not it was because the others let her or she was just that good, Julie won just about every game. It had just gotten dark when Lily's sister Christine showed up to get her.

While Julie went upstairs to bed, Lucas hung around downstairs washing the dinner dishes and hoping to hear what his parents thought of Lily. Eavesdropping was never his strong suit though and he missed the entire conversation while he was lost in his own thoughts.

His mother walked in while he was putting the dishes away. "Ah, there you are Lucas," she said coming to help him. "I thought you'd already gone to bed." Her eyes twinkled like she knew something that he didn't.

He narrowed his eyes, "No, I stayed to clean up. After all, it was my guest."

His mother nearly laughed at him. "Stayed to clean up? That's what you're going with?" She dried off a plate and put it neatly away in the cabinet.

Lucas hung his head, "So what did you think?" He eyed his mother warily.

"Well, your father doesn't like her but he doesn't like anyone so I wouldn't waste sleep on it," she answered, her eyes still twinkling merrily.

When she didn't continue, Lucas peered at his mother again, "But what about you, mom?"

Anne sighed, "Truly, Lucas, there is something magical about her. Something I just can't put my finger on." She paused for a moment before adding, "What's more is that she likes you too." She placed the last dish in the cabinet and turned to leave. "Don't stay up too late."

Lucas stood there all alone in the kitchen completely stunned. There was no way that Lily felt the same for him as Lucas felt for her. He was positive that Lily only saw him as a friend. Yet here Lucas was still standing in the kitchen wondering if the mysterious Lily might want more than just a friendship.

CHAPTER 5

FAMILY
(THE DEMON THAT SHAPE-SHIFTED)

The train had been slowing for the past five minutes in preparation for stopping just outside the ancient city of Demont. "Don't look like you're going to a funeral, Annabeth," a short stout woman spoke to her daughter.

Annabeth was not happy about this move. She liked her old house and her old school and now she was being forced to go live in Demont of all cities and attend a secondary school that had a lousy reputation. "I told you I didn't want to go here," she grumbled to her mother.

"Not this again!" her mother said exasperated with her stubborn daughter. She shook her head in frustration before standing. They'd gotten a private room on the train. "I'm going to see how much longer before the train stops. Stay out of trouble!" Her mother left the cabin, shutting the door softly behind her.

Months ago, Annabeth resigned herself to the fact that she was going to a dreadful town and decided if she had to go, she was going on her own terms. So Annabeth began changing her appearance to something the young shape-shifter would like. Annabeth thought maybe she'd leave her wings as they were and just fold them over her shoulders like she'd been told most demons did. They looked like a cloak that way.

For as long as she could remember, her mother made her shift them away as shape-shifters were more acceptable than demons. Or rather, they could blend in better with normal humans when they kept their emotions in check. The slightest slip could expose a shape-shifter in a heartbeat.

Annabeth's hair was as dark as night and though she could shift at will, her wings were a deep red as they should be with her age. She knew that as she got older, her wings would continue to darken but she also knew that they wouldn't develop properly if she couldn't use them.

While in Troale, the teen was never allowed to fly unless her mom took her away for the weekend to a friend's country home. Annabeth's mother hired a private tutor to teach her how to fly and control flame as all demons were capable of. Meanwhile, Annabeth learned the shifting bit from her own mother.

"No one ever listens to me," she grumbled before leaving the cabin. She needed something to occupy herself that wouldn't get her in trouble with her mother. Granted, it might still get her in trouble with someone else but Annabeth wasn't picky. She made her way down the corridor and into the dining car.

"What can I get you?" the counter attendant asked, spotting the black haired girl.

Annabeth startled, not expecting to encounter anyone, before a slow sly smile appeared on her face. She sauntered to the counter trying to feign an air of maturity, "How 'bout some whiskey?"

The attendant laughed, "Nice try kid but not buying it."

"Worth a shot," Annabeth shrugged before sitting on a stool at the counter. "Can't blame a girl for trying, can you?" She smiled weakly.

Rolling his eyes, the attendant shook his head, "I can but I won't just this time because you're so cute." He was flirting with her now.

Annabeth looked up sharply surprised. The man was old enough to be her dad or so she assumed. The younger shape-shifting demon had never actually met her own father.

The attendant roared into laughter. "I'm only joking!" he gushed out trying to catch his breath again. Once the man calmed down, he brought a lemonade over to Annabeth. "The name's Jake, by the way. This drink is on the house."

She muttered thanks and sipped slowly on the drink in front of her. She was still in a bad mood because of the move. "You ever feel like no one listens to you?" she asked.

Jake nodded, "All the time. Why do you ask?"

"It's just..." she trailed off.

"Come on, sweetheart, what's got you so bothered?"

Annabeth sighed, "I don't want to move to Demont. I liked my old home but my mother's forcing us to move all the way to the other end of Jodacai! She thinks Demont is what is best for us." She rolled her eyes.

Jake nodded, "Sometimes, we are forced to do stuff we don't want to." He thought a moment before adding, "You may not be happy now but give it time. You might find what you're looking for in Demont."

Annabeth nodded sadly clearly not believing him.

Jake patted her hand lightly, "How old are you? Fifteen? Sixteen? Look at it this way, you only have a few years left in secondary and you can go back to whatever city your from afterward."

Annabeth brightened a little. "I never thought about it like that. Thank you!"

Suddenly, Annabeth's mother came through. "There you are! I've been looking everywhere. Time to gather our things, the train will be at the station in a few minutes." Her mother dragged her off back to the cabin.

Annabeth and her mother gathered their things and left the train when it stopped. Her mother had arranged for an apartment in advance. Unfortunately, it was just a small one-bedroom apartment and the mother and daughter pair would have to share the tiny bedroom.

The next day found Annabeth being gawked at by some of her classmates while she pretended to work on props for the upcoming performance in her theater class. At least this new school had a somewhat decent theater program as far as she could see.

"Hey, Lucas!" Lily whispered, thumping him lightly on the arm as she came to stand next to him. "Did you notice how much the new girl looks like you?" she asked.

Lucas glanced over toward the new girl and frowned. "What do you mean?"

Lily eyed the two, "Well, she's got the same kind of hair - straight and black just like you."

"Big deal. Plenty of people have straight black hair," Lucas interrupted.

She rolled her eyes, "You didn't let me finish. Her eyes are shaped like yours and they're the same shade of gray." Lily paused, another pair of gray eyes coming to mind. "Eyes just like your dad."

Lucas blinked, eyeing the new girl again. "Hmm, I don't know. Maybe she's a cousin or something? I'll ask my parents if I've got any cousins in the area later."

Lily still wore a frown. "There's more.." Lily's hand reached out and lightly touched one of Lucas's wings currently laying flat on his back like a cloak.

Lucas blushed lightly but turned to look at the new transfer student. She wore a light cloak or so it appeared. Annabeth's was almost the same shade as Lucas's wings. Was it really just a cloak?

The day dragged on, much to the displeasure of most of the student body and at least a small portion of the instructors. Lucas was both looking forward to getting home and dreading it all at once. He was eager to find out if the new girl, Annabeth, was a cousin or some other distant relative; but was not so eager to ask his father.

Lucas didn't get a chance to talk to his parents for almost a week after Annabeth arrived. The girl was making friends easier than he ever had. Lucas envied her charismatic personality and friendly nature. One morning, he overheard Annabeth discussing a sleepover at Nightshade Cavern with Lily and her sisters. He rolled his eyes at the thought. As the conversation continued, Lucas learned that Annabeth's father wasn't in the picture and she didn't know who he was.

That just meant that she might be related on her father's side and the only one that might know would be her mother or his own parents possibly. She was a demon just like him and based on her physical traits, her father and his father were the family connection as far as Lucas could tell. The news just furthered Lucas's need to talk to his parents: they must know something.

When Lucas got home that evening, he discovered his mother had gone shopping and wouldn't be back until late. Lucien was in his study working on some odd job he'd been hired for. Working in the study meant that he was doing preparatory work for the real job – a job that his father would be going out of town for.

Lucas approached his father's study quietly. Since Anne was gone, he only had to ask his father about possible relatives in the area. He thought about just not bothering to ask but his curiosity was getting the better of him. Steeling his nerves, he knocked before opening the door slowly. "Father?" he called.

His father looked up from the papers he was looking over and snarled moodily. "What?"

Lucien's attitude almost made Lucas bolt right then and there; however, he did have a reason for disturbing his father. "I'm sorry to bother you," he apologized quickly. "I just wondered if we had any other relatives in this area. There was a new student at school that looks a lot like us: same hair, same eyes, and she's a demon." Lucas looked at his father hopefully. He wondered if he'd get an answer or a reprimand for disturbing the older demon over nonsense.

"You bother me over a new student?" Lucien spat with disgust. He stood suddenly, shoving his chair backward.

Lucas nearly ran for the door. He knew what would happen if he stayed put and had no desire to accept punishment for being curious. He tore from the room and up the stairs quick as a flash, slamming his bedroom door behind him.

Meanwhile, Lucien sat back in his chair. His anger spent, he reached into a drawer and pulled out a small bottle and glass. Pouring himself half a glass, he sipped calmly. He knew his son didn't deserve the anger but a part of him was angry. So very angry and no matter the problem, he couldn't shake the anger. Often he overreacted to little things because of the lingering anger.

More than a decade past, he'd been happy. Anne had

just given birth to their son and life had looked so promising. Lucien's thoughts suddenly snapped back to what his son had asked. Had they any relatives? Without thought, Lucien left the house, his wings hanging loosely upon his shoulders in his hasty departure.

It didn't take Lucien long to find what or rather who he was looking for. News traveled fast in Demont and all the demon had to do was inquire at one of the local taverns about new faces.

Genevieve Decatur paced the small one bedroom apartment she shared with her teen-aged daughter. Her daughter was spending the night with a new friend and Genevieve was left to her own devices. She wondered if she had made a mistake in coming to Demont. She had left the town more than a decade before due to scandal and heartache. She'd vowed to never return and never to be a victim of such heartache again. She'd succeeded mostly but everything seemed so different now.

Genevieve was not well and she had yet to tell her daughter. Her first priority was ensuring that Annabeth was taken care of when the time came. Eventually, Genevieve would have to tell Annabeth but for now she was playing a very dangerous game. Her strength was ebbing every day.

"Knock! Knock!" the door sounded loudly causing Genevieve to jump.

Genevieve wasn't expecting company and wondered who it could be. She made her way to the front door, smoothing her clothes as she went. Genevieve was shocked speechless when she opened the door. Standing before her was a man that she'd not seen in more than fifteen years. "Genevieve," he said stepping into her apartment.

She glared at him. "What are you doing here?" she demanded angrily, nearly slamming the door shut. She swung around to face him.

He turned on her, "What am I doing here? Shouldn't I be asking you that? You swore to Anne that you would never come back here but here you are," he uttered nastily. He was advancing toward her.

"Oh, no you don't!" she railed at him, side stepping

away. "I'm not here to ruin your perfect little family if that's what you're thinking." Genevieve crossed her arms in front of her chest. "If circumstances were different I wouldn't have even bothered, you miserable demon!" she spat.

Lucien towered over her. Anger radiated from him, "Then what did you come back for?" he demanded.

Suddenly, she didn't seem as sure of herself as she moved to sit on the sofa. She didn't speak at first but rubbed her hands up and down her arms as if trying to warm up. "I'm dying, Lucien," she finally burst out as she stared at her hands. A moment later, she glared up at him defiantly.

He moved to sit as well, having not expected to hear that. Lucien was normally a cold man with little feelings for anyone including his family but he had loved once upon a time and the woman before him was one of his loves. "Are you sure? Have you seen a mage?" he questioned almost frantically.

Genevieve laughed. "How ironic!" she cried out. "I only wanted you to show the care and concern that you always did for Anne and you finally do but it's too late to enjoy it." She shook her head trying to dispel the sadness that had seemed to pervade her very essence. "I've seen dozens and there are no cures for this."

"Then why did you come?" he questioned confused. "I would think that you came for money but if there is no cure, why now?" Lucien got down on one knee, tilting Genevieve's face upward.

She cried ever so slightly, "I came so our daughter could get to know her father and her brother so she wouldn't feel so alone when I'm gone."

He kept blinking, not comprehending what he was hearing. When the news finally sunk in, he stared open mouthed at Genevieve. "We have a daughter?"

Afraid of the backlash, the situation would cause in his personal and professional life, Lucien didn't stick around Demont after the conversation to meet his daughter. He didn't have any intention on getting to know her right away. Instead, he left Demont for work again as if he'd never heard the news. Then again, work always came before everyone and everything. Lucien didn't even bother to let his wife know about Genevieve and the daughter they shared.

       Hurt, Genevieve prepared her affairs for the end. She knew she didn't have much longer and she didn't want her daughter having to worry about the details. As the days passed by, her illness continued spreading throughout her body and her condition deteriorated rapidly.

       Genevieve didn't want to worry her daughter Annabeth so she played practical jokes and pretended like nothing was wrong with her. By the time Annabeth learned the truth, she'd be angry at her mother but at least Genevieve didn't have to see her hurting on her behalf. It was a tough decision but she felt it was for the best.

       When she reached the final stages, she wrote out a letter to explain her actions and sent it out with a courier to be delivered upon her death. When that time came, Annabeth's future guardian would be tasked with informing the teen and caring for her in Genevieve's steed.

CHAPTER 6

DISRUPTION
(HOLES IN THE WALL)

Five months into the class, Mrs. Quaid's mirror had long since disappeared and she was at her wits end. At one point, she tried to punish the whole class by assigning them all detention after a particularly heinous afternoon. One of the students had the audacity to put a sign on her back without her knowledge. The trick was an innocent enough prank but the snickers and looks hurt her pride.

It didn't help matters when one student actually did what the paper said and kissed her in front of the rest of her class! Mrs. Quaid was beyond embarrassed. The worst part is that if the wrong person saw or heard about the student kissing her, she could be fired and refused employment as an instructor at every institute of learning all across Jodacai.

"Get out! Get out of my class at once!" the history instructor screamed at her class. Sick and tired of being sick and tired, Mrs. Quaid had enough, "Get out!" she yelled again, practically pushing the students out of her class. She suspected that one of the students in this class was the special one she'd been sent to find but she couldn't be sure.

Mrs. Quaid still had to report back to the mage on her findings and hope she was still paid in full for the job she did. The history instructor just could not handle teaching these students anymore. She wondered if the mystery student she was searching for might have learned of Mrs. Quaid's motive and deliberately sabotaged her career.

As the last student left her class, she slammed the

door shut and locked it. No one else would be coming in. For once, she'd have peace and quiet. No interruptions, no holes knocked in her walls, no stolen journals, and no students! She moved back to her desk where she unlocked a hidden drawer. Inside the drawer was a mostly empty jar of potion and a hand-held mirror.

All of the trouble had made it harder for her to investigate for the special being hiding out in the student population. When she cheated a bit and purchased the special potion on the black market, her job had gotten a little easier.

She now had a list of students who were not normal humans: Of about twelve hundred students, only about two hundred were non-humans. The potion had turned out to be exactly what she needed to distinguish the normal humans from the non-humans. Learning that some students were non-humans was no big deal to her while others took her completely by surprise. The only downside to the potion was that there was no way to know what type of non-humans the non-humans were.

The last jar was mostly empty now because she'd slipped the potion one way or another to every student in the student body: tables, chairs, books. The potion was topical and reacted with their magical cores or so it had been explained to her.

As a normal human, the potion had no effect on her; however, non-humans came down with headaches and stomach cramps along with a red rash that lasted for about an hour. Of course the headaches and stomach cramps were a side effect of another ingredient being added to the mix.

That ingredient had taken a bit longer to acquire as Mrs. Quaid was forced to go far away from Demont to avoid suspicion. But at least it made the freaks miserable, she thought.

The small hand-held mirror was actually a two-way communications device that allowed her to contact her benefactor regarding the information and leads she'd come across. Mrs. Quaid lifted the mirror from her drawer and tapped the glass three times with her fingernail as she'd done countless times before.

The mirror flashed briefly until the glass no longer reflected herself. A dark shadow replaced her reflection on the other side of the glass. "Master," she greeted cordially.

"Quaid, why have you contacted me?" the shadow demanded. "Did you find the child?" He sounded impatient.

She looked flustered, "I've found all I can. I can't handle these students anymore but I've narrowed my search down to exclude regular humans. One of them is bound to be the one you are looking for." Mrs. Quaid held up a paper, "I've got a list of the non-humans right here."

Somehow the shadow looked more menacing than it had a moment before, "I sent you there to find but a needle in the haystack and you think you can pass the haystack off as the needle?" he demanded angrily. "One child!"

"You don't know how bad it is here!" she whined at the shadow in the mirror. She wasn't looking at the mirror but rather looking at the ceiling. If anyone saw her they'd tell you she gave the distinct impression that she was going to cry. "I've eliminated the obvious non-humans, they can't possibly be the special child you seek. I've already crossed them off the list."

"This is what I get for sending a simpleton to do a mage's job," the shadow spat in disgust. "I could have done as much if I didn't want found out!"

Her eyes flashed angrily, "Wait one stinking minute! You promised me a fee for finding that which you sought. Granted I didn't quite find it but I narrowed your search so I do deserve something!"

The shadow grew darker, "You want something for a job unfinished? Fine." The sound of fingers snapping could be heard through the mirror and suddenly Mrs. Quaid dropped the mirror she held. It fell to the floor and the glass shattered. "Oh!" she cried scattering to the floor to clean it up.

"BANG! BANG!" the door pounded loudly.

"Open up, Mrs. Quaid. We need to discuss this latest infraction." The principal stood outside her classroom door demanding to be let inside.

Mrs. Quaid swore loudly. She had planned to quit and run off with the money promised her in exchange for her finding that blasted child. However, now it seemed she'd have to kiss up a bit to save her job. She regretted taking the job in the first place but mostly she hated the child she'd been sent to find. This should have been easy money.

She was still cleaning up glass when the locked door came unlocked and swung open. The angry principal came in straight away. "What do you think you're doing?" Mr. Henderson demanded.

"At the moment, cleaning up this broken glass," she uttered sarcastically.

"What?" he asked, not quite hearing her.
She looked up, large fake tears coursing down her face, "I'm sorry! I just couldn't take it anymore!" Mrs. Quaid threw her hands up to cover her face feigning like she was really upset. "Those rotten kids are always doing something to me or my stuff. They keep destroying school property, stealing from me, they're constantly cheating on all their lessons! It was too much!" she pleaded.

The principal was still glaring at her, "Even if that is so, you could have come to someone rather than kicking the students out to wander the halls and disrupt the other classes!"

"I was at my wits end. You wouldn't do anything about them but send them back to me!" she shouted, her tears stopping at once.

Mr. Henderson just glared at her, "How dare you accuse me of turning a blind eye to student delinquency! If there was any truth to half the things you accuse, then why is no other instructor complaining similar or any of the honor students complaining about the interruptions in their lessons?" he queried, his voice deadly calm. "Furthermore, why is there no proof to your accusations?"

She looked at him wide-eyed; she was being accused of lying about everything. Who did he think he was? "How dare I? How dare you!" she yelled. "I thought a student kissing me was the worst of my troubles but apparently, I was wrong!" Mrs. Quaid turned away from him opening her desk to start gathering her things. There was no way she was going to beg for her job back now. She would just have to apply at another school.

The principal's purple face turned white in shock. He'd been told she was having trouble handling her class yet like he'd said, there was no proof of half of what she claimed. In fact, numerous student complaints about her claimed she made special tests for students she deemed needed the extra help while leaving other students to flounder. Some even complained that students that refused to do the work made better grades than those that actually did their assignments.

There were complaints from other instructors that one could hear her shouting so loud at her classes that it permeated the walls when her students were quiet. Now was different, the teacher in question was claiming a student had initiated a romantic relationship which was forbidden at this level and below. A relationship between an educator and student was one thing he just could not ignore.

"Clean out your desk immediately, Mrs. Quaid. I will personally escort you off school property and this will go in your employment file. Never let it be said that I sat back and let something like this take place under my watch!" Mr. Henderson's face was chalk white; he was beyond angry at this point. "I should never have hired an ill-qualified nut job to teach here!"

"Ill-qualified nut job?" So angry, she was seeing spots, Mrs. Quaid growled at the principal. "You insufferable pig! I've done nothing wrong!" she shouted at him. "Just you wait; you haven't heard the last from me! I'll have this whole school shut down!"

Mr. Henderson ignored her threats as she continued shouting all the way off school property. He had to call the police because Mrs. Quaid's behavior bordered on unruly as she was led from the school. However, Mr. Henderson did exactly as he said he would do and personally escorted Mrs. Quaid from the school property to ensure the crazed woman would not come into contact with another student.

Afterward, the principal noted the disgraced teacher's file and passed the word around about Mrs. Quaid. She would never teach at another school ever again.

As for Mrs. Quaid, her threats landed her in jail for a

time before she was released under the condition that she never darken the city of Demont with her ill-temper and presence again.

Of the students kicked out of class, Lucas and Lily were two of them. The pair found themselves wandering through the cemetery next to the school waiting for the next bell to ring signaling the end of the lesson. Lily was reading old headstones and grave markers looking for anything worthwhile.

"Lucas, look at this!" Lily exclaimed in surprise. Before her on the ground were grave markers with the family name of Daemione. The dates purported that if related, they must be ancestors.

Lucas glanced at the graves, confusion stealing through his mind. "What the..." he trailed. "My family has lived here for many generations is what my Father has always told us. This one here is my grandfather Dominic and my grandmother Marie." He was examining the grave markers around his grandparents. Lily joined him. It appeared that all of the grave markers in the area were members of the Daemione family with bunches from the same time periods.

"There are so many! Did you know your family used to be so large?"

"Actually, I didn't," Lucas responded, perplexed.

"Let's head over to the library and look it up. There's bound to be something there," Lily suggested.

"Sure, couldn't hurt and then I can ask my parents more about them. Maybe I have some relatives still alive," Lucas sounded hopeful. "Maybe Annabeth is a cousin after all?"

Looking through different volumes in the library, Lucas and Lily didn't find much. It wasn't until Lily asked the librarian, that they were handed a book on the most prominent families in Demont in the 2800s. The Daemione family dated back to the founding of the city itself with Lucas's great great great grandfather Desmond Daemione for whom the town was named. Demont had been a play on the demon heritage and Desmond's name.

Suddenly Lucas was interested in his family history.

If his father wouldn't give him answers, he would have to search for them himself! That afternoon, Lucas came home to find that his father was out of town yet again on business. Lucien hadn't even said so much as a goodbye or see you later to his wife and children.

Lucas wondered if his father's sudden departure had anything to do with their family history but dismissed the thought. Lucas only just discovered the information by chance that day. There couldn't possibly be any skeletons in his family closet.

His mother Anne was in the library reading like she normally did when his father was away. She never had much time to read when her husband was home. It didn't take Lucas long to tell his mother about the graves or the information he found at the library.

For her part, Anne didn't seem surprised. In fact, she was quite happy he was interested in his ancestry. "I had hoped your father would be here to show you this but," she paused, "we all know how his work schedule runs." Anne led her son to a section of their private library that seemed different than the rest.

The section was dusty as if it had not been touched in years strange as that might seem. The newly rebuilt manor had only been standing for about seven months. The shelf in the center of the section was blackened and looked like it came through a fire at some point. The books themselves looked singed but otherwise unharmed.

"What's going on?" Lucas asked, curious about this section that he didn't remember being in the library.

Anne laughed, "Ah, it is definitely time. Magic has protected this section of the library since before the manor burnt down."

"But I saw the manor after the fire! There was nothing left. How did the library on the second floor survive?" Lucas was eyeing the books and the shelf with amazement. "Wait, I've been in here a dozen times and have never once seen this section before. I think I would remember a burnt bookcase."

His mother did not touch the shelf or the books but

beckoned him to do so. "These books have been passed down from generation to generation. They are our family history. Of course, your ancestors found ways to protect their secrets and protect their legacies," Anne took a scroll from the wall and brought it to the lectern for perusing. "The shelf is hidden from view by anyone except someone of our blood and only when you seek the knowledge does it show itself."

Lucas followed his mother to the lectern, "What's that one?"

"This is our family tree. It magically updates itself when knowledge is made known to members of the family." Anne unrolled the scroll and laid it out flat scanning the document, "See here is Desmond Daemione. He was co-founder of Demont. And here on this side is the other co-founder Jason Deaumont."

"Wait, that traces down to you!" Lucas exclaimed. "Does that mean, Julie and I are descended from both founders?"

Anne laughed again, "Yes, it does. I was the first female born in the Deaumont line as far back as this tree goes. To be honest, there was a prophecy made in Desmond and Jason's time that purported that the two families would one day be one. It was the reason they settled and founded Demont. The two treated each other as brothers." Anne explained noticing a branch of the tree that did not exist the last time she saw the scroll.

The last time she'd looked at the scroll was just after Julie was born and the branch hadn't been there then. Before Lucas could see the new information, she rolled up the scroll and sent him off to do homework. "Lucas, you need to go do your homework. There will be plenty of time to look through this information later."

Though Lucas felt somewhat overwhelmed with the new information, he was excited that he would be learning more about his family history now. Granted, something else was bothering him. At the back of his mind, a small grain wormed through his defenses and he knew something else was wrong. Something was about to happen that would change everything and Lucas just wished he knew what it was.

CHAPTER 7

BODIES
(THE SCHOOL NEWSPAPER)

In the past, the school hosted a class to put together a short newspaper that was three to four pages long for the student population. The newspaper shared the goings on at the school from new students to sport information. There was even an advice column where students could write in and ask for advice. Of course, what newspaper would be complete without a community section that shared community related news as well.

At the end of the last school year, the principal and teacher in charge of the class decided that the newspaper didn't garner enough support among the student body and wasn't worth continuing. Of course, not everyone agreed with the decision.

Meagan Tiller was one such student. She loved the school newspaper but felt that the school could improve upon it in several ways. So when the school announced it would no longer be funding or publishing the papers, Meagan decided something needed to be done. She needed to get a staff together to work on an improved version of the paper and she needed sponsors within the community to fund the project.

"Hey, Lily!" called Meagan. Once upon a time, Meagan considered Lily her best friend. That had all been before Lucas enrolled. Now the two were lucky if they even spoke to each other once a week as their schedules permitted.

Lily jumped in surprise but smiled at her friend,

"Hello Meagan. How are you?" She'd been about to head to the library where she normally spent her lunch period away from everyone.

"Did you here about the bodies found at the pier?" she questioned, making small talk so she could lead into the discussion on reviving the newspaper.

"Yes, I heard the police are ruling the deaths a homicide given the number of bodies found. All of them were on a research team together, weren't they?" Lily responded, proving she was following the latest news in Demont.

"I know! Their families must be devastated!" Meagan exclaimed, pausing for a few seconds. "Hey, you know what would be really cool?"

"Hmm?" Lily murmured, a pencil in her mouth as she opened her locker.

"What if we started a newspaper here at the school and wrote about it to keep the student body up to date? I mean, it sounds like a serial killer or something," Meagan suggested, affecting an air of innocence.

"That would be awesome!" agreed Lily. "I know a couple people that might be interested in helping if you don't mind."

Meagan's smile was strained when she responded but she really wanted Lily involved in this. She wanted to reclaim her friend but that might mean putting up with some of Lily's strange friends until she could turn them against each other. "That's fine," she muttered. "Umm but only a couple, I've already got a full staff lined up."

That hadn't been entirely a lie. Meagan did make a list of who she wanted on the newspaper staff when she was given permission to re-create the newspaper. Of course, most of the students she wanted on staff were fairly popular and would guarantee interest and would also put Meagan in more popular social circles.

Lily was excited about the revamped newspaper. She and Meagan once shared a journalism class as first years when they came over to secondary school from primary. The two friends enjoyed the class with Dr. Logan so Lily was confident that they would be able to produce a great newspaper.

She didn't know who Meagan asked to join the staff but Lily intended on asking Danah to help some by illustrating certain articles and sections of the paper.

The downside was that Danah was home-schooled, given her predicament, and that might make things a bit difficult. Lily's sister couldn't very well go out during the day and sometimes the moonlight bothered her as well. The plight of vampires really was understated and morbidly exaggerated on some fronts.

Jonah might be interested in the newspaper. It was one way to get his name out there and possibly to give him more popularity. That was Jonah's greatest desire: to be popular among his peers. Lily thought about asking Lucas to join but wasn't sure. The demon already had a lot on his plate with his music competitions and experiments.

That evening Lily talked to Danah about joining the newspaper staff as an artist. The vampire girl agreed enthusiastically before suggesting they ask Annabeth. Lily only smiled knowingly in response: Annabeth was the first person she asked.

It took two weeks before Meagan produced a list of staff members. Lily and Meagan were to be co-editors with Mrs. Tuttle being their teacher sponsor, a requirement by the principal when they took on the task.

Lily's eyes bulged when she looked over the list. Half of the students weren't even passing let alone intelligent enough to write articles. Lily gave them the benefit of the doubt for her friend's sake. It didn't help Meagan's cause when only two of the six students showed up for the first official meeting of the newspaper staff. More surprising was that not only did Jonah show up but also Lucas and Annabeth. Since Danah wasn't in school, Lily managed to bring some of her sample artwork for Meagan's approval.

Meagan grumbled about everything at the meeting and forced all 'potential' staff members to fill out forms detailing their schedules, contact information, ideas they might have for the paper, and articles they might be interested in writing. Personally, Lily, felt she was going a bit overboard with all the information sharing but she didn't say anything in front of everyone.

"Look, all I'm saying is that you don't need to know their class schedule or where they live to decide whether or not they can be on the staff. None of that should matter," Lily protested after everyone left.

"Honestly, Lily. What if we need them out of class during the day to work on newspaper stuff? Or they get sick before a deadline and we have to travel to their house to pick up their article? You never know," she explained, treating Lily as if she were stupid.

One of the reasons, the pair had drifted apart in the first place was Meagan's tendency to treat Lily like an idiot all the time. Lily gritted her teeth. Another reason was Meagan's constant need to be right no matter that no one agreed with her. Sifting through the papers, Lily pulled out two that were incomplete and started to throw them away.

"What are you doing ?" yelped Meagan snatching the papers from Lily's hand.

"You said they had to fill out the forms completely or they couldn't be on the staff. They didn't finish filling them out." Lily grabbed a paper back and laughed, "This one couldn't even spell 'lunch'." Lily just shook her head.

Meagan glanced through the rest of the forms, noticing that Lily's other friends had done exactly as they'd been asked. She almost groaned out loud. She was being a stickler for the sole sake of eliminating them before the newspaper even got off the ground.

Two weeks later, Meagan and Lily mustered enough sponsors to support the new school paper. All the pair had to do was put small advertisements in the newspaper for the student body and educational staff to see. It wasn't really a bad deal. Meagan decided to ditch her two staffers and replace them with three who claimed to actually want to be a part of the newspaper staff. Only time would tell if Lewis, Mandy, and Brian would last.

"I think we should assign that Daemione boy the music section since he's into that type of thing," Meagan suggested. The girl had a bigger problem with Lucas than she did anyone else.

"That sounds good but we should let Lucas write some informative pieces every now and then too. Annabeth would be great with community events - she's so involved in everything!" Lily volunteered.

"Fair enough. What about Jonah?" Meagan asked.

"Well, he's always hanging around different groups and knows all the latest gossip. Why not put him in charge of the 'What's Going On' section? You know so he can do the rumor mill column," Lily rolled her eyes, "and announcements about good grades and attendance."

Meagan smiled, "Sounds like a plan! I'm going to put Lewis in charge of the sports section. He is an athlete, after all." She was practically drooling just thinking of the boy.

"Is he even going to have time with all the sports he's in?" Lily questioned, writing down everything so they'd have it for later.

"Give it a rest," Meagan answered quickly, "He'll have plenty of time and if he needs any help then I'll happily be available." A goofy grin was plastered across her face.

Lily laughed, "I suppose that if he needs a girlfriend, you'll be available for that too?"

Meagan glared at Lily. "Ha ha!" she said sarcastically. "At least, I'm not in denial about why I want a cute guy like Lewis on the staff."

"I only asked people that I felt had a shot of writing decent articles. Not my fault I happen to like one of them. Besides, I thought you liked Daniel?" Lily questioned.

"I do but I'm getting no where with him. I think it's too soon," Meagan answered, her entire demeanor reflecting hurt.

"Too soon!" exclaimed Lily. "We split up more than a year and a half ago!"

Meagan nodded glumly, "I know but he just doesn't seem to notice me. I think he's still hung up on you."

Lily shook her head, "I don't see why he should be. Us splitting up was his idea." Shrugging, Lily wrote down the other sections needed for the newspaper. "Who do you want to give the holiday and birthday sections?"

"How about Mandy? She's really enthusiastic," Meagan grimaced. "And Mandy knows just about everyone!"

"If you say so," Lily agreed. "That just leaves the community news, advice column, 'who's who', staff section, and the other school events page. I'm not to keen on school events so I guess I'll take the advice column and the 'who's who'. What do you want?"

Meagan smiled, "I'll take the community news and staff section. Brian can have the other school events." She hesitated and looked uneasy. "There was one more thing I wanted to talk to you about. I think we should ask Marcus to take pictures for us since your sister doesn't go to school here." Meagan eyed Lily to check her reaction. "Besides, you said Danah was most talented in drawing things. We can have her illustrate the stuff that doesn't have pictures."

Lily shrugged. "That sounds fair," she agreed. "Better than fair, Meagan. Thank you for giving her a chance. It means the world to Danah and me." Lily was sincere about that. Danah didn't have friends except for Lily's friends that came to the cavern and she couldn't just go out and meet new people. This was a step in the positive direction for her little sister. "When's the next meeting?" She was cleaning up her mess and putting her notes away.

"About that," Meagan winced, looking at the clock.

Sighing loudly, Lily put her notes back out. "It's right now, isn't it?"

"I figured we were already up here so we might as well." the other girl offered by way of explanation. "Besides, you didn't have anything better to do."

Jonah and Annabeth walked in together talking amicably. If only Lucas and Jonah could get along that well. A minute later, Lucas rushed in carrying an instrument case. "Sorry, almost couldn't make it!" he apologized.

Lewis, Mandy, and Brian came in shortly after chatting like they hadn't a care in the world. And maybe they didn't. All three were humans like Meagan. They didn't have to suffer the prejudices of others if they found out.

"Great, everyone's here. We'll have to catch Marcus later," Lily started before the boy in question walked through the door. Not for the first time, Lily wondered if she was really the co-editor or just another puppet with Meagan pulling the strings.

"Okay, welcome to the newspaper staff everyone!" Meagan said enthusiastically. "I'm happy each of you could make it. Lily and I have met and discussed where each of you would serve the paper best so here are your assignments for the first issue." Meagan handed the assignments to Lily to pass out.

"Assignments are due at the beginning of each week so we have time to put everything together and get it approved prior to the printing at the end of the week. If you have a problem with the deadline or need assistance, contact one of us," Lily said, passing the papers around. "And we will try to help. Are there any questions?"

"So do we get paid for this?" Brian asked, examining his finger nails. The boy actually came from a family with a lot of money and often flaunted that fact.

Lily closed her eyes and took a deep breath. "No, we do not, Brian," Lily smiled and turned to Meagan. "Let's make this a little simpler! Brian, Mandy, and Lewis, you three have been assigned to Meagan. Any questions you have, please feel free to ask her." She nodded her head and smiled. The three didn't seem bothered by the new plan. "And I'll take Annabeth, Jonah, and Lucas under my wings." She spread her arms wide to imitate actual wings. "This way, neither of us should be too overwhelmed."

Meagan's smile could not have gotten any bigger. "That sounds like a plan!" she agreed wholeheartedly. "Oh, and we've included examples of what kind of articles we're looking forward to reading from everyone. Are there any other questions?"

"Actually, yes! Are we going to cover the recent murders at the pier?" Annabeth questioned. She looked genuinely interested in the answer and possibly the actual murders as well.

"I was wondering the same thing," Marcus asked. 'I could go down there and get some pictures or something."

Lily looked to Meagan for an answer but she didn't

miss the look on Jonah's face. Rather, Lily saw the look in his eyes that told another story altogether. Jonah had seen or heard something important with regards to the murders.

Meagan revealed that she was going after the meeting to speak with detectives about the investigation and would be writing an article to go in their first edition of the newspaper. She was excited and wished everyone luck on their first assignments.

"We'll meet again the same time next week," Lily announced. "See you all later." She smiled at everyone warmly as she dismissed them. Meagan had a meeting to make and Lily needed to talk to Jonah and get him to open up about what he knew.

"Spill the beans!" she commanded softly. "I know you know something."

Jonah shook his head, "I never could hide anything from you."

Lily smiled, "I'm fairly good at reading people but you had that look in your eyes. What's going on? What do you know?"

"It's just that group of people they found were investigating the 'Great Fire'. Their leader interviewed me about what I knew," Jonah revealed evenly. "They were poisoned because of what they knew. Someone is searching and he doesn't want anyone getting out a warning."

"Vision?" Lily asked.

Jonah nodded. "We better let Christine know."

CHAPTER 8

RESTRICTIONS
(SCHOOL YARD PRANK)

Lucas loved practical jokes, more often known as pranks when he was involved. The demon boy never had much reason to laugh and felt it was only fitting to make something to laugh about. The pranks were harmless and generally garnered laughter from everyone involved and not involved. Of course there were exceptions, like certain school officials when he pulled a prank that resulted in school being canceled.

His most recent prank involved a combination of snow and water. Lucas was trying to block all routes to the school by building snow blocks around the entrances and exits. That alone wasn't enough to get school canceled so he also intended to water the snow blocks so the snow would turn to solid ice. The city and school would spend days trying to tear all of them down unless the weather suddenly warmed up again.

"You're going to get in trouble!" Lily warned.

Lucas smiled, "No we won't, promise."

Lily blinked owlishly. "Wait!" she cried out. "'We'? I'm not helping you with this." Lily was bundled up in a somewhat heavy coat complete with a knitted scarf, probably made by Danah.

The demon boy on the other hand was not. His body temperature tended to run a little higher than normal humans and most of the non-humans as well. Fortunately, his wings did look like a cloak draped across his shoulders so he didn't have to worry about looking odd without any protection from the cold weather. "It's okay, I'm not asking for your help. I enlisted others," Lucas smiled mischievously.

"We're here monkey!" called out Jonah, stepping into view with Danah and Annabeth.

Lily glared back and forth between Lucas and Jonah, "What have you two juveniles gotten my sister into?"

"Lighten up, Lil," Danah chimed in. "I wanted to do this. Besides, I'm free for the night if only for a few hours." Danah rarely left the safety of the cavern, far enough underground to protect herself from the harsh rays of the sunlight and occasionally the moon. Tonight, the moon was over shadowed by numerous clouds which just meant that Danah was safe from the harmful rays for now.

Lily sighed. "Fine, let's get this over with so we can get out of here quicker." Like her companions, she started small with a snowball that she rolled into something larger. If one didn't know better, they would assume the group was making snowmen.

The large snowballs, they moved in front of all the entrances of the secondary school. The group piled the snowballs three layers thick and at least six layers high. When they were finished putting snowballs on top, they started shoving snow in the holes to make the snow block more solid.

The snow almost touched the roof of the school before Lucas began spraying the blocks with water. It didn't take too much water or too much time really before all eight entrances and exits were completely blocked. However, blocking the doors with snow had taken quite a bit of their time and light was starting to permeate their lovely overcast night. It would not be long before morning overtook the night.

"Talk later, okay?" Lily suggested. "Home, now!" She pulled her sister to her side and took off. Lily did not want to take any chances.

Jonah and Annabeth took off in the opposite direction toward their own homes while Lucas chased after Lily and Danah. Generally, Lily traveled in the same direction as Lucas and cut off into Flamewood Forest right before they reached his house. This time, Lily and Danah cut into the forest much sooner, racing the clock to get Danah back underground before the light cleared the clouds.

Lucas followed right behind them, not intending on going home. He'd lied to his parents the night before and told them he was spending the night at Jonah's place. If only the faerie knew, Jonah would have a fit. The demon boy wasn't above lying every once and awhile. Lucas was careful about when he did lie as he didn't want to make it a serious habit. To be honest, his mother knew exactly where he planned on being that night. It was his father that he'd lied to.

Though he hadn't mustered the courage to tell his best friend the truth: Lucas's father hated Lily. Lucien thought there was something off about her. The older demon ordered his son to find a new friend claiming Lily was a bad influence.

The whole argument had been weird especially when you took in that Lucas's grades were the best they had been in years. His homework was always finished on time. Lucas even found time to write articles in the school paper thanks to his friendship with Lily and non-friendship with Jonah. Lucas was even participating in more music concerts thanks to extra time spent practicing. The young demon was staying out of trouble mostly.

Lucas did not understand where his father got the notion that Lily was bad. The whole mess was unnerving and Lucas refused to give up his first real friend because his father hated her. So, the demon talked it over with his mother while Lucien was out of town. Anne would keep his secret and even help him from time to time when needed. She held a better opinion of Lily.

Lucas could never invite Lily back to the Manor again and he had to pretend he was going to see Jonah when he really was going to see her. Sometimes, he told the truth and was rewarded with dark looks from his father and rude comments about his choices in life.

The demon had taken to hiding out in the family library to read about his ancestry in spare time. He was so excited about what he was learning, he started hanging out with his friends less and less. The prank had actually been a way to give them more time together. And blow off some steam.

When the three arrived back in the darkness of the cavern, Lily turned on her best friend. "You could have got her killed!" Lily railed at Lucas much to his surprise.

"Killed? How do you figure? It was just a harmless prank that will get us out of school for a few days," he replied perplexed at his best friend's anger. "I asked her to help so we could all spend more time together since we hardly get to spend more than a couple hours a week with each other. I thought you'd be happy about it all!"

Lily started to retort when Danah interrupted her.

"It's okay, Lily. I'm fine, really!" Danah piped up. She put her hand on Lily's shoulder to calm the other girl down.

Lily shook her head, "That's not the point! You could have died today." She looked forlornly at her sister. "I don't know what I'd do if anything happened to you." Lily hugged Danah.

Lucas just stared at the two, a bit confused. "What is she allergic to the cold or something?"

Stepping back away from Lily, Danah stared at the demon boy confused. "You mean you don't know?" she asked looking between him and her sister.

"I never told him. It was your secret to tell, not mine," Lily answered for Lucas. "I don't want people treating you differently because of what you are." Only Lily could look angry and guilty both at the same time.

"Ah, now I get it. You must be a vampire," Lucas was watching the pair closely. "Makes sense as to why you're not in school with the rest of us. I thought vampires were safe after dark though." He sat on the couch and made himself comfortable. He had a lot of questions to ask Danah. If Lucas was lucky, he'd find out what non-human Lily was.

Danah frowned, "Not entirely. The moonlight can hurt us too. I rarely get to leave the cavern unless the moon is covered by clouds like last night. Cissy and Lily are really protective and they tend to overreact to every little thing though," she glared at her sister.

Lily stuck out her tongue. "We are only trying to protect you. There's nothing wrong with wanting to protect your family. In any case, Cissy has a book on vampires in her library if you want to know more."

Lucas rolled his eyes, "Most of that stuff is tripe! You can't ever find a book that tells the truth about the different non-humans."

"You'll find hers are quite accurate," Lily laughed nervously. "Cissy only took up potion making about twenty-eight years ago. Before that she was a Historian Mage. Of course, she had to research the potions first and she's improved on a great number but her real passion is researching the different species of non-humans."

"Seriously?" Lucas questioned. "Haha, I bet she'd go wild if she ever got her hands on a phoenix!"

Lily and Danah both grimaced. "You have no idea." Danah responded.

"What's it like living with her? I mean, Christine has to have potions for everything, doesn't she?" Lucas asked enthusiastically.

"Not everything," Danah answered. "She doesn't have a potion for me to go out in the light."

It was Lucas's turn to look guilty. He quickly apologized and decided it was time to stop asking questions to keep from putting his foot back in his mouth.

"I'm going to go lay down for a few hours," Lily interrupted the awkward silence. She left the large cavern to return to her room wondering what she was going to do. Sooner or later, Lily would have to share her secret with Lucas.

School ended up being closed for three days while city officials worked to break down the ice blocks. By the end of the second day, they had to call in mages to melt the ice using weather magic. Unfortunately, that meant another heat wave brought on by weather magic gone awry. Lucas almost regretted his prank. Almost.

In the end, he learned a great deal about vampires through Danah and Christine's books. Lucas even borrowed some of Christine's books on demons to peruse at a later time.

In return, Christine wanted to study more about demons via him. Lucas told her that he was fine being a research subject so long as she didn't start poking and prodding him with needles.

It was another hot afternoon when Jonah walked up grumbling about how the heat was melting the colored wax in his hair. The faerie loved coloring his own hair but didn't want anything permanent as he changed his mind too much. Jonah used different colored waxes and spiked his hair every morning. The day before, his hair had been red and today it was blue. "You'd think they'd have perfected the weather spells by now as many times as they've had to fix your messes!"

"It's not that simple, Jonah," Lily said. "Weather magic falls under elemental magic and requires the mastery of at least two elements: sky and water. According to Cissy, two elements aren't even enough and three or four would be best when practicing weather magic but it's almost impossible to master beyond two elements."

"Thank you, Ms. Encyclopedia," Jonah responded sarcastically. "Now that we've got that nifty little lesson on elemental magic under our belts, let's retreat to our corners and get started trying to master the elements."
He rolled his eyes.

Lily blushed and looked toward the ground. She was great at standing up for her family or even her friends but Lily could not stand up for herself if her life depended on it.

Lucas, on the other hand, glared at Jonah. "Some of us like hearing about magic and we don't think she's an encyclopedia either! Now if you wish to remain ignorant, you can leave," he said harshly to the faerie. "Before I make you."

Jonah shrugged and walked away. "Not worth it," he muttered under his breath.

The demon turned to Lily, "Don't worry about him, Lil. He's a stupid jerk and his opinion doesn't matter one bit!"

Lily smiled sadly, "It's fine. Sometimes I'm just over sensitive." The red in her cheeks faded a little. "Did you know I used to be home-schooled like Danah? Yes and then when I started school, I had trouble keeping friends. I can't exactly go to friend's houses or bring many people home. Given what we are," Lily was testing Lucas. She needed to know she could trust him with her secret.

Lucas nodded. "Story of my life!" he agreed wholeheartedly. "Why don't we get out of here? I have an idea for the newspaper and I wanted to show you."

"Sure. Where to, your highness?" Lily mocked playfully.

"To our secret spot!" he crowed triumphantly as Lucas headed toward the old auditorium building. Lucas's idea involved his family history and the history of Demont itself. He borrowed a couple books from home that he intended to show Lily.

He just hoped he didn't get caught because his dad specifically told him the books could not leave the house. The older demon warned that the magic protecting the books inside the manor didn't work on the books if they were taken out of the manor. With a little bit of perfect timing and a whole lot of luck, Lucas could get the books back before anyone noticed.

"I don't know," Lily said after he explained his idea and showed her his sources. "I mean, writing this article could expose us all as non-humans or at the very least your entire family. It doesn't sound like a very good risk."

"People need to know the truth about this town though and the truth about all of these cities. They need to know that our ancestors were the founders of this world and we shouldn't have to hide in the shadows cowering to the humans in charge!" the demon boy argued.

Lily shook her head sadly. "It's not so easy. The Council is working with the humans to bring equality to Jodacai a little at a time. Too much, too soon will only scare everyone involved. No one wants another massacre like the Phoenix Wars."

Lucas shrugged, not really agreeing or disagreeing.

"Look," she said, taking his hands. "One day, the world will know what we are and we won't have to fear what they might do to us."

"I'll be waiting for that day," Lucas responded, the

same serious look in his eyes.

The pair stood that way for a moment more before Lily blinked and quickly let his hands go. She stepped back away from her best friend. "I think the school could deal with a toned down version of the history. Maybe, we could have a series of articles about the history?" she suggested. "But I'd leave out any non-human or human references for now, anyway."

Lucas nodded. Now he just had to get the books back home and into the library before his parents noticed.

When the young demon returned home, he couldn't find either parent. Lucas assumed his mother was out and that his father wasn't back from his business trip yet. It was the perfect time to return the books. The library seemed empty so Lucas crept to the magically safe-guarded section of the library, his school pack in hand. Just as he was pulling the first book from his pack, the deadly calm voice of his father made him pause.

"And just what do you think you're doing, young man?"

Lucas winced, his timing hadn't been so good after all. He would have done better to invite Lily over while his father was away on business if his mother didn't protest him sharing their family history so much. "I was just putting them back."

"I can't believe you would be so irresponsible!" railed Lucien. The older demon was red in the face from shouting. "Taking those books from the library where they are safe and protected! You could have exposed our entire family if anyone had seen them!" Lucien's eyes narrowed, "Did they?"

"I only wanted to keep reading and I couldn't stay in here all night and day!" Lucas tried to explain.

"Did anyone see the book, boy?" his father growled.

Lucas rolled his eyes, resentfully. "No," he grumbled. There was no telling what he parents might do if they knew the truth.

"It doesn't matter. We told you the books could not leave the manor and should not leave the library! This is the only place they are protected and you deliberately disobeyed!

I'll bet it was for that stupid girl! You're not allowed to see her and this time I mean it!" Lucien declared.

Lucas started to protest that Lily had nothing do with his actions but at the mention of Lily's name, Lucien's eyes flashed dangerously. Only his father could make the connection without there being any mention of Lily. He didn't understand why the older demon hated his best friend so much. Lily helped him with his school work often making it easier for him to understand. Thanks to his best friend, he was writing articles for a school newspaper! So why then did Lucien hate such a helpful person?

"And you're not going to see Jonah either," Anne added, all humor gone. She'd gone out on a limb for him. "You're grounded, young man and no amount of excuses or apologies will suffice here. You're to go straight to school and come straight home."

"What about my music competitions?" he protested. Lucas had been looking forward to the events since he started at Demont. His last school wasn't nearly as involved in the arts as Demont Secondary. For that reason alone, Lucas was glad his parents forced him to come back to this place.

Anne started to retort that he should have thought about the competitions before he disobeyed them but Lucien stopped her. "No, he can go to that. After all, it was a prior engagement that will better his future." He smiled maliciously, "Besides, that girl will not be there and unless I'm mistaken neither will that faerie," he answered, his voice full of disgust. "Time out of school and away from that pair.

Lucas was going to be miserable until the grounding was lifted.

CHAPTER 9

CREEP
(SCIENCE OF MAGIC)

Christine spent many sleepless nights thinking about the different talents she and her charges possessed and how better to understand them. Of course, it wasn't just her charges for which she was curious about. Thanks to Lily, she now had a demon and a half-ling within her power as well.

The inquisitive mage read all the books -both the accurate and the not-so-accurate. The more accurate books were informative but still lacked something that she couldn't quite put her finger on. So to make up for the missing pieces, she decided to study the other non-humans separately to discover the secrets of each species. She published her own findings for her very private library. Sometimes, she even loaned the books out to people.

Today, she was experimenting to find a cure for Danah's problems. Unfortunately, Danah was a vampire. Unlike the vampire lore brought over from the old Earth, Danah could not change into a bat nor any other creature. Nor was she highly sensitive to garlic or crucifixes. The rubbish brought forth by the humans was ridiculous. Holy water or any water, for that matter, did nothing but get the vampire girl wet.

Danah did need blood regularly as her body could not produce it as regular humans or other non-humans did. Generally, Christine acquired blood through her underground business dealings when necessary. It was much easier than 'borrowing' blood from humans whenever she required it. And a lot safer since non-human blood was potentially fatal. Non-human blood did not mix well with other non-human blood unless the species were the same.

It seemed that of all the twisted rumors and legends about vampires, at least one held true in it's entirety: the sun was to be feared.

Vampires were highly allergic to the sun. Their skin burned and blistered depending on how long they were exposed to it. If outside for too long, the burning blisters opened to bleeding masses of pain. Eventually, the vampire afflicted died a slow painful death. So naturally, most vampires chose to live indoors during the day and came out sparingly at night.

Some vampires, like Danah, were even sensitive to the moon light. For her entire life, Danah lived away from the sun and moon. Truly, she'd led a lonely life except for Christine and Lily.

Danah wanted to be normal or at least as normal as possible. She wanted to go to school with Lily, Annabeth, Lucas, and Jonah. More than anything, she just wanted to be free to wander wherever no matter the time of day or night.

Other mages and non-humans alike had tried to find a cure for the light problem for years but no one had ever been successful. Granted, the research was currently banned by the human government. They figured that by keeping the vampires in the dark, they would be better protected.

Banning the research only caused more mages to search for a cure; however, no one came close to solving the problem at hand. Christine had already spent more time than any other on finding a remedy for Danah's problem. Her work did get much easier when she stopped trying to find a permanent solution and moved to just trying to find a temporary solution. Maybe that was where everyone else tended to go wrong.

That same day, frustration poured from Lily in waves. They'd gotten a substitute in her favorite science class this week to fill in for Dr. Saffron while he was away for a conference. The new instructor had no love for anyone remotely different. Unfortunately, that meant most of her friends who could not hide the fact that they were different were singled out and picked on one way or another.

Oh, the instructor never made mention of how they were different or even that they were different at all because he'd found ways around that. He singled them out for imagined infractions and minuscule mistakes found in their lessons for the week.

What made matters worse was that Lucas, aside from being a demon, was a musical prodigy! Granted, that was great for Lucas. It just wasn't so great for Lily because it meant she had to face Mr. Pikeron all alone.

Lucas was away for the week doing concerts for Demont Secondary with other musical adept students in the neighbor city of Yashae. The superintendent of students was trying her best to improve Demont's reputation by showing how truly gifted the students here were.

At the moment, Lily hated the superintendent.

Lily hated Mr. Pikeron more than she thought possible because she knew that he was not a normal human like he pretended. Lily was gifted at seeing beyond appearances - you could call it a gift of her own heritage. She often had to study someone for a time to discern what exactly they were but she could always tell right away when the person was normal or not. And Mr. Pikeron was far from human.

Right away, he'd singled Lily out but Lily's secret was so closely guarded, there was no way he could know what she was. In fact, Lily had never even shared her secret with Lucas, her best friend. Granted, she did hang around with non-humans.

What exactly was Mr. Pikeron's problem and what was he doing in Demont?

When the bell sounded, Lily looked up to see that the instructor was staring at her again with something akin to anger on his face. She flinched and gathered her things, shoving them into her bag as fast as she could. It didn't matter that she'd been quick; she still managed to be the last student out.

Mr. Pikeron had enough time to make his way to the

door before Lily could escape. "All alone?" he whispered.

A chill went down Lily's spine and she didn't respond out loud.

"You should be more careful so someone doesn't snatch you," he continued maliciously as she passed.

Lily's heart raced as she practically flew from the room. Her first instinct was to get home but even with her thoughts jumbled, she knew better than to let it show that the crazy remark the substitute uttered had affected her.
Did he know about the secret she guarded so closely?

Lily went to her next class and continued the rest of her lessons. That afternoon, she asked Jonah to walk home with her, not willing to be caught unawares.

Christine was working in the lab when Lily came in. She had meant to tell Christine everything but instead got caught up in helping her sister. "Why not use these?" Lily asked, holding up a small vial with a silvery substance in it.

Christine glanced at the vial, puzzlement crossing her face. "That only works for healing open wounds." She was shaking her head.

"Only if it's from the human form," Lily argued. "These are from the original form, aren't they?

"Yes, they are," Christine answered, a frown on her face.

"Besides, even in human form, the tears collected heal the mind and that's not exactly an open wound," Lily argued.

"No, the mind is another matter altogether and nightmares brought on by real life events is an open wound of the mind."

"Yeah but maybe by using these in the formula, you can prevent the outside wound from manifesting altogether?" Lily reasoned.

Christine looked thoughtful, "Hmm, I never thought of it that way." She started scribbling furiously in her journal, marking figures and outcomes. "Indeed, an interesting experiment. Is Danah up to a test?"

"If it'll allow me to go to school with Lily and Annabeth, then yes!" piped up the little vampire. "How come no one else has worked on a day walker formula for vampires like me?" she asked curiously.

Lily frowned and looked to Christine expectantly. "I suspect that it has more to do with people being afraid you'll drink them dry of their blood. Silly superstitious humans don't understand you have other means of getting sustenance and needn't drain a person of all their blood just to survive."

Christine was grumbling while she mixed together different ingredients. Finally, she stepped back just a little and added a single drop of the silvery liquid. Quick as lightning, she threw up an umbrella type shield to protect her two charges and herself in case of an explosion.

"That's why they invented stakes and made up the exaggerated rumors of holy water and garlic. Let's not forget the stake through the heart!" Lily added, picking up a stick and miming like she'd been stabbed through the heart.

"No, those two specific instances only originated because humans came across vampires allergic to water and another vampire allergic to garlic," Christine responded with distaste. "As for a stake through the heart, that would kill anyone."

When there was no explosion, Christine took the umbrella shield down and eyed the concoction in front of her. It was a pale flesh color and Christine hoped it would be what she'd been working toward all along. She swished the concoction around a little in the beaker before sniffing it. Taking a syringe from the drawer below the table, Christine carefully extracted a very small portion from the beaker.

"Wait!" Lily exclaimed. "How do you know that won't kill her?" she was almost frantic.
Startled, Danah stepped back away from both of her siblings.

Christine merely shook her head, "I've been testing her for the last few months with the different ingredients in preparation for the different concoctions I was going to have her try. None of them are harmful to her. Not to mention, the last ingredient should be more than sufficient enough to ensure she won't die from this," she answered matter-of-factually.

Lily and Danah both eyed her skeptically.

"Plus," Christine added, "if this potion works, she'll be able to live a normal life!"

"Mostly normal life," Danah piped up again. "I still have to have blood at least twice a week." She held out her right arm for her sister to try.

Christine grabbed Danah's arm, turning it this way and that before dropping it and reaching for the other. "The veins in this one won't do," she uttered and Danah offered her other arm. When Christine found one she liked for the shot, she carefully sterilized her arm and then injected the sample amount into Danah's arm. "You'll need to feed soon."

Danah nodded slightly. "How will I know if it works?" asked Danah hopefully.

Lily hugged her sister. "Give the stuff time to work through your system, little sister. Then I'm sure Cissy has a whole slew of tests to perform over a period of time so that we know you'll be safe out in the sun with us," Lily answered, imitating Christine.

Christine glared at Lily briefly before her expression softened turning to Danah, "She's right. We have to make sure your body can tolerate the sun before you can start leaving during the day. I also need to find out how long it lasts before you have to have another dose of this stuff or if it even works at all. My figures say it will work but you never know till you try it."

"It should be in her system by now, right Cissy? Can we check her now?" Lily begged, clearly excited that Danah might get to go outside.

Christine just rolled her eyes, "It's already dark outside and there's no moon tonight. There is no way we will know till tomorrow. We'll go early, when the light isn't too bright." When the other two girls groaned, she just shook her head. "It's for the best because the potion will have a full night to get in her system and should be more potent."

The two nodded and started to leave before Christine called them back. "I don't think so, you two!" she nearly growled. "I know what that look means and you're not doing it! I need to be present when she goes out in daylight and even still, we have to do it in slow doses otherwise it could cause irreparable harm even with the special ingredient that we added."

"Yes, ma'am," Lily replied cheekily.

Christine glared. "Go to bed!" she told Lily. "Oh and Danah, to answer your question: People have been trying to find a cure for this problem for as long as I've been alive. Probably longer still. Unless this works, we'll still be searching. I won't give up though."

Danah nodded in understanding, a sad look on her face. "Good night, Cissy," she said before heading from the room after Lily.

While Christine cleaned up the lab, both Danah and Lily made their way to the very back of the cavern where a few large extensions had been made to form rooms underground. The whole cavern was natural with a few man-made parts to help the little family along. Of course, a bit of magic had been used to ensure the whole thing wouldn't collapse on them. It was quite the unusual place for people to live but the family of three was anything but usual. It was perfect for just them.

Christine was a stickler for procedure. She didn't leave anything to chance and everything was carefully thought out and planned before anyone had a chance to jump right in. Before she'd come to live there with Danah and Lily, Christine had been among a group of mages that did as they pleased and encouraged others of their kind to do the same. While Christine had never agreed, she wasn't keen to be caught all alone by those unkind to mages. So she stayed with the other mages for protection of sorts.

Unfortunately, since the mages neither planned nor thought their actions through, most ended up caught by a group of magic-hating humans or dead by their own experiments. Christine, on the other hand, had always been careful.

Her time with the other mages ended when a young mage apprenticed to her wound up dead due to the actions of the rest of the group. Christine tried to teach the young one the right way to do things with forethought and knowledge. The young one chose to listen to the other mages instead.

Christine denounced the other mages for their actions and left them forever behind to start again. It angered a lot of the ones left but most if not all were dead now because of their actions.

Somehow or another, Christine came across a badly injured vampire orphan in her travels after her fellowship with the mages. She took Danah in without question and has been caring for her ever since.

The two traveled all around Jodacai before Christine was called to Demont where she found a young Lily without guardians and more or less living on her own. Quite familiar with the area because Lily lived with a caravan of faeries for a time, Lily knew of the caverns hidden safely in the mountains and beneath the lake.

Though the three acted as sisters, Christine was more like a mother to them than anyone ever could be. Here they all were: Christine the planner, Lily the compassionate, and Danah the shy one. Christine took care of them all, making medicines and potions designed to help people. She ran a pharmacy for normal humans and non-humans alike.

That night, when Lily laid her head down to sleep, she remembered that she forgot to tell her sister about the creepy substitute and what he had said to her. By that time, she was far too comfortable in her own bed to get up. Lily told herself that she would tell Christine in the morning. With any luck, Lucas would be back soon and she wouldn't feel so alone.

CHAPTER 10

BLOOD
(CAUSE OF DEATH)

Meagan really outdone herself on her community news article plastered across the front page of the school newspaper. There had been no updates to the case of the five bodies found at the pier since the story originally broke.

After weeks of begging, Lily did share with Meagan what she knew about the five being investigators hired to investigate the Great Fire. Meagan hadn't even uttered a thank you before she went on her way interviewing people that could confirm the information.

Imagine Meagan's luck that she would contact the investigators responsible for finding out about the murders on the day their cause of death was released. In truth, luck had little to do with it because Meagan contacted them every day - sometimes, twice a day.

All five victims died with traces of Vampire's Curse in their system. There was clearly an epidemic in Demont - someone was using the most powerful and lethal poison in Jodacai to kill people. Rather, someone was killing off non-humans. A sixth victim - a student - turned up in the quad after school let out the day of the article.

Making use of vampire's blood, the poison was banned more than a decade beforehand when it was used to kill high ranking officials believed to be humans. At the time, humans were lead to believe it was a poison for humans too.

Later it was discovered, the poison was only lethal to non-humans. Normal humans experienced stomach pains among other symptoms but recovered with medical care and time.

Generally, the Vampire's Curse poison was ingested in one's food or drink. Due to the amount of time it took for the first five bodies to be found, it was unknown how the first five victims were given the poison but the sixth student was found to have food tampered with prior to ingestion.

Patty Daiglow, a fourth year shape-shifter, ate her lunch like normal but never left her table when it was time to go to class. The poison weakened her until she put her head down and closed her eyes like in slumber. She never woke up again. The poison took just long enough so that she was alone when she died.

It was cruel.

Patty had her whole life ahead of her but now she would never marry or have children of her own. Her parents would have to bury their daughter and a community would be mourning one of their youth. Part of their future.

The worst part was that it revealed to those familiar with the poison, that the Daiglows were not normal humans. Exposed, the mourning parents fled Demont after the news story about the poison broke.

For those that didn't know the connection, they saw the murders as a threat and tightened security around the school. Students started bringing their own lunches from home not wishing to be another victim of the killer.

Strangely, Meagan assigned the article about Patty to Lily. For her part, Lily interviewed Patty's parents and her friends and wrote a beautiful if not heartbreaking article to memorialize the young shape-shifter taken too soon. No parent should have to bury their own child. It just wasn't the natural order of things.

With one student dead and five adults dead, it only seemed to be getting worse. People were panicking. "Christine, you have to pull her out!" Dr. Saffron called, coming into the main room of the cavern.

"What are you talking about?" Christine asked the dragon, confused. The mage tended to stay to herself in the cavern with Danah and Lily. She only ever came up to run the local pharmacy. Most of the time, she left that to hired help. Christine had anxiety issues and did not like being around people.

Dr. Saffron looked between Christine and a glaring Lily. "You don't know about the murders?" he asked staring pointedly at Lily.

"Murders?" Christine eyed her charge, "Something you forgot to tell me?"

"No," Lily responded quickly and rudely. "Nothing to worry about." She was still glaring at her instructor.

The dragon laughed. "Nothing to worry about!" he roared. "Six people have been murdered! One of them a student at the secondary school and there's nothing to worry about?"

"A student was murdered? What's going on, Joffrey?" Christine asked the instructor.

"Someone is using the Vampire's Curse to kill people. The first five victims were all killed at the same time and then dumped at the pier." Dr. Saffron filled in.

"They were investigating the Great Fire," Lily mumbled, looking away from Christine and her instructor.

"Wait! Why am I just now hearing about this?" Christine asked. "You should have come to me as soon as you found out they were murdered!" the mage accused Lily.

"I was going to tell you about them but I forgot. Jonah saw how they died. They're employer killed them to keep them from revealing their findings on the Great Fire."

Christine blinked rapidly, processing the information. "That's it! I am signing you out of that school and you're coming back home!"

"I refuse to do the homeschooling thing again!" Lily yelled angrily at Christine from across the cavern.

"Why are you fighting me on this? I'm just trying to protect you!" Christine yelled back.

Lily glared, "Protect me from what? Some stupid poison that can only kill me if someone can slip me it? What makes you think I'd be dumb enough to eat or drink something that someone else gives me?" She threw her arms up in disgust. "I don't even eat or drink at school! I hide out in the library during lunch period so I don't have to deal with Meagan's constant chatter about wanting to be more popular, or which boy she currently likes, or how she wants to quit doing the newspaper because the three people she chose to be on the staff don't do their assignments."

"I don't know, Lily. If anything happened to you," Christine said softly, her head down.

Lily walked over to embrace her sister, "You worry too much. Nothing is going to happen to me or my friends, if I can help it. We'll figure out who's doing this and stop them before they get a chance to come after us. Promise Cissy."

"I'll do what I can from here. I'll check my black market contacts and find out who's been asking for the Curse or at the very least vampire's blood. We've got to get to the bottom of this before it's too late," Christine declared.

"You won't take her out then?" Dr. Saffron questioned.

Christine frowned and shook her head, "Wouldn't that just arouse suspicion? Is there even any proof that the killer will go after another student?"

Dr. Saffron just stared at her, an 'are you kidding me?' look upon his face. "There is no proof but I think the signs speak for themselves. First the 'Revealer Potion' and now 'Vampire's Curse'. And add the five researchers hired to investigate the Great Fire. It can only mean one thing, Christine. We have to.."

Christine looked panicked, "No! Not yet! We can handle this." She nodded as if trying to convince herself, "We'll just have to take some extra precautions. You said you don't eat at the school?" When Lily nodded, the mage continued, "For now on, you and your little group are to take your lunch with Joffrey. No food from outside of the cavern not even if your friends offer you it. No chances!" she ordered. To the dragon she said, "I'm sorry, my friend but we can't pull her out. That might just be what they're waiting for."

"I understand, Cissy," he answered. "I think you should reconsider about the council though! They should know."

Christine shook her head again, "No, they'll only complicate matters. We have to handle this ourselves if we want to avoid detection." The mage turned to her sister, "You make one mistake and I'm pulling you out faster than a demon can fly. Do you understand me?"

A dark look on her face, Lily nodded. The young woman was not happy about this in the least. Her whole routine would be thrown off all in the name of her best interests. Well, news flash,Lily could protect herself. It was a matter of showing her sister and Dr. Saffron that she could. Maybe the answer was in sharing her secret with her best friend.

Christine could not object to Lucas knowing. Jonah could see the demon boy in their future so the demon would remain a mainstay in their lives for some time. In a way, Lucas already knew - he just had to remember. Lily just had to decide when was the best time to discuss the situation with her sister.

The next day, Lily found herself listening to meaningless prattle from Meagan while she waited for Lucas and Annabeth. Jonah was out of school sick or so he claimed. Truthfully, he was probably faking.

"Come on, we're having lunch with Dragon-breath!" Lily growled, still in a bad mood. She grabbed hold of Annabeth and Lucas's arms at the same time and locked her arms underneath theirs in order to lead them away. The trio made their way from the cafeteria to the last classroom in the science wing.

"Since when?" Annabeth squeaked in surprise.

"Since Cissy was going to pull me out of school unless I agreed to her stipulations." The small group was in Dr. Saffron's classroom now. The dragon instructor was sitting at his desk eating his own lunch. Lily glared at him.

The magic talking staff which seemed to be hovering at the moment seemed to spin around as if coming to face them, "Ah, a new addition to the fruit basket."

Lily's glare slid to the staff, "Behave yourself or else." She never said what she would do to the staff or how but she didn't need to: It heeded her warning.

"How does this staff work exactly?" Lucas asked, eyeing his angry best friend.

Dr. Saffron frowned, "I can still push to have you taken out if you want to continue, young one." He'd been speaking to Lily, who was still glaring at him.

"What are you talking about?" Annabeth interrupted.

"Oh, did I forget to mention that Dr. Saffron was the one trying to get Cissy to pull me out of school and now I get to sit in here when I'm not in classes."

"But if your sister pulls you from school, I won't see you again," Lucas admitted.

Lily blinked, "You can still come to the cavern."

"Still grounded?" asked Dr. Saffron.

"Grounded? For what?"

Given the music competitions and other events Lucas participated in, the demon didn't have time to spend with his friends. Conveniently, it meant that he didn't have to share that he was grounded or even why. He definitely didn't want to share the exact nature of the grounding. "I just did something stupid is all and then got caught," Lucas explained. "Don't know when my parents will lift the punishment. Seems like it'll be forever. All this mess with Patty and the other murders is making things worse."

"Is that why your sister is thinking of taking you out of school?" Annabeth asked quietly to Lily.

Lily nodded, "She means well. I just don't want to go back to homeschooling. It's lonely and I'd miss everyone too much." She smiled sadly before tacking on, "Including dragon breath."

"Watch it!" warned Dr. Saffron, a slow smile creeping across his snout.

Annabeth laughed and put her arm around the other girl. "Don't worry, I doubt anyone else will be killed. I mean, the authorities are bound to catch whoever killed Patty."

She was wrong. Two weeks later, a mage child in first year was discovered, head down in his reading class. James Cochran had lunch detention in his math class. His lunch was in his locker. The young mage practically ran to his locker to scarf down his food. He didn't pay attention to the signs that his locker had been forced open or that his lunch had been tampered with.

When James's head started to hurt during class, he just put his head down and closed his eyes. Like Patty, he never woke up again.

It took a full month for Christine to find out anything from her black market contacts and the information learned was not much to go on. "Apparently, a woman with two-toned red hair purchased the revealer potion and then a few months later, she came back for the vampire's blood."

Dr. Saffron frowned, "So, this woman found out what the students were first so she would know who to target. But why the researchers?"

Christine frowned, "I don't think we're dealing with a single murderer. I spoke with Jonah about his vision of the first five murders. They were meeting because they knew someone was after them. The research team was killed to protect the secret of the Great Fire."

"The secret?" Dr. Saffron asked. "What is the secret?"

The mage sighed, "The secret is that humans started that fire but the phoenix made it so much worse."

The dragon's snout fell open, taken completely by shock. "How can that be?"

"I don't know. It was before I arrived and not even Jonah will speak of it,"Christine answered. "I believe, Lucas and his sister were involved as well."

"How can you be sure?"

The mage shook her head in answer. "Julie, his little sister, came back to Demont with nightmares. Their parents told me that the nightmares started after the Great Fire. The family lived in Demont and their home was destroyed in the fire. Actually, if what Lucas told me was true, it was the first home destroyed."

Dr. Saffron blinked and shook his head, trying to process the information. "What did he say?"

Christine frowned, "He was only a child so he doesn't remember everything and his parents don't believe him at all. Then again, they could be right and he might have made it all up."

"Except you don't think he did," the dragon stated.

"No, I don't. It was like a tale from the 2700s when

the humans found their way to Jodacai. He was exposed as a demon after school and then the humans came to kill him."

"And he lived to tell the tale?" Dr. Saffron asked skeptically. "I want to hear this!"

"I don't know how he did. He doesn't even know but that's why Julie was having nightmares. Somehow or another, Lucas and Julie ended up with the faeries for a short time before he returned to his parents who'd left town right before the humans attacked."

"Seems too unreal," the dragon responded, shaking his head. "How was the phoenix involved then?"

"I'm not sure. None of the four will even speak of it especially not her. All I've managed to get out of them was that the times before I came were rough on her. Regardless, all four were involved somehow and so only those four know the real secret of the Great Fire," Christine uttered completely serious.

"Have you shared any of this with the Council?"

Christine shook her head. "Eventually, they will have to know so the past will not repeat itself; however, until we know the facts, it does no good to even discuss it."

CHAPTER 11

FRIENDS
(WHEN PUPPETS COME ALIVE)

In years past, the theater class performed one play at the end of every semester. This year was different. Their instructor decided everyone needed to shine: really, she made a deal with the Nursery and had to fulfill her end of the bargain.

Earlier in the year, she assigned a vampire play as the play for the second semester performance while telling them she had something else in mind for the first semester. She didn't bring up the matter again until a week before their deadline.

Ms. Maecott split the class into groups and each group was given an assignment. The students were to write and direct their own play involving some form of puppets. The groups even had to perform their play in front of the rest of the groups and an audience - specifically, the young children at Demont Nursery.

The assignment was easier said than done. The class was given a list of puppet types and each group had to choose from the list. No two groups could use the same type of puppet. That wasn't the hard part because each group wanted their play to be different. The first group chose to use wooden puppets on strings that you manipulated to get the puppets to move. The second group used the most common type of puppet - hand puppets. The third group chose finger puppets and the fourth chose stick puppets. Faced with no other choice, Lily had to take the only option left: life-sized puppets.

Lucas was away again for a music trip. Lily wasn't familiar with the rest in her group though she knew that at least one was a non-human.

Jade Nightingale was a faerie like Jonah. Unlike Jonah, Jade was only in her third year at Demont Secondary. Theater was the only class the young faerie shared with Lily or any of their group. Unfortunately for her, Jonah, Lucas, and Annabeth tended to take up most of her time. Today was different since none of Lily's friends were in class.

"I'm Lily," she introduced herself to the skittish faerie.

The faerie girl nodded, "I know who you are."

Lily frowned, "Yeah, we've been in this class together since the beginning of the semester. Sorry, the boys usually keep me pretty busy playing referee. Annabeth tries but she can never keep them quiet for long."

Jade smiled, "Yes, they are quite a handful even when they're not fighting with each other." The faerie's smile turned into a wince, "Sorry, I shouldn't have said that."

Lily laughed and only shook her head, "No, it's true. Jonah and Lucas are something else." Without thinking, Lily blurted, "Hey, do you want to meet up after school? I mean we can hash out ideas for the play or just visit?" Lily had started drawing on a small slip of paper.

Frowning, Jade started to decline, "I don't think I can. Family stuff." It was a lame excuse but Jade didn't want to be found out and the only way to protect her secret was to keep to herself. While Jade had been a faerie all her life, the secret of her being one was something she had lived with for at least the past ten years. Jade learned early on what the harsh realities of sharing that detail of her life with anyone caused. "I'm not like you," Jade uttered under her breath.

Finished with her picture, Lily slipped it across the table to Jade. "No, you're not like me but that's the beauty of it: We're all different."

Jade looked at the picture and then looked up alarmed at Lily.

"If you change your mind, I'll be around," Lily smiled.

The rest of the lesson featured examples of professional puppet plays and tips on how to create a successful play. Needless to say, the rest of class was quite boring.

Lily chose to forgo her torture session with her favorite instructor in favor of hanging out with her new 'friend' Jade in the cafeteria. She was somewhat saddened to learn that Jade didn't seem to have any friends. "Hey lady!" Lily waved, a smile adorning her face. "Mind if I join you?"

Jade nearly jumped out of her skin in surprise and then shook her head by way of answer. She was writing a story, one of her favorite past times. Jade saw fantastical things in her mind attributing them to having an overactive imagination. If she had friends, she knew they would love the stories she wrote. Except Jade didn't have friends and she never shared her stories.

"What are you working on?" Lily asked, curiously. She sat her pack down on the table and took a seat.

"Just some stuff," Jade responded, scribbling furiously as she tried to finish before the inspiration left her.

Lily reached over and grabbed a page to read.

Shocked, it took a few minutes before Jade could react. The faerie girl started to grab the paper back when she noticed the expression on Lily's face. Jade waited.

The fiery-headed girl finished reading a moment later and passed the paper back, "This is really good. Have you thought about getting published?"

Jade shrugged. "They don't always have happy endings," she tacked on as if the admission would make a difference.

"People aren't always looking for happy endings," Lily responded. "Sometimes people just want a story that will catch their eye or pull on their heartstrings." She held her hand out for another page.

Unsure of herself, Jade thought about just gathering her stories and running away. Another part of her screamed in protest at the idea. Someone wanted to be Jade's friend and more than anything, Jade wanted to be Lily's friend. She picked up the rest of the story and handed it over. "Be gentle!" Jade pleaded in mock humor. Somehow, this all seemed familiar.

Half of their lunch period went by before Dr. Saffron appeared looking for Lily who smiled mischievously at him before uttering, "I forgot."

The dragon instructor glared at her. "Come along then," he ordered.

Lily shrugged and gathered up the other girl's papers. As she handed the papers back to the confused Jade, Lily grabbed her hand and pulled her from the chair. "I refuse to go alone."

"Let go, Lily," Jade said alarmed, trying to pull her hand back. "I don't want to get in trouble."

"You're not going to get in trouble. Dr. Saffron is in cahoots with my guardian," Lily had no idea why she'd referred to her sister as her guardian as she'd never done so before now. "My friends and I go to his class every day for lunch: It's quieter."

Jade looked to Dr. Saffron for confirmation. He nodded and gestured on the two to follow him as he turned his back to them and headed back toward his classroom.

"Where did that come from?" Lily asked suddenly.

"What?" Jade asked.

Lily pointed at a fruit sitting on the desk. She could have sworn it wasn't there the moment before.

"Oh, this?" Jade picked it up. "I swiped it from the cafeteria on the way out." She brought the fruit to her mouth to take a bite.

The other girl quickly knocked it from her hand, a frightened look on her face. "You can't eat the school food!"

Jade's expressive eyes showed alarm again. "Why not?" she asked.

"Haven't you been reading the school paper? Someone's poisoning the food with Vampire's Curse. Two students have already been killed!" Lily exclaimed.

"Seriously?" Jade asked, shock all over her face.

"You really do live in your own little world, Nightingale," the talking staff remarked.

Lily turned to glare at the staff. "Not helping," she said to it.

Dr. Saffron glared at his own staff, "I can lock you back in the cabinet if you want to keep it up."

The staff seemed to pale but didn't respond.

"I thought you would see it my way," the dragon said, a mischievous look spreading across his snout.

Lily shook her head. It was going to be a long week.

The next day, Lily and Jade found themselves alone again. Jonah was away for a cosmetology conference, Lucas was at another school for music again, and Annabeth was away with her mother. None of the three would be back until the night before the performance.

"Ms. Maecott, we're having trouble with this. Half our group won't even be back until the day of the performance," Jade informed their instructor. The faerie girl was starting to open up a little but she still shied away from most everyone.

The instructor shrugged, "Well since your grade depends on you performing on that day, I suggest you make it work."

"Seriously?" Jade squeaked but Ms. Maecott already walked off.

Sighing, Lily just shook her head and then glared at the instructor's back. "I guess we'll have to make it up as we go along. It won't do any good to give out lines. We'll just have to get the costumes and props ready and go from there."

Jade nodded. This was going to be challenging. Fortunately, Eliot Prentiss was also in their group and helped them with the large project.

The day of the production dawned bright and early. The theater class took a field trip to the nursery school to perform their plays in front of the small children.

"So, what are we doing?" Lucas asked, coming up behind Lily and Jade.

"Winging it," Jade answered, surprising everyone except Lily.

Lily smiled, "If we don't perform today, we fail so Jade and I made up costumes and props for everyone."

Jade started pulling clothes from a large box painted pink with polka dots. She had a small slip of paper with names and that person's role in the life-sized puppet play.

"Annabeth is the ballerina and Lucas is the knight. Jonah doesn't have to change because he's playing the birthday boy except I need you to put on that!" She pointed toward the small party hat that Lily held up triumphantly.

Jonah looked horrified at the thought of putting the hat on his head. He wasn't horrified because the hat was bright pink or that it had a puffy green ball on top. "It will mess up my hair!" he whined.

"Here, take this," Annabeth handed Lucas his costume complete with a fake sword. Annabeth left the group to change in a small closet to the right of the back stage area. Lucas waited outside to change next.

When she was dressed, Lily decided it was time to explain what they were doing exactly. "So, we couldn't attempt to write lines since no one would have time to learn them. Instead we just hashed out a synopsis for what the play is about and we'll just make up things as we go. First rule is to watch what you say since our audience is little children." Lily was dressed from head to toe in a black and white cat costume.

Strangely enough, Jade the faerie was dressed as an angel, giant fluffy white wings and all. Of course the wings were fake - a faerie's wings are multicolored and translucent. "We're toys and stuff in a toy store. A little boy comes in to buy a present for his friend. He talks to the clerk about it and he's directed to us in toy form."

"I'm the clerk," Eliot volunteered.

"The curtain will close and then reopen to us coming 'alive'. We are supposed to bicker and argue about which one of us the boy will choose for his friend before the curtain closes again. When it opens back up, our actual toy counterparts will be on the counter and Jonah will be there to choose," Jade filled in.

"We don't care which one of the toys you choose, just pick one and that is how the play will end," Lily finished. "Annabeth, don't forget your box. You're supposed to be a ballerina in a jewelry box." Lily shared a quick look with Jonah who nodded in understanding.

"Eliot will be writing down everything we say for our

script book that we have to turn in as part of the assignment," Jade spoke up again.

"I don't think I've seen you speak this much in forever!" blurted Annabeth.

Jade shrugged, "I've never really had much reason to speak before now."

Lily put her arm around the younger girl. "Places everyone!" she called. "It's almost time to start."

The group listened as their play was introduced and the instructor stepped off stage. The curtain opened to Eliot the clerk standing behind a counter. There were shelves around the stage that held random toys and books for children. Jonah the child walked over to the counter.

"It's my best friend's birthday today, sir," Jonah the child told the clerk. "But I don't have much money." The child held out a small amount of bronze coins, a red hair bow, a button, and a piece of unwrapped candy.

Eliot the clerk nodded, "Ah! You're in luck. I have a very nice selection for just that price." The clerk winked at Jonah. "Give me a moment and I'll get the toys for you to choose from." Eliot the clerk moved to the shelf and took down four toys: A child's jewelry box, a black cat plush toy, a toy soldier, and an angel doll. He presented the items to Jonah: "Just one toy. Choose wisely," the clerk advised.

The curtain closed and then re-opened to reveal life-sized replicas of the toys.

Lily, the cat plush toy, yawned and stretched out like a cat would, kneading the nearest object with her front paws. "It's been so long since I was off that shelf," she commented.

"Ouch!" shouted the soldier as the cat's paws came into contact with his face. Lucas the toy soldier quickly backed away. "You're not the only one that's been up there a long time. It's been ages! I had forgotten what it was like to be picked up," he complained.

Music began playing as the jewelry box opened, "I can't wait to go home with a child!" the twirling ballerina inside enthused.

"Haha! Don't make me laugh!" said Lucas, "What boy in their right mind would choose something pink and polka dotted. Let alone a music box!"

"Hey!" Jade the angel protested. "Don't be so rude. You don't know if his friend is a girl or boy. That nice boy could choose any one of us," she informed, hopeful of being chosen herself.

"Meow!" Lily the cat plush toy said, batting at one of Jade's angel wings.

Horrified, the angel grabbed the soldier's sword and swatted the cat's paw away. "What are you doing?" Jade demanded, perplexed by the unplanned attack.

"He won't want you if you're not in one piece," threatened Lily the cat, smiling cruelly. Lily was still in character and advanced on Annabeth the ballerina who immediately dived back down into her jewelry box and shut the lid.

Lucas the soldier yelped and hid behind the sword-wielding angel. "Get her!" he ordered, annoyed to be asking someone else to fight his battle.

Jade the angel swiped at Lily the cat plush toy, fearful of actually hurting her friend.

Lily meowed again and held her paws up in defense. Without actually meaning to, Jade's sword slashed Lily's right paw, ripping it. Fortunately, it didn't actually hurt Lily and only stuffing fell from the 'wound'. Rolling with it, Lily cried out in pain. "My paw!" Lily the cat plush toy shouted.

Surprised both Jade and Lucas just looked back and forth between Lily, the sword, and each other. Jade recovered first and ran over to Lily. "I'm sorry!" she cried. "I didn't mean to!"

Lily threw herself to the stage floor, mewing and crying loudly, "He'll never choose me now! Who could ever want a ripped plush toy!" Truly, Lily was overacting but that was the only way to get genuine reactions from the others in her group since they hadn't been given sufficient time to rehearse.

The curtain closed with Jade the angel doll trying to help Lily the cat plush toy. A moment later, it opened again to Jonah the boy and Eliot the clerk again.

When Jonah reached for a toy, he picked up the angel

holding a little sword. In his eyes, it was by far the very best toy there was. "I think Cindy will like the angel best," he told the clerk and handed over his money.

The clerk smiled and grabbed the rest of the toys to put back on the shelf. Eliot the clerk looked down at the toys and was surprised to find the paw torn on the cat plush and the sword missing from the soldier. "How did this happen?" he asked quietly.

The curtain closed with Jonah the child walking off stage with the angel doll.

CHAPTER 12

SECRETS
(WITNESS TO A BURNING)

Lily walked the long way to school alone. She'd spent most of the night before arguing with Christine about sharing her big secret with Lucas. Lily finally got the nerve up to talk to her sister.

Fortunately, she'd had the common sense to not have Jonah over when they had the discussion. Christine was completely against informing the demon boy. She said enough people knew but then another student turned up dead from the Vampire's Curse poison. Lily argued that it would afford better protection if her best friend knew the truth of the entire situation.

The newest victim killed was a faerie named Carmen Hollander. She was a sweet girl in her second year at Demont Secondary. Carmen was also one of Jonah's cousins. Jonah was beyond upset and wouldn't talk to anyone because he felt guilty about not seeing the death ahead of time. Mostly, Jonah was ashamed that he'd never been close to Carmen or even took the time to get close to her though they were so close in age.

Lily and Danah tried to cheer him up but their attempt only ended with him isolating himself from everyone by steering clear of school and the cavern. Carmen's death and Jonah's subsequent reaction did convince Christine that Lily should share her secret with Lucas.

So Danah and Christine were home, preparing the

cavern for the burning tonight while Lily made the trek to school. So close to a burning, Lily always felt drained and would normally stay home. However, today was the big day and she needed to make sure Lucas was there. Lily pushed the fatigue from her mind, concentrating on the task at hand. She needed to pretend like everything was okay, that nothing was wrong.

Lily walked through the school doors, the sound of her feet on the ground pounded in her head and she cringed in pain. The noise coming from the other students as they talked and shouted almost made her turn around and go back home but that wouldn't accomplish her goal. Lily continued down the main hall to the history wing where her locker was. She knew she'd see Lucas because his locker was in the same row. She tapped him on the shoulder as she moved passed him. "Hey, Lucas!" Lily said, a forced smile plastered on her face.

Lucas glanced up from his locker and smiled warmly at his best friend, "What's on your mind, Lil?"

Her smile softened immediately, never growing tired of his nickname for her. "Are you still grounded? Are you busy?" Lily's attention was focused on her locker and the lock that she always had trouble with. The lock was old and required a key that was rusted over. She had been able to clean it up a little but it still was hard to fit in the lock.

"I'm always busy," Lucas responded smiling. He'd already removed his books that he needed and now stood, leaning against the locker next to hers. Lucas watched the other students as they passed by.

Seeing him out of the corner of her eye, she frowned but kept trying to force the key. She really should just take the key to Christine and have her clean it up. Christine had a potion just for removing rust. "Is it important?"

Lucas almost laughed at her question but settled for a huge toothy grin. "Sleeping is always important."

Her expression turned icy as she turned to glare which caused him to laugh. At that exact moment, the key finally turned and the lock snapped open. Lily just turned back to the locker to exchange books for the ones she would need.

Lucas frowned, eyeing Lily's pale face. "What's wrong?" he asked her. She wasn't even acting like her normal self. Something was definitely wrong.

Lily looked unsure of herself, which was more unusual. "Nothing's wrong," she responded squeezing her eyes shut and holding her breath for long enough to shut her locker back. "Look, if you're not busy, meet me at the usual place after school."

Lucas nodded but Lily still wasn't looking at him. "Are you sure you're okay?" Lucas asked concerned.

She muttered something noncommittal before opening her eyes again. Lily was too pale and her eyes were too bright and glossy.

"I'll meet you here. I don't trust you to get home on your own," Lucas volunteered.

Lily nodded once and walked off toward their shared chemistry class. Mr. Pikeron was substituting for Dr. Saffron again which meant that Lily and Lucas couldn't so much as sit together. The temporary instructor insisted that Lily sit all the way across the room with a girl named Tracy while Lucas was forced to sit alone.

Every time, Mr. Pikeron substituted, Tracy spent the lesson staring at him. The girl had the hugest crush on Mr. Pikeron and everyone could see it except Mr. Pikeron. She'd been caught more than once by other classmates writing 'Mrs. Tracy Pikeron' on her notes with doodled hearts. Lily thought it was disgusting. Then again, Lily had reasons for not liking Mr. Pikeron.

Mr. Pikeron, for his attentiveness to non-human students, completely ignored Tracy and her poor attempts to get his attention. In fact, the substitute spent so much time glowering at Lily and Lucas that Tracy misconstrued his hate for something akin to love. Though the attention was unwanted, Tracy was jealous of Lily and hated her because of it.

Mr. Pikeron assigned the students to read a chapter from their textbooks for the lesson. Lily shielded her eyes with her hands the entire time and pretended to read. Actually, she had her eyes closed and was trying to block out as much light as possible since noise wasn't an issue at the moment; however, Tracy would have none of that.

The angry girl kept bumping one of Lily's arms off the table. A couple times, Lily nearly smacked her head on the table. By the end of class, Lily was furious with Tracy but didn't have the energy to argue about it. Not to mention, it wouldn't do any good. If she accused the other girl of doing it on purpose and Mr. Pikeron got involved, he would just take Tracy's side.

Worried about his best friend, Lucas kept an eye out for Lily off and on all class period. He caught on right away when he noticed the malicious smirk on Tracy's face when she bumped Lily's arm. Lucas actually witnessed her doing so several times through the corner of his eyes. So he decided a little payback was in order. Time would only tell how she was made to suffer for her terrible behavior.

When the period ended, Lily was one of the first students to leave. Now that Lucas thought about, any time they had this substitute, Lily was nearly always one of the first students to get out of the class. Lucas wouldn't see Lily again till fourth period when they shared history class together.

As it turned out, he didn't get another chance to talk to Lily. She managed to worm her way out of history by claiming she had research to do in the library. Lucas couldn't skip out of the lesson like his best friend and was forced to sit through the entirety of it. Lucas was distracted all lesson and was unable to answer a question the instructor posed when he was called upon. The demon boy was just too worried about Lily.

When Lucas made it to his next class, Lily was already speaking to the instructor about a headache. She asked to see the school nurse and then was gone before the lesson even started. Lucas thought it might be true judging by the tension around her eyes. He wondered if a headache was what had been bothering his friend all day. Thinking back, Lucas pushed the explanation away; this hadn't been Lily's first headache. As far as he knew, his best friend had never reacted this way before to a headache so it had to be something more.

He swung by the nurses office on his way to trigonometry hoping to catch Lily. It would be Lily's free period and there was no telling where she'd hide out till her next class. Unfortunately, he had no such luck as the nurse refused to let him in. However, the nurse did give him an excuse to give to her next instructor. On his way down the hall, he unfolded the slip to see what the excuse was. Lily's sister and guardian Christine picked Lily up midway through their last lesson together.

Lucas figured that meant she probably wasn't feeling up to visitors that afternoon. All the same, he had agreed to meet her. Lily knew she was sick then and still had him agree. After his last class, Lucas was surprised to find Lily leaning up against her locker when he went to put up his books. "I thought you went home," he said confused. She looked much the same as she did before: pale and glassy-eyed.

"I did," she answered, "but you said you would meet me here so I thought I should come back." Lily's eyes were clenched shut against the light and she did her best to drown out the noise.

"Lead the way," Lucas said, shutting and locking his locker.

If it were possible, her eyes clenched shut even tighter. The halls were clearing out and Lily didn't move at first. Finally, she pushed off the locker and opened her eyes. Lily smiled just a moment before turning and hurrying from the school. The pair made their way through the forest to the lake and then took the hidden trail across the lake to the island. From the island, they descended into the cavern.

Arriving, Lucas took a seat on one of the couches figuring Lily would sit near him. Christine was standing, her hands resting on the back of a recliner. His half-sister Annabeth was sitting on the other couch next to Danah. The only other person there was Jonah who was lounging long ways on the love seat, his feet resting on the arm. Lucas rolled his eyes. He really didn't see why Jonah had to be there but it wasn't his decision to make.

The rest of the group seemed tense like they knew

something was going to happen. Only Lucas was out of the loop on this secret. Even Annabeth looked excited and expectant.

"You're sure about this?" Christine asked Lily.

Lily nodded. "It's time," she answered. Instead of sitting on one of the many pieces of furniture, Lily moved to the very center of the room. The furniture formed a ring around the center with a few side tables on either side of each piece. Lily promptly sat in the floor, folding her legs underneath her.

Lucas eyed her confused, "Why don't you sit up here on the couch?"

Lily shook her head in answer before squeezing her eyes closed. She put her head down against her chest and within seconds a flame surrounded her. In a flash of fire, Lily was replaced by a large bird, burning from head to claw in a magical fire the like of which Lucas had only ever seen once before in his life.

Lucas jumped from his seat, his eyes wide in shock. The memory of the great fire resurfaced and he remembered the small bird he'd been forced to get rid of. When his mind flashed back to the here and now, he stood watching entranced by the burning.

As the magical fire burned, the bird keened sadly. The golden red bird's feathers burned away, taking the bird with it. Slowly the flames began to dwindle away to reveal a pile of ash. Tears pooled in his eyes realizing the bird was gone. Surely, she couldn't come back from that. He looked up to the rest of the people in the cavern. They all still stared at the spot where the magical fire had burned.

Christine caught Lucas's eyes and pointed back toward the pile of ashes. "Watch," she directed quietly.

Obeying, Lucas turned back to watch the ashes only to see a hatchling bird pushing its way out of the ash. He smiled, the hatchling had Lily's beautiful brown eyes.

It was chirping softly, growing golden red feathers and growing slightly as she did so. She spread her wings out slowly and carefully, as if readying herself to fly. Judging by her wingspan, the hatchling probably was capable of flying.

Lucas moved closer, itching to hold the bird in his hands but stopped short thinking better of it.

"Go ahead," Christine told him. "She won't mind."

Lucas scooted closer, holding out his hands for the bird to hop into. The little hatchling chirped happily and hopped into his hands, a magical fire still burning around her. Lucas, as a demon, was unaffected by fire, magical or otherwise.

"She's a closely guarded secret in the midst of our group but she wanted you to know," Christine told him. "Really, it's much like the secret you keep, demon boy."

Lucas froze from petting the bird, his eyes wide in surprise. "Lily told you?" he asked.

Christine laughed, "She doesn't keep secrets from us." She pointed to the bird in his hand. She had grown yet again and was no longer a fledgling.

"She's known you were a demon since the first time she saw you. It's kind of one of her talents," Danah piped up.

Lucas nodded in understanding, though the whole thing was still a mass of confusion to him. "I thought y'all were sisters?" He put the fiery bird back on the ground and turned toward Lily's sisters.

Christine laughed, "No, not quite. While we pretend to be sisters, I am just their guardian and protector." She grinned enthusiastically. Christine had moved to stand behind the couch that Danah and Annabeth sat on. She rested her hands on Danah's shoulders. "Danah was my first charge."

"Cissy found me when I was still little and took me in. The council sent us to Demont so we could protect Lily. She was all alone when we got here but now we have each other. We're family," Danah told him.

Again Lucas nodded the look of confusion still on his face. "Okay, I think I understand but what is she?" he pointed toward the fiery bird that was eyeing him strangely and trilling softly.

"She is a secret that we're not allowed to share with anyone including our parents," Annabeth responded looking up at Christine to confirm what she'd said.

Christine and Danah both nodded. "We're only telling

you now to help protect her. We suspect that the murderer on the loose is after her or at least one of the murderers is," Christine revealed evenly.

Lucas's expression turned to annoyance, "That still doesn't answer my question: What is she?" The demon boy looked down at the bird he'd placed on the large coffee table.

The fiery bird seemed to smile at him and Danah commanded him to put her back down on the floor away from the pile of ash.

The bird started to grow again; only this time, she didn't grow bigger as a bird. There was a small fiery explosion like before and sitting curled up on the floor was the girl that had disappeared.

He averted his eyes quickly and Christine threw a robe over her. When Lucas looked around at everyone else, he noticed that everyone seemed to be looking elsewhere except for Danah who had moved to help her sister.

A moment later, he felt a light tap on his shoulder and turned to see Lily. "You," he said softly, his face a mask of confusion.

Lily smiled sadly. "Me." Her head dropped to look at the floor again. Lucas wanted to embrace her but something held him back. "I am a phoenix," she whispered before looking back up again, "The very last one."

EVE

OF

BLOOD

CHAPTER 1

TRAGEDY
(SKELETONS IN THE CLOSET)

Lily nearly cackled with glee: her little sister was finally going to get to join them in the sun! Over the last few months, Christine conducted test after test to ensure that Danah wouldn't end up dead from exposure to main light source: the sun.

Christine's new potion allowed a vampire to live a somewhat normal life in the sun for up to five weeks. At that point, a vampire only needed to get another shot of Day Walker potion. Since Lily had been the key to the final ingredient, Lily was given free reign to name the new potion.

According to the research Christine conducted, the silvery substance, more specifically known as phoenix tears, worked as a healing agent simultaneously healing the skin before the sun could burn it. The dragon scales fortified her skin from the light and acted as a better protector than could normally be found. Lastly, the phoenix blood harvested while Lily was in human form allowed the skin to reform after it was burned.

Together the three powerful ingredients acted together to both prevent Danah from burning and allowed her a freedom from light that she had never enjoyed as a vampire. Granted, Danah still would have to feed on blood but she could easily get that when she wasn't in school.

Danah walked with Lily, excited to start in public school for the first time. Christine's home-schooling curriculum was sufficient in the past to educate her but the lessons were boring and she was lonely. Danah always wanted to get out of the cavern and interact with other people. Granted, Lily brought Danah friends in the form of Jonah, Lucas, and Annabeth but it wasn't the same. Now, thanks to the Daiglow potion, she would be able to do exactly as she wanted and much more.

First thing was first, Lily took Danah straight to the front office so they could finish filling out forms to get her schedule. Christine's home-schooling curriculum put her a year behind Lily which was unfortunate but Danah recognized it as a chance to shine as her own unique person. She would find a group of friends to call her own and pretend to be normal or at least as normal as she could.

The two did share a theater class which was a compromise at best. Lily loved acting and pretending to be other people and other things; Danah wasn't so keen on being in front of an audience. Lily planned to introduce Danah to all of her friends that she'd not yet met, but it would have to wait till their shared class.

Danah's first day was everything she'd dreamed of and more! While she didn't make a whole lot of friends, she did find a subject that she really loved and was happy to see that Annabeth shared three classes with her besides theater. Of course, she also made fast friends with Jade the faerie who shared two classes besides theater. Jade, Annabeth, and Danah all shared their last period class in the art department. Apparently, the three non-humans all had a passion for artwork, both making and admiring.

Jade and Annabeth were both gifted in the ability to draw whatever they wanted. As the day rolled on better than she'd ever imagined it could be, Danah seemed to be floating on clouds. However, the day wasn't so magical for others.

At Daemione Manor, Anne flipped through the mail, sorting what went to which family member. Her daughter had a pen pal that she liked to stay in contact with and her husband was always getting requests for his weapons expertise. It was how he made his living. Lucien was capable of forging any weapon out of just about any material. As for Lucas, her son received some correspondence from former instructors in Troale where they'd lived for nearly eight years.

Anne placed each stack in a cubbyhole on the desk in the hall. The routine they'd set up years before worked well with the busy little family. It allowed each the freedom to sort through their own mail and respond in due course. She was proud that she didn't have to nag her family to respond to letters.

She looked through her stack of mail, glancing at the newsletters sparingly finding nothing of great importance. She was about to go back into the kitchen when she heard the knock at the door. Anne wasn't expecting anyone but went back into the entrance room to answer.

The matriarch of the demon family was surprised to find a courier standing on her porch, a letter in hand. Typically, couriers were only used to notify next of kin after someone died. Although, it wasn't unheard of for important messages to be sent via couriers too. She wondered briefly if there had been an accident with her husband before dismissing the idea. Lucien only left just that morning for his latest trip.

The courier handed her an envelope addressed to her with no sender listed. She frowned but knew from past experiences that letters like these were written in the event of a death. Anne could swear there was something familiar about the hand writing. Someone that used to be close to her had sent the letter but she just couldn't place the handwriting.

The courier only waited long enough to ensure he'd delivered the letter to the correct person before he turned and left. Shutting the door, Anne went back to the desk where she picked up a letter opener. Carefully slitting open the top of the envelope, Anne pulled out a single folded paper. Slowly she opened it and her eyes flashed in recognition. This letter was from Genevieve.

Dearest Anne,

If you're reading this, then it means I've succumbed to my illness. I so hoped a cure would be found and I might beat this but I guess it wasn't to be. I wanted to tell you in person but I couldn't work up the courage.

Forgive me. I must apologize profusely. I never meant to cause you any pain or trouble. I meant to stay gone forever like we agreed; however, circumstances being what they are now, I had no choice.

After I left Demont, I discovered I was with child - Lucien's child. I couldn't bare to cause you any more grief and decided to raise Annabeth on my own.

Please Anne, don't be angry. I never meant to hurt you. Whatever that has happened between us was entirely my fault and I understand if you can't forgive me but don't let Annabeth suffer for my sins. Please take care of my daughter in my stead. She will need help in the days to come.

I spoke with Lucien a month to the date of this letter when he discovered I was back in Demont. I felt I owed an explanation to him for keeping Annabeth a secret for so long and choosing now of all times to come out with it. Annabeth still does not know about my past actions, her father, or my illness.

Annabeth will need someone to lean on that is strong and compassionate. I need you to deliver the news to her. She should hear it from someone that knew me. Someone I trust implicitly.

All my love and regret,
Genevieve Decatur

Anne read and re-read the letter a dozen times, half-crying all the while: Genevieve used to be her best friend. Anne and Genevieve grew up together. They went to primary and secondary school together. Anne and Genevieve always thought they'd grow up and live next door to each other. They each planned on marrying and having children. Anne always thought their kids would be more like siblings than just friends. How ironic that they were exactly that.

Genevieve and Anne had the same taste in men and as it turned out the same man. When Anne caught her husband with Genevieve, Anne was furious. She demanded that Genevieve leave and never return. She didn't know that Genevieve was carrying a child at the time. No one knew she was. It definitely would have changed things back then but not necessarily for the better.

Ever since the affair, she and Lucien had done nothing but fight. Her husband was so angry and resentful that one would have thought he'd been married to Genevieve instead of Anne. Yet, Anne did her best to maintain their marriage for their son and then daughter's sake. All these years, Anne missed her friend. She never got close with anyone else because she feared it would just happen all over again. Anne didn't think she'd ever be close to anyone again.

The only question left to answer was whether or not she'd be able to put all her animosity aside for Genevieve's daughter. The girl would have no place else to go and truly the best place was with family no matter if none of them really knew each other. Truly, Anne had been the wronged party in the whole mess but she felt guilty nonetheless.

Maybe her guilt was for forcing Genevieve into a complete upheaval of her entire life. Maybe the guilt was because a child had grown up without her father or siblings. Or maybe Anne was just too softhearted for her own good.

One thing was certain, all the trouble was caused by Lucien when he couldn't be bothered to respect his marriage to Anne. Based on his actions, she would wager that the affair might have been instigated by her husband seducing Genevieve. It took years for Anne to even be open to that scenario and she'd been so angry at Lucien that she constantly picked fights with him. Where had her life gone so wrong?

The clock chimed loudly and Anne knew she had work to take care of. First, she was off to the mortuary or hospital. She needed to confirm that Genevieve was actually dead and the letter wasn't a hoax - someone's idea of a cruel joke.

It took longer than she expected to cut through all the red tape and find out that Genevieve died that morning after spending the night in the hospital. She learned from someone on staff that Genevieve's daughter didn't even know her mother had been in the hospital. The girl was spending a few days with a friend on her mother's request.

Anne decided that the best course of action was to meet Genevieve's daughter at the school on familiar territory before bringing her back to the manor. The letter in hand, Anne practically flew from the hospital and to the school just a few blocks down the road.

When, Anne arrived at the office just before classes were scheduled to let out. She explained to the secretary that she was there to speak to her son's instructors. Ms. Juniper handed her a visitor's pass and pulled a large binder full of schedules out from under the desk. "You'll find your son's schedule in there. Just search by family name," the secretary directed, going back to her desk.

Anne flipped to her own family name and marked it while she continued flipping till she came across Genevieve's last name: Decatur. Though Genevieve's daughter was named in the letter, it didn't dawn on Anne what the name was until she found the girl in the master book of schedules. Sadness nearly overtook as she silently read the name: Annabeth Decatur. Genevieve named her daughter after Anne and suddenly the whole mess seemed all the more heartbreaking in her own mind. Anne felt guiltier.

According to the master schedule, Annabeth was in Art class which was down the hall in the math wing. Anne closed the book quickly before heading out of the office and down the hall to the art class. As she came to the door around the corner, she noticed that the door was open. She walked up quietly and stood just outside the door, watching the students inside interact.

She glanced about trying to figure out which one was Annabeth before her eyes widened slightly seeing features that could only belong to a child with Daemione blood. Annabeth was seated with two other girls, a blond with sad eyes and a brunette with shadowed eyes. Anne got the distinct impression that the brunette was a vampire but she shook her head at the notion. Vampires could not be out during the day, after all.

Annabeth looked to be wearing a thin cloak over her shoulders but Anne knew the cloak was actually her wings. Given Annabeth's heritage, the older woman knew the girl was quite capable of shifting them away. She had long black hair, the same color as Lucien's but the straightness and length of Genevieve's. Her eyes were a dark shade of gray just like Lucien and Lucas. Anne nearly cried looking at her. Other than her hair and eyes, she looked just like Genevieve. She wondered briefly if the girl knew about her mother's death or if the girl knew anything about the rest of her family. If Annabeth didn't know, she was about to find out.

Anne knocked on the door drawing the entire class's attention to her. The instructor walked over to see what she needed. They spoke briefly before Annabeth was called to get her things to leave. Together Anne and Annabeth walked down the hall.

"Ma'am, did I do something wrong?" the girl asked her.

Anne smiled sadly, "No, Annabeth. Come sit down with me. There are some things we need to discuss." Anne led her across the hall to the auditorium where she knew they'd be away from prying eyes. The bell rang as they made their way there and the hall soon filled with students.

The two stepped into the quiet auditorium and took seats about midway down the aisle. Anne made sure the girl was comfortable and tried to figure out how she was going to tell the girl about her mother.

"What's this about?" Annabeth asked before Anne could come up with the right thing to say.

Sighing, Anne turned to face the girl, "My name is Anne. I am..." She started to say she was a friend but given how she treated Genevieve the last time she saw her, it just didn't seem appropriate. "I was a friend of your mother." That was more accurate as they did used to be friends and apparently Genevieve still had seen her as one after all these years apart. "Did your mom ever tell you how much she loved performing? We used to compete for the lead parts all the time. We could never be mad at each other when we beat each other out for the leads," Anne laughed. "It was almost like we'd take turns with the parts. Genevieve and I used to have so much fun in our theater class."

Annabeth frowned, a bit confused. "Okay. What does that have to do with anything?" She was eyeing Anne like she'd turned into a monster.

Anne just sighed. "I don't know how to tell you this but your mother was very sick," Anne told the girl. "She was sick for a long time and didn't want you to know in case a cure was found. Your mother just wanted to protect you from getting hurt." Tears pooled in Anne's eyes.

Annabeth stared at her as if she had grown another head. "No, she's not." she responded. Then suddenly, as if understanding what Anne was trying to say, Annabeth asked, "Wait a minute, is this some sick kind of joke? Did Mom put you up to this?" The girl laughed and shook her head. "Ever since we came here, she's done nothing but play practical jokes. I swear, this is a bit much though."

Anne nearly cried, remembering their childhood spent pulling pranks on each other. She'd pushed it all away with the hurt she'd felt at the time. "I'm sorry, Annabeth," she choked out.

"No," shouted the girl. "Mom's fine! She's just playing another joke," she pleaded.

Anne reached out to embrace the girl. Already, her heart aching for the child in front of her but she had to be strong. There would be time to grieve later, she thought as she wiped her own eyes. "I came to bring you home. I've already arranged for your things to be delivered to the manor."

"Wait, what? I don't even know you!" she cried out. "I want to go home to momma!" She backed away from Anne with tears streaking down her face. Annabeth bolted from the auditorium.

Anne knew she'd have to go after the girl but her heart had other plans. The emotions, she'd been trying to hide, burst forth and she sobbed into her hands. She still had to tell Annabeth about her father and siblings. Anne still had so much more to discuss with her, including the funeral arrangements. Anne sighed; she truly did not want to do this. If only things had been different, she told herself. Slowly, she calmed herself down before going after Annabeth.

When Lucas arrived home from school with Julie, his parents weren't home. His dad was away on another business trip and his mother was who knows where. He made a small snack for himself and Julie and then went to do his homework. Thirty minutes later, Lucas fell asleep at the desk, a tiny trail of drool making its way down the side of his face.

CHAPTER 2

GRIEVING
(LITTLE SISTER TROUBLES)

Anne tracked Annabeth back to Genevieve's small apartment. It was empty now, save the boxes and bags that had been packed up that very day by a hired servant. Annabeth had thrown a temper tantrum and forced the servant to leave. Under the circumstances, it had been understandable.

All the same, Anne asked the servant to wait downstairs while she calmed the distraught girl down. Anne would signal for the servant when he could return to finish his job.

A few hours later, Anne finished relaying the story of Annabeth's parentage, the affair, Genevieve's amends to Anne, and now Anne's amends to her former friend. After the long discussion, Annabeth agreed to come home with her. She was curious about her father and little sister. As it turned out, she was friends with Lucas at school.

"Lucas! Julie!" Anne called as she stepped into the entrance room with Annabeth. The real test was going to be explaining to her children that they had a sister. Briefly, she wondered if Lucien already knew that Annabeth would be coming to live with them or if he even cared. "Come on, you can help me with dinner while we wait for Julie and Lucas to come down," Anne suggested. Still holding the girl's hand, Anne led her across the entrance hall and then down the hall to the kitchen.

Upstairs, Lucas awoke suddenly, wiping the drool from his chin and grumbling. What time was it? He checked the clock and swore loudly; he'd slept the afternoon away and hadn't finished his homework. Lucas was going to have to start all over as he'd accidentally drooled all over the pages. He blinked wondering what had woken him up?

Julie came skipping through the hall. She poked her head into Lucas's room. "Come on, big brother!" She smiled happily at him. "Mommy's home!" she exclaimed excitedly.

Lucas stood, stretching. That must have been what woke him. He left his room, heading down the stairs and into the living room. The fire was roaring but his mother wasn't in here. She must be in the kitchen. Maybe she'd been at the market. He puzzled at that thought as his mother was gone for an awfully long time.

Lucas trailed slowly behind Julie who was still skipping happily through the manor. She skidded to a stop in the kitchen and Lucas almost walked into her. He looked up to see what had her so baffled to find his friend Annabeth in the kitchen with his mom. "Uh, hi," he uttered to Annabeth.

Anne turned from the stove. "Finally!" she said exasperated. "Lucas, come help! I need you to cut up a head of cabbage."

Lucas moved to the cold box to grab the cabbage but was stopped by Annabeth who already had the head of cabbage out. She placed it on the cutting board next to a knife. He blinked but moved to do as he was told.

Anne smiled as Julie came around to hug her. "Hello love. Come here, I want you to meet someone." She took Julie's hand in her own and moved across the room to where Annabeth stood by herself. Anne bent down to Julie's level and stuck her arm forward. "Julie, this is your sister Annabeth."

The knife clattered to the floor behind them and Anne knew Lucas heard loud and clear.

Julie smiled, not really understanding. "Hello Annabeth! I'm Julie. I always wanted a sister!" she exclaimed excitedly. "Want to play dolls?" Julie asked hopeful.

Annabeth smiled down at her. "I always wanted a sister too," she whispered. She choked up thinking about how her mother only ever got the chance to have her before the illness must have taken hold of her.

Frowning, Julie hugged the older girl. "Don't cry. We don't have to play dollies. We can play something that you want to play."

Anne smiled sadly. It was just like a small child to think that dolls would make someone cry. Her heart hurt from the emotional day and she knew it would get worse before it got better.

That evening after dinner, the four demons retreated to their respective rooms or the living room as was the case with Anne. Normally, she could be found in the library but with so much on her mind, she just wanted to sit in front of the fire and do nothing.

That was how Lucas found her, curled up in a chair in front of the fire. Anne was half-asleep. "Mom," he called, tapping her shoulder.

She startled back fully awake, her hand going to her heart. "Don't scare me like that!" She cried out.

Lucas shook his head, "Sorry, mom."

"What did you need, honey?" his mother asked.

Lucas sat across from her in the other recliner. "Mom, what did you mean earlier? You know, telling Julie that Annabeth was her sister?" He was wringing his hands together.

Anne sighed. "I had hoped to postpone this conversation a bit longer."

"Is it true then? Is she our sister?" Lucas asked her.

She nodded. "Your father had an affair while I was pregnant with you. I walked in on them together."

Lucas nodded as a piece of the puzzle slid into place. "So that's why you two fight so much! I always thought Dad just had a bad temper."

Shaking her head, Anne frowned again. "When your father and I married, I was young and he was a lot older than me. Still, he wasn't used to being with only one person and that was a problem we had to work through." She paused trying her best to ensure their son didn't have a negative opinion of his father. "Now, I don't want you to think badly of him. That was the way he was raised and it was a different time."

"Oh, mom!" he complained. "I don't want to hear about that!" He replied, mild disgust in his voice.

Anne gave her son a dark look. "Anyhow, I was hurt and forced Genevieve to leave Demont. She promised that she'd never come back." She sighed, "I was a fool. We didn't even think there was a possibility that Genevieve could be with child." Anne sighed again. "Oh, what a mess! I think everything would still have been a big secret if Genevieve hadn't passed away unexpectedly."

Lucas's eyes went wide, "Wait! Annabeth's mom died?" He was shaking his head, "Poor Annabeth. Does she know?"

Anne's head was down, "She's already been informed. We have to make the final funeral arrangements. Of course, Genevieve took care of most of that," she muttered. "Annabeth will live here from now on."

"Does Dad know?" he asked suddenly.

She couldn't lie to her son but all the same, she didn't know the answer herself. Surely, her husband hadn't known prior to all this but the letter had said otherwise. "I don't know, Lucas. He was out of town when the letter came from the courier. He won't be back for another week."

Lucas nodded in understanding. He liked Annabeth enough but he didn't know how to act around her anymore now that he knew the truth. "What do we do now, Mom?" he asked hoping she would have the answer.

She sighed again, "We give her time. She's grieving and she's got to get used to us. She didn't know anything about her father- your father. She didn't know anything about you or your sister. And she knew very little about me only because Genevieve mentioned growing up with me." Anne paused a moment and reached out to put her hand on her son's knee, "Just be there for her, sweetheart. It's all we can do right now."

Annabeth sat in her new room; her clothes and things already delivered now sat in the corner waiting for her to unpack them. Anne offered to help her unpack and go through her mother's things but Annabeth didn't want or need her help. To go through her mother's stuff felt like it was making her mother's death that much more real. She didn't want it to be true. Surely, it had to be some cruel joke that someone was playing on her.

She glanced about her new room again. She didn't even know these people yet she already hated them. She hated Anne because she could have grown up with her father and siblings. She hated her father because aside from not being there her entire life, he still wasn't there. As for Lucas, she hated him because she'd hate herself in his place but he didn't hate her.

Then, there was poor little Julie who had never done anything wrong: Annabeth hated her most of all. It wasn't fair that Julie had grown up with her mother and father right there the entire time. The young demon had never had to lay in bed at night, wondering who her father was or why he wasn't in her life. Annabeth was crying again.

Throwing herself on the bed, Annabeth cried herself to sleep. The next few weeks were going to be a blur. Between funeral arrangements, going through her mother's things, and settling into life with the Daemione family, Annabeth had more than enough on her schedule to last a lifetime in her opinion.

It wasn't until three weeks later that she had a chance to breathe again. Lucas took her out to the cliff that he and Julie jumped from to fly. It was secluded enough from the rest of Flamewood Forest and far enough outside Demont that Annabeth could take time to be by herself and just fly lazily through the air.

Lucas left her there to meet up with Lily at the cavern. Annabeth didn't understand why Lucas didn't just ask his best friend out. Her brother practically spent every waking moment with the phoenix girl.

Annabeth liked the phoenix girl because Lily befriended her when she first moved to Demont. Aside from Anne, Lily and her sisters were the only ones that knew Annabeth wasn't just a demon but a shape-shifter as well. Lucas and Julie didn't even know the truth. They thought her mother had been a demon. Her new siblings were so unsure of making any mention of Annabeth's mother that they might never know the truth. Truly, that was to Annabeth's liking; she didn't feel like talking about her mother to anyone.

It still hurt to think, let alone talk, about it all. Annabeth was just so hurt that her mother didn't give her a chance to say goodbye. Genevieve was sick for so long and always kept it from her daughter and Annabeth was so angry. Annabeth loved her mother and felt guilty about her mother dying all alone in the hospital. She should have been there and would have if her mother hadn't kept her illness a secret.

The truth was that Annabeth didn't want to see it but who would? No person in their right mind would want to see someone they love sick and getting worse day after day. Annabeth ignored all the signs because she didn't want to believe anything could ever happen to her mother.

Annabeth was flying about leisurely when she heard it. It was a high pitched keen coming from a little further in the forest. She followed the sound, moving cautiously. You never knew what you would find in the forest especially Flamewood. This particular forest was notorious for dangerous animals. She reached a small clearing partially hidden by underbrush.

Something orange caught her eye and she moved in that direction where she heard a whimpering. She crept forward as quietly as possible, listening to the sound get louder as she moved closer.

When she parted the underbrush, she was assaulted by a nauseating smell. There on the forest floor was a dead fox. Horrified, she started to back away when she heard the whimpering again. She blinked and looked again at the fox and saw that a baby fox was hidden underneath the big fox's paw.

The sight rocked her on her feet. The dead fox had been a mother and her baby was orphaned now. It wasn't even lucky enough to have a second family it didn't know to go to. She reached out and picked the little kit up. "Poor little kit!" she cooed as she cradled the little baby fox to her chest. The baby fox stopped whimpering and seemed to purr a little at her. Annabeth smiled and decided she would take it home to the manor. The half-demon would just have to convince Anne to let her keep the poor thing.

As it turned out, Annabeth only needed to show Anne the baby fox for her guardian to agree to let Annabeth keep it. At first, Anne laughed and accused her of being just like Lucas.

"What do you mean?" Annabeth asked.

Anne sighed, "He was about eight, I believe. Your father and I went out of town for a few days and left Lucas here with Julie. A sitter was supposed to join them but I don't think she ever made it before the Great Fire."
Anne frowned, remembering the dark time in their past.

Annabeth was a captivated audience. "You mean you were here for the Great Fire?" she asked, her voice full of curiosity.

Her guardian shook her head, "No, we didn't make it back until the fire was over but the manor was gone. Burned to the ground in our absence. We were trying to track where Lucas and Julie might have gone when he just walked out of Flamewood Forest." Anne described the scene just as she remembered it. "He was holding Julie in his arms and there was the strangest bird just sitting there on his shoulder." Her frown deepened as she remembered all over again.

"That seems a bit odd," remarked Annabeth.

"It was!" laughed Anne. "That bird seemed so intelligent like it understood what was going on and what was being said. It was all so strange. Of course, Lucas wanted to keep it but Lucien forbid it. Our home was destroyed and we had to find a new place to live. Just so much going on!"

Annabeth nodded in understanding.

"Lucas was heartbroken about having to get rid of his pet. I wonder what ever happened to that bird.." Anne trailed off. The older demon sided with her husband that day but now it was time for a change.

While Anne was telling the story, she examined the kit for signs of injury or disease. She even told Annabeth it was female and asked what she was going to name her. "I don't know. I didn't really think that far ahead. What do you think?"

Anne thought for a moment, "How about Jenny?" A second later, she quietly murmured,"In memory of your mother..."

Annabeth turned the name over in her head, giving it a little thought. Her mother had liked foxes when she was alive and the little kit did need a name. "I like it," Annabeth admitted.

Her guardian smiled at her and then preceded to instruct Annabeth on how to feed the baby fox. Since it was still so young, it required bottle feeding around the clock. Eventually, they would have to return it to the forest.

"How do you know so much about taking care of baby foxes?" Annabeth asked her.

Anne merely smiled, "When I was younger, your mother and I studied to help animals. She went on to finish her studies but I had to drop out after I got pregnant with Lucas."

The two continued to converse with each other and share stories as they cared for the baby fox. For the first time since the whole nightmare started, Annabeth felt like everything might be okay.

CHAPTER 3

MAGIC
(PUSHING THE RULES)

Christine frowned, going over the figures in her notebook. It shouldn't be possible but according to her research, it was entirely probable. If the information she recorded was correct, any being - human or non-human could do magic so long as they were able to acquire blood from a mage like herself.

The blood was the easy part, the problem came in finding a willing participant who she could trust not to double cross her or reveal her findings to anyone.

Her first thoughts were of Lily and Danah: No matter what, neither could know of this research in case it went bad and she was caught. Neither deserved to suffer for her curiosity. Still that didn't solve her problem of a trustworthy and willing participant. Christine couldn't test her research and theories without finding someone she could trust.

Humans were too greedy for Christine to even entertain the idea of asking. Not to mention the whole sticky situation of the person finding out what Lily was. Christine would have to choose from the people that knew the secret or else risk far more than just her own freedom.

Dragons were often too clumsy with their added appendages and robust size. Of course, that meant that her friend Dr. Saffron was out of the running. He might have been willing too since he loved a good experiment.

Faeries could foresee the outcomes and generally wouldn't participate in something that could get them in trouble. Christine winced, some faeries were better at that gift than others. Jonah's gift was particularly strong and Christine relied on it far too much. She shook her head, where was the fun in following the rules?

Outside of Danah, Christine didn't know any other vampires which automatically ruled them out. Granted, vampire's were too fragile where non-human blood was concerned. Instituting non-human blood into their diet could and often did kill them. That was why vampires had to be careful to only drink human blood.

Christine feared the very nature of shape-shifters might influence the outcome of the experiments. If they could change at will, then what stopped them from changing into a mage when they were exposed to a sample of blood? The idea was improbable but Christine wasn't so sure it was impossible. That left Annabeth out, even though she was still half-demon.

Which brought her to her only option if the demon boy Lucas agreed. He was smart, Christine would give him credit for that but was he open enough to try this particular experiment? He was already proving how trustworthy he could be by not sharing the phoenix secret.

"Lucas, can I speak with you a moment?" Christine stopped him one day while Lily was in her room. Fortunately, Jonah was not here today to interfere. The mage had been waiting for just this moment when all the pieces would fall into place.

Lucas nodded and followed the mage into her lab. Lily warned him she would be a little while. "What do you need, Cissy?" he asked, adopting the same nickname that Danah and Lily used with her.

Christine glared and just shook her head. She really did hate that nickname but it could be worse. Sighing, she brought a notepad out. "I need help with an experiment," Christine told him.

"What kind of help?" he asked nervously. "Nothing to do with needles, I hope." Lucas glanced around the room suspiciously for unseen sharp objects.

The mage laughed, surprised that a demon would be afraid of

needles. "No," Christine responded, "No needles - at least not for you."

"Then what do you need?" Lucas asked apathetically as he folded his hands across the smooth lab table.

Christine hesitated, debating on whether she was making the right choice. Finally, she sighed before laying all her cards out. "I'm conducting an experiment on the ability of other races such as demons, humans, etc to do magic if they have mage blood at their disposal therefore proving that while magic is passed down from mage to mage through the blood, magic is possible even if you weren't born to the race of mage."

Lucas's mouth dropped open as he listened. When she stopped, he shook his head to clear the fog. "Wait, are you saying that I can do magic?"

"If my theory is correct, then yes," Christine admitted. "But in order to prove that I need a willing participant," she added worried he might not agree.

"I'll do it!" Lucas said. "When do we start?" he asked enthusiastically.

Astonished with his clear excitement, Christine almost told him immediately before the severity of consequences for performing this experiment hit her in the stomach. "First, there are some things you need to know," she told him, an air of seriousness in her voice.

Lucas frowned but nodded for Christine to continue.

"This has to be our secret - you can't even share it with Lily!" Christine warned before continuing. "We could get into serious trouble for this but so long as we keep it to ourselves, we should be fine."

Lucas's frown deepened, "Is it really that bad?"

"You have no idea," Christine answered. "My research alone could get me in trouble without conducting any tests."

"Lucas, there you are!" Lily exclaimed, stepping into the lab doorway. "Cissy, I thought we could go hang out at the cliffs for a bit. Danah is trying to darken her complexion since she can get out during the day," she rolled her eyes.

Christine nodded. "Have fun and be careful!" the mage said.

Lucas and Christine shared a look before Lucas

nodded his understanding and joined his best friend and her little sister for an afternoon in the sun.

The next few weeks found Lucas making various excuses to get out of spending time with Lily, Danah, and Annabeth. Most of the time, he pretended to have a lot of school work to make up due to his recent absences for musical excursions. Other times, he just excused himself as being tired.

After leaving he would detour to Christine's shop downtown where the mage waited for him.

Christine didn't like her sisters to be at the shop since it was too exposed to other non-humans and humans alike. She didn't want anyone putting the pieces together about Lily being a phoenix. All it took was one slip-up.

Both Danah and Lily rarely visited the shop unless it was an emergency. Generally, the pair went straight to the cavern which was big enough and hidden enough that they could be themselves without any fears.

On the other hand, Christine often had to work in the shop just to get the potions finished and on the shelf since good help was hard to find. Help was harder to find given the secrets she kept. Fortunately, Christine had a secret room in her shop where she could conduct experiments and do research far from prying eyes.

"Okay, what do I need to do?" Lucas questioned leaning on the large center table.

Christine and Lucas started meeting at the shop when the experimentation stage started. "Here comes the part you don't want to watch," she warned.

"Ah, the needles!" Lucas exclaimed. "I'll just be over here when you get finished," the demon started to turn away when he noticed she wasn't pulling out a needle but a small knife. He frowned, "What are you doing?"

Shrugging, Christine put the small knife to her hand where she sliced her palm open. "This method is quicker," she explained, collecting the dripping blood in a small vial. When the vial was half full, she moved her hand away from the vial and poured the silver substance made up of phoenix tears on it. The open cut closed into a scab. "Odd, I thought I'd grabbed the other one."

"What?" Lucas questioned, a memory lapping at the back of his mind. He remembered Jonah pouring a similar substance on his wings when he was a child. Only the silver was brighter than the substance in the vial Christine was using. "What is that?"

Christine blinked, coming back to herself. "Umm," she grimaced, "these are phoenix tears harvested in human form. They don't work as well as the tears harvested in phoenix form but she doesn't stay in that form long. I have to take what she'll give me, you know?" she said by way of explanation.

"How hard are they to obtain?" he questioned, a faint suspicion creeping into his mind.

Christine laughed thinking the demon boy was joking. "Seriously?" she asked when Lucas didn't laugh. "She's the only phoenix and you can't market the product without letting the cat out of the bag, so to speak."

Lucas nodded, his suspicions confirmed. Jonah and Lily were closer friends than he realized at first. The pair knew each other at the time of the Great Fire but how was it that he only ever saw Jonah back then. She had to have been around in order for him to get the tears. He shrugged and pushed the thoughts from his head, "What's next?"

"Well, I thought we could try blood from different sources to see if the magic is actually in my blood or something else," she offered. "What do you think?"

"Personally, I think the magic is in your blood but you're the mage, not me. It could be in your skin, hair, or even your mind," Lucas responded. "But how could you know for sure? I mean, every bit of that runs through your blood some way. If you cut your skin off, you bleed because its under the surface."

"My hair grows through the skin and my mind operates solely because of the blood pumping through it. So I guess that eliminates the need to even bother with other ingredients," Christine sighed to herself and then nodded. "Let's do this!" Grabbing Lucas's hands, she poured the blood straight onto his skin.

Lucas quickly jerked his hands back, "What are you doing?"

Christine rolled her eyes, "You already attempted the spell on your own so it's time see if the mage blood will make a difference. The easiest way is to put my blood in direct contact with you without mixing your blood and mine." She was shaking her head in exasperation. "We've been over this already!"

"Sorry," he apologized. "Same spell?" Lucas put his hands together to coat the entire palm of both hands. He needed to coat the entire surface if he hoped to get the magic to work for him.

She nodded, "Same spell."

On the table in front of Lucas sat a basic healing potion that didn't take long to make. None of the ingredients were volatile nor would any of them react to being mixed with mage blood. Neither was any of the potion ingredients valuable. As a precaution, Christine had removed all other potions from the room and used her magic to place a magical barrier about the room to keep the magic from leaving should the spell go awry.

Three small bowls sat around the healing potion just for the purpose of the spell. If the spell worked right, the potion would separate into the bowls and back into their original ingredients.

Lucas brought his hands up right above the potion and bowls and commanded nervously, "Pesot!"

Christine and Lucas both dived down under the table when the potion exploded outwards in different directions, the bowls shattering in the wake of the spell. When the ingredients hit the walls, Christine looked up excitedly, "It worked!"

Hesitantly, Lucas poked his head out from under the table to survey the damage, "Yeah, maybe we used too much blood?"

Laughing as she crawled out from under the table, Christine surveyed the damage. ".Just a tad."

"That was amazing!" Lucas exclaimed, standing back up. "Can you fix this?" he asked gesturing to the damaged mess of the secret lab.

Christine shrugged, "I prefer to use normal methods to fix these kind of messes. Stray magic tends to effect potions and other spells when you use it so loosely."

It took nearly two weeks for Christine and Lucas to learn that a single drop of blood was sufficient enough to allow the magic to flow as if the caster had magic of their own. Of course some larger spells required a little more blood but none required more than a few drops of mage blood.

Sworn to secrecy, Lucas didn't bring up the matter after the testing was complete. It was enough to know that it was possible if he should ever need a spell. Christine was even thankful enough to allow him a very small vial with ten drops of blood to be used only in case of an emergency. The mage taught him some simple but effective spells that might come in handy.

Christine returned to the cavern earlier than she planned in order to brew some Day Walker potion for Danah. While she waited on the potion, she recorded observations and other random notes on the blood magic experiments.

"Tisk tisk," uttered Waylon Radcliffe coming into the cavern's lab.

Christine looked up sharply, "What are you doing here?" she demanded, moving quickly to hide what she was working on.

"I'm disappointed in you, Christine," Waylon answered.

She blinked not really comprehending. "What are you talking about?" Christine questioned.

"This work is forbidden!" he exclaimed. "Anything to do with blood magic is highly illegal now warranting swift and immediate action," the elder mage continued, a stern look on his face.

The younger mage looked worried but not guilty: Christine needed to stay calm to ensure damage control was taken care of. The last thing she wanted was for Lily or Danah to have to clean up her mess. Christine knew the risks of her research long before she took them. "I don't know what you're talking about!" she lied.

Waylon shook his head, "I had to keep close tabs on you and your magic because of the precious being I set you to guarding."

Outraged, Christine was speechless. The young mage just kept opening and closing her mouth.

"Don't worry, no one else knows," Waylon confided, stepping up to the table and peering at Christine's notes. "Yet," he added. "That will depend on you and your actions from this point onward. You do understand why no one can know what you've discovered, right?" Waylon asked.

Christine glared, "These notes are for me and me alone. I do not share them with even my young charges."

Waylon eyed her skeptically before asking, "And what of your test subject? Has your volunteer the same discretion?"

It took a moment for Christine to find the right words to voice her answer. "My 'test subject', as you put it, is a protector or the 'precious being' you set me to guarding. I dare say that he or she will have the utmost secrecy regarding the research I conducted into magic in the blood."

The elder mage nodded. "Good but the research and testing is finished. No more, Christine, or I won't be able to protect you." Waylon turned from her to leave, "No matter what powerful being you have on your side."

The comment had been a direct reference to the phoenix siding with Christine given the relationship but the threat was still a threat. Either Christine stop her current research or risk punishment through the council. As it turned out, the matter was taken completely out of her hands when another student was poisoned.

Derrick Vitroli was a fourth year student who frequented the pharmacy because he was interested in taking up potion making for a living after he graduated. The young mage always had hundreds of questions for Christine about the education required to be a medical mage, what kind of apprenticeship was necessary, potion ingredients and reactions to other ingredients, and just about everything else one could think of.

If nothing else, Derrick was thorough in what he wanted for his future. He was discovered at home the morning before school. Apparently, he'd had a late night snack that he'd carried with him from the school.

In his name, Christine intended on finding a cure for the lethal poison known as Vampire's Curse. When she succeeded, it would be known as Vitroli in memory of the young mage and she would make sure that he was never forgotten.

CHAPTER 4

SUSPECTS
(SECOND THOUGHTS)

"Whoever is killing the non-human students is stepping up their attacks! The deaths are getting more frequent. Just last week Isabelle Lakrice was poisoned with the Vampire's Curse and now her best friend Molly Ingram is dead too. Something's got to give," the vampire girl stated.

Isabelle Lakrice was the first dragon student to enroll at Demont thanks largely to the efforts of Dr. Saffron. Now, no one was sure if another dragon would ever come to this forsaken city. Isabelle's little brother was scared to come back to school and her parents were discussing returning to their hometown in Daraigone.

Isabelle and Molly had been inseparable when the dragon girl started at Demont and Molly was devastated when her best friend turned up dead. Molly's death was self-inflicted; a botched spell to get justice for her friend's death. The idea was sound but Molly wasn't strong enough in her powers to cast a spell of that magnitude. Molly's parents were keeping the cause of her death a secret, letting people believe she had been killed just like Isabelle.

Being a mage, Christine was both familiar with Molly's parents and privy to the big secret of her death; however, Christine wasn't sharing that information with Danah, Lily, or any of the small group. For the moment, it was best the teenagers believed the girl was just another victim of the murderer.

Danah didn't start school just to start losing friends.

While she barely knew Molly, she'd made quick friends with Isabelle who was eager to be friends with the vampire girl. Granted, she didn't know that Danah was a vampire but not many did.

"Did you find out anything from your contacts, Cissy?" asked Lily.

Christine shrugged, "Just that a woman with two-toned red hair purchased vampire's blood on the market a few months into the new school year. That was the only distinctive trait the contact mentioned."

The mage was trying to invent a cure for the Vampire's Curse poison. The only problem was that in order to find a cure, you had to have a living victim that already took it or a volunteer willing to ingest the poison. No one would volunteer for such an experiment and Christine wasn't willing to ask anyone. It was too risky. So, finding a cure was slow going.

"My contact didn't know if the woman was human or non-human like us," Christine added suddenly.

"Two-toned?" Lucas asked suddenly, looking to Lily. "It couldn't be her, could it?"

Lily shook her head, " Couldn't be, could it? I mean Mrs. Quaid's been gone for a long time now. I overheard the principal just after she left and she's not even allowed back in Demont."

Lucas shrugged, "Only person I knew of with two-toned hair."

Christine looked up, "There's that name again!"

"Huh?" Danah asked.

"Nothing," Christine answered. The mage almost forgot all about the Revealer Potion and who brought in that little piece of evidence. The woman named Quaid had worked at the school and apparently had two-toned red hair just like the unknown suspect behind the murders. Christine didn't believe in coincidences. "Tell me more about her."

"There's not much to tell," Lily said. "She only taught at the secondary school for half of the semester before she was fired for an inappropriate relationship with a student."

"She wasn't having a relationship with a student,"

Lucas said, disgusted at the thought.

"No but she was in the middle of a nervous breakdown and told the principal a student kissed her," Lily responded, shrugging. "That was more than enough for him to believe she was."

"Nervous breakdown?" Christine asked.

"Well, she was always shouting at us and threatening the rest of the students for no reason," Lily explained.

Lucas nodded, "Sometimes, she sent us to the office claiming we were disrupting the class or something but we never really did anything."

Lily laughed, "She accused Lucas of stealing her journal but it was right there in her trash can the whole time. He tried to tell her she must have knocked it in the can but she refused to even look. It was kind of weird." Lily's expression turned to perplexed. If she remembered that particular incident correctly, Lucas had been polite in his dealings with that instructor but Mrs. Quaid was altogether unruly. She completely ignored him like he wasn't even there and told other students that he stole her journal. "Come to think of it, she ignored us."

Blinking, Lucas thought back to the class. "She didn't act that way at first though. It was about a quarter of the way into the semester when Mrs. Quaid's behavior changed. Right after she started using that new citrus cleaner," he volunteered.

Lily laughed, "You remember that stuff?"

"How could I not?" Lucas asked. "She used so much that it always gave me headaches."

Christine blinked, "Of course!" The mage rushed from her lab and the cavern before any of the three teenagers could ask where she was going or what was going on. The Quaid woman displayed definite proof of overexposure to the Revealer Potion. Not many knew that side effect because not many were ever around the potion long enough to suffer from it. Christine was a medical mage now and saw her fair share of overexposure cases but not just to that potion.

While non-humans only reacted once in a year-long

span from that potion, humans tended to suffer delusions and other side effects. The potion wasn't even meant to effect regular humans but then again, most potions didn't have a small trace of vampire's blood. Christine discovered it shortly after Dr. Saffron left that day. The amount was so insignificant that she had all but forgotten.

Vampire's blood added to that particular potion was known to speed up the reaction time to side effects. It was truly a dangerous potion and was illegal to manufacture, buy, or sale the potion by the council's laws. A non-human had to of broken that law for Quaid to get her hands on it.

Lily and Lucas looked at each other. "You don't think Mrs. Quaid is behind the murders, do you?" Lily asked.
"I didn't but it is possible. We should probably let Cissy and Dr. Saffron handle it though." Lucas came to stand next to Lily. "But in case that quack comes after you, I've got you covered," he offered sincerely putting his hand on her shoulder.

If there was nothing else to be known about the phoenix girl, it was that she lived the first seven years of her life virtually alone. Lily survived without any help before she ever knew she was a phoenix. Granted, she lived in an orphanage prior to finding out she was a phoenix too but she was also the youngest by at least five years. Lily had no friends and no on looked out for her.

Picked on and belittled for anything and everything, Lily had to learn to stand up for her own self or suffer. So while Lucas meant well by his comment, it didn't sit well with Lily. She shrugged his hand away and stepped back from him. "Like I told my sister, I can take care of myself," she told her best friend.

Shaking his head, Lucas tried to explain, "What I'm saying is that you don't have to. I've got your back."

"I can protect myself," Lily said, her voice full of hostility. She took another step back and away from Lucas.

"You're not alone anymore!" he tried again.

Lily shook her head and smiled sadly, "But I am alone."

"No, you're not. You've got us," Lucas gestured to

himself and Danah. Neither Jonah nor Annabeth were visiting today.

"Don't you get it?" she asked, her voice full of resentment. "I'm the last phoenix! Not the second-to-last or the first-of-many. I am the very last one of my species! And nothing you or anyone else does can change that," she finished, tears pooling in her eyes. Lily shook her head and looked to the ground before turning and running from the room.

"I'm not sure I understand what just happened," the confused demon boy stated as he looked to Danah to explain.

"I don't know!" the vampire girl threw her hands in the air. "Don't ask me!" she exclaimed before taking off in a different direction.

Lucas growled in frustration before leaving the cavern to return home. If you were close enough to him on his walk home, you would hear him muttering about how all girls were crazy and how he was never going to understand them.

Christine left the cavern and rushed to see her fellow guardian: Dr. Saffron. Not only did Christine suspect the former instructor of using the modified Revealer Potion on the students but she also suspected the woman was using the Vampire's Curse to kill non-human students in revenge. If the modified potion caused the woman to go prematurely insane due to exposure, the hostile Quaid would blame the students she singled out with the first potion.

It was very likely that she was responsible for the murders and that she wouldn't stop unless someone caught her or she killed all the innocent non-human children. Even if she killed her intended targets at the secondary school, what was to stop the mad woman from killing at the primary or even the nursery? Someone had to stop Quaid before she could kill again.

"That doesn't seem like her, Christine," Dr. Saffron said. He was completely aghast at the idea of another instructor poisoning the students. Former instructor or not, the idea was beyond insane and the dragon couldn't wrap his head around it.

Joffrey Saffron started his career in teaching several

decades before in the small town of Aiquad where he was born and raised. Originally, he came to teach there to help the other dragon children that could not attend regular school. Several years into the field, Dr. Saffron was able to get a law passed that allowed dragons to enjoy the same freedom as humans where education was concerned.

Of course, dragons were far from dangerous: they only looked scary. Mostly the myths from the old earth carried over to Gaeshar when the humans migrated to the planet. It was only in the current century that the humans were finding out that not everything about the native inhabitants was what it seemed or what the humans believed.

Being a devoted instructor, the dragon could not understand how another instructor like himself could carry out such an evil and despicable act. The very notion made him sick to even think about. Another teacher!

"I realize that," Christine argued, "but the potion had a very small amount of vampire's blood in it. According to my own research and the research of other mages in my field, that alone would have accelerated and enhanced the effect of the potion on her mental state. The modified Revealer Potion would have caused her to go insane."

"I don't know," the dragon said, "It's all so surreal! Plus, she was banned from Demont that same day. How would she have sneaked back in so easily? The walls block entrance from everywhere except the train station and you have to pass through the checkpoint to get here from there." Dr. Saffron was making excuses now, trying to find some way to disprove Christine's theory.

Christine shook her head, "All I'm saying is she fits the description my contact gave me and her behavior suggests an overexposure to the modified Revealer Potion that she just so happened to find." The mage woman rolled her eyes at the last part because she didn't believe Quaid found the potion. Rather, Christine believed Quaid bought the potion herself.

Dr. Saffron was still shaking his head in denial. "I need more proof. These kind of accusations could ruin a person's life."

"Yes, well, so can being murdered," she retorted

harshly. "Just keep your eyes open, Joffrey. If you see her or anyone fitting the description, let me know. We have to stop the murders and save the children. Not just the phoenix and her friends."

"I understand," he said, nodding. If the dragon did see Quaid or anyone else matching the description, he would let the mage know. Guarding the phoenix child wasn't just her job. He too had been assigned to protect the child phoenix from any who wished to do her harm.

Christine had been assigned as her primary guardian and protector while Dr. Saffron was assigned to be a regional protector. A guardian was selected in each city to protect the child phoenix should she reside in that area. Her primary guardian was to keep traveling with her from area to area so as to not draw too much attention to her. That was the original plan, anyhow.

Now Waylon, the head of the council knew that the phoenix child could not leave Demont for very long and so she could not follow that plan. Ancient magic kept Lily right where she was and no amount of magic used thus far had been able to remove the ancient spell that was keeping her in Demont.

Rather than share the information with the rest of the council, Waylon felt he should keep it to himself. In his estimation, the phoenix child was safer if the truth wasn't divulged to everyone. In fact, only Waylon knew who her primary guardian was. While Christine was required to report to the council on Lily's health and knowledge, that task fell to her regional guardian so that her identity would remain a secret for the phoenix child's protection.

Eight years ago, the council called upon him to uproot his family and move to Demont where he may or may not get a chance to teach the phoenix child. Dr. Saffron wouldn't be able to live with himself if something happened to Lily or one of the other students he'd grown fond of because of their connection to the phoenix girl.

The dragon instructor enjoyed teaching but over time he'd lost much of his spark to injustices forced upon his non-human students. Dr. Saffron never thought he would enjoy teaching as much as he used to until Lily, Lucas, and Jonah came to be in his classes. Though, Jade, Danah, and Annabeth were not in one of his classes this year, Dr. Saffron looked forward to teaching them the following year.

Even arguments between his magical talking staff and himself paled in comparison to the conversations he had with these young minds so ready to learn. They were like sponges, absorbing any bit of information he threw their way.

Dr. Saffron didn't want things to go back to how they were before. The dragon instructor had to be on the lookout because the murderer had to be stopped before she could kill again. Especially before she killed one of the students he'd taken under his wings. Even worse, the murderer had to be stopped before she moved on to easier targets like the non-humans at the primary school.

Quaid or whoever was killing the non-human students could not be allowed to keep killing. Someone had to catch her before it was too late.

CHAPTER 5

POISONED
(THE WINGLESS FAERIE)

Her first sleepover! Jade had been invited to her first sleepover ever. The faerie was ecstatic about the sleepover with Danah. Lily and Annabeth were already at home waiting for them. It was girls only - Jonah and Lucas were not invited but that never stopped the two before.

Danah and Jade had an afternoon fashion show immediately after school let out for the day. Their afternoon fashion class required they show off their original designs. They were graded on how well they presented the fashions and the creativity of their works.

Meanwhile, Lily and Annabeth were already at home setting up for the sleepover to come. They'd been planning this sleepover for a good month deciding that they needed it right now to escape from the constant fear of poison, homework, and life in general. The group just wanted to enjoy themselves a little.

"I'm so sleepy," Jade yawned as the pair walked.

"It's not even time for bed yet!" exclaimed Danah. "Home is just a little bit further. You'll love it!" The pair walked on in silence, taking a right into Flamewood Forest.

"I thought no one went into this forest," Jade commented, yawning again. "Rumors say the forest is haunted by the victims of the Great Fire."

Danah laughed, "No, just a rumor. I can't believe this is the first time you'll be coming over!" The vampire girl was ecstatic. Usually, it was Lily and her friends over but like

Jade, this was a first for her as well. Danah was finally able to have her own friends over! Granted, they were also Lily's friends but since the vampire girl could leave the cavern now, she was a lot closer to the friends she did have.

Jade felt like she was getting weaker all of a sudden. Her energy was draining away. "I feel so weird," she muttered.

Danah glanced at her friend. "You do look a little off color," she commented. "Have you eaten anything lately?" Danah asked worried about her friend.

The faerie girl shrugged, "I grabbed an apple from the cafeteria after the fashion show."

Eyes wide, Danah nearly stopped walking to stare at Jade, "You didn't?" Her voice came as a strangled gasp in her fright of the situation.

"What's the big deal? An apple's healthy enough," Jade argued, yawning again. "Oh! This stupid yawning! I'm just so tired all of a sudden." The tired faerie yawned yet again and then growled in frustration.

"The big deal is that someone is poisoning the food with Vampire's Curse! If we ingest it, we'll die!" Danah tried to get through to her best friend. "How long ago did you eat the apple?"

Jade stopped walking to think a moment, "Right before you came back from your locker. So maybe fifteen minutes ago?" Jade yawned again, she really didn't feel like walking anymore and wanted to just sit down and rest. That tree in front of her looked comfortable enough. She started to move toward it when her thoughts were interrupted by a shout.

"Concentrate!" screamed Danah grabbing Jade's hand. "You've been poisoned! Come on, I have to get you to the cavern. Cissy will be able to help." She pulled the other girl along through the trees to the lake.

"Vampire's Curse?" Jade asked, her mind getting sluggish. "But there isn't a cure." It was getting harder to focus and her limbs were getting heavier. "Can we just lay down here and catch a nap?"

"No!" Danah responded. "That's the poison talking, fight it!" she demanded of her friend. "Please," Danah pleaded, dragging Jade across the invisible bridge.

Jade was so out of it now that she didn't even realize they were walking across the water of a lake without getting wet. Her movements were getting sluggish and she had several scratches from trees and brush in the forest. "'m tired," Jade murmured, her eyes closing of their own accord.

"Don't fall asleep!" Danah shouted. When the pair made it across the lake to the small island entrance, Danah had to maneuver her friend so they could go into the tunnel together.

Jade collapsed just in the entrance of the tunnel that led into the cavern. Her limp form collapsed to the ground, dragging Danah down with her.

The pair slid the rest of the way down the tunnel as if it were a slide. When the pair came to a stop at the foot of the tunnel, Danah knew she wouldn't be able to move her friend alone. "Help!" Danah cried out. "Lily! Christine!" she screamed hysterically. "Annabeth!" Briefly, she wondered if Jonah or Lucas came over even though they weren't invited. "Somebody help!" she screamed again as she clung to Jade's unconscious body.

A moment later, Christine and Lily ran into view, followed closely by Jonah, Annabeth, and Lucas. "What's going on?" Lily asked before she spotted the unconscious faerie laying across her sister's lap.

"She's been poisoned!" exclaimed Danah. "Cissy, you have to help her! Please!" she pleaded, tears in her eyes. Jade was her first friend outside of Lily's friends.

Christine went into medical mage mode: "Get her to the couch," she ordered Jonah and Lucas.

The pair lifted the smaller faerie easily enough and carried her down the rest of the short length of tunnel left and into the main cavern. "I think you better hurry, Cissy," Lucas said. "Her breathing is slowing down," he added as the two laid her out on the couch.

Christine rushed to her lab to get the latest version of the antidote she'd created. She wasn't sure if it would work but it was the best hope they had. She practically flew from the lab to the couch and Jade. "This is going to be difficult.

Jonah, hold her legs in place. Lily, hold her arms. I can't restrain her with a spell or it might interact with the antidote." She took a deep breath. "When I pour this into her mouth, I need you to hold her mouth closed so she can't spit it out involuntarily. She has to drink it!"

Lucas nodded and moved to the end of the couch her head was at. Danah stood to the side out of the way so Christine could work. Tears coursed down the young vampire girl's face as she worried over her friend.

"Let's hope this works," Christine uttered just before she pulled the stopper from the vial and tipped it into Jade's mouth. Lucas immediately clamped his hand over her mouth and forced it closed while Christine massaged her throat to force the liquid down.

Unconscious, Jade's body tried to reject the potion at first and a tiny bit escaped from her mouth onto Lucas's hand. Suddenly, Jade's breathing stopped altogether.

A silver light glowed from the faerie's back where wings suddenly started to grow from the scar tissue there. They were beautiful and showed all of the colors of the rainbow. They weren't translucent like other faeries' wings but they were whole again like they hadn't been since she was a small child.

Jade's step-father Albert was a cruel man that was terrified of anyone finding out that he was married to a faerie and that his children were all faeries due to their mother's blood coursing through their veins.

Serena Nightingale-Daviane, Jade's mother, grew up thinking she was human. Her own parents feared the prejudices of humans and had her wings surgically removed after her birth. Serena grew into a beautiful woman and never even had a scar from the surgery. Of course, things changed when Jade came along.

Serena met Trevor, Jade's father, when she was still in school. It was a tale of young love and tragedy. Before the two ever knew that Jade was on the way, the love birds planned on marrying and raising a family together. The best laid plans of faeries rarely go astray but Trevor was killed in some kind of accident.

That's where Serena met Albert - a special investigator called in to decipher the clues in Trevor's death. Six months to the day of Trevor's death, Serena gave birth to her oldest child and learned about Trevor's secret.

By then, Albert knew the truth too: Trevor was murdered because he was a faerie. The police had no leads as to who killed him and the murderer was never caught. In love with Serena, Albert proposed to her using the excuse that it was the only way to keep baby Jade safe.

The whole affair was too much for Serena but she agreed to protect her child. Serena eventually gave her husband three sons. All three boys were born with faerie wings that Serena had removed at birth to hide the secret she never knew she had.

Just after her last brother was born, her step-father found out the big secret after witnessing the birth of his final son, little Albert. Little Albert, his namesake, was born with glowing wings in magnificent blues and greens. Big Albert felt betrayed by his wife whom he loved even before Trevor died but then the former police officer was furious.

That was when Jade found out the truth about her step-father. At six-years-old, Jade's wings were violently ripped from her little body by a very angry Albert. In his rage, he revealed his own secret: Albert was responsible for Trevor's murder. He threatened to do the same to her if she ever told anyone.

Through Jade's pain and fear, she blocked the entire episode from her mind and Albert managed to cover it all up with the help of a couple good friends. Serena didn't learn about any of it until she came home from the hospital with the wingless little Albert. Big Albert truthfully revealed that Jade was attacked by the same person that killed Trevor; however, he claimed the man got away and would come back to kill Jade if they didn't leave Sievere.

By the time the family moved to Demont, the family had been "discovered by Trevor's murderer" at least a dozen times all ending up with Jade beaten to a bloody pulp while Serena was at work or away from the home for something. Though Jade didn't remember the first time, the young faerie never forgot the subsequent beatings that followed ever again.

So when her wings cut through the fabric of her shirt and regrew where they'd been torn off, that blocked out memory became crystal clear in her mind and she remembered when the pain started and why it started. Jade sucked in a breath before she let out a blood curdling scream of agony as the pain washed through her all over again.

When the pain finally left her, Jade sat up on the couch, where she was crowded by the rest of their group worried about her. Most of them backed away to give her room but there was Lily - her first friend - and Danah - her best friend.

"Are you alright?" Danah asked, her voice full of concern.

Jade shook her head, her eyes filling with tears.

"What's wrong?" Danah felt powerless to help her best friend as she threw her arm around her shoulders, being careful to avoid the other girl's wings.

"Don't you see?" cried Jade.

"You've got wings?" Lucas asked, confused.

Lily gave him a disapproving look before shaking her head, "What are you talking about, Jade?"

"They're not stories!" Jade had a pained look in her eyes. It was like her whole world was falling apart. "I guess I'm not as imaginative as I thought." She shrugged Danah's arm off her shoulders.

Danah frowned, "I don't understand, Jade. What's going on?" Danah felt hurt at the dismissal.

"All these years, I've been writing these stories about every day people. Fantastical tales of daring and bravery. I've even written stories of heartbreak and woe but it wasn't me!"

"Okay, now you've really lost us," Annabeth blurted without thinking.

"It's the faerie in me trying to come out," Jade answered.

"That still doesn't make any sense," Danah responded quickly.

Lily looked thoughtful for a moment. "Ah, that does make sense. I wondered why you never had visions."

"I did though! I just didn't know them for visions since they came in a different form," Jade responded to the half-asked question.

"I wonder why they took that form," Jonah pondered from his corner of the room.

Christine stood in the door to her lab, looking torn between going into her lab to make notes or going to Jade to run tests. Finally, she settled on making sure the faerie girl was okay. She quickly ran a diagnostic spell to see if the poison was out of the girl's system. Breathing a sigh of relief, she nodded to Danah and Lily. "That was a close call but the antidote worked!"

"Great!" Lucas exclaimed. "We can get it to the rest of the non-humans now, right?" he asked before taking in the remorseful look on Lily's face. "Right?" he asked again.

"It's not that simple, Lucas," Lily answered, her head down. "The main ingredient in the antidote is phoenix tears."

"So?" Lucas said, perplexed why there would be issues. "Go cry or something," he ordered, ever the optimist.

Lily shook her head sadly and didn't respond verbally.

"Phoenix tears harvested while in phoenix form," Christine clarified.

Surprised, Lucas simply uttered, "Oh."

"If there were more phoenixes, I might be able to make enough to give to the rest of the non-humans. As it stands, we'll barely have enough poison antidote for everyone here right now," the mage informed. "Now that I know what will work, I'll have the antidotes for everyone by tomorrow. This was too close for comfort."

"Wait a minute," Jade said, a surprised look on her face, "you're a phoenix?"

Lucas winced, "Oops."

"And you thought it was safe to tell him," Jonah said dryly.

Lily glared at her friend, "Shut it!"

"I was only saying that stupid demons ought to keep their fat mouths shut," Jonah said before putting his hands up in surrender.

"I am," Lily admitted to Jade. "You can't tell anyone

and its best not to ever mention it again. Even here where we feel safe."

"Why did your wings rip through your clothes like that?" Annabeth asked, changing the subject.

"Because she didn't have wings before," Christine answered. "Am I right?" she looked to Jade for confirmation.

Jade nodded, her head hanging as she remembered losing them in the first place. "I think that's why my visions took such an unusual form," she hypothesized.

"Do you want to talk about it?" Lily asked, picking up on the distressed feelings radiating off the newly healed faerie.

Jade shook her head vehemently not trusting herself to speak anymore.

"We're here for you when you're ready," Danah volunteered putting her arm around her best friend again.

Jade nodded and laid her head on Danah's shoulder. She would talk when she was ready and not before. The only thing she was certain of was that things would not continue like they were. Her step-father wouldn't lay another hand on her and he wouldn't be taking her wings away ever again.

CHAPTER 6

GUARDIANS
(VISIONS NEVER LIE)

Christine was beyond frustrated at this point. If it wasn't one thing, it was another! Without even asking, Jonah revealed the newest vision of what was to come.

Sometimes, Christine thought she relied on the young faerie's talents far more than she should. His power of precognition was far stronger than most faeries and it was a lot more accurate than the three faeries on the council thought possible especially given that his gift was far greater than their own.

The mage had to visit her fellow guardian - Dr. Saffron - regarding a life or death matter according to the most recent vision. If she didn't warn the good dragon now, then it could very well mean his life.

"What's going on?" Joffrey asked when he opened the front door of his home.

Christine's serious expression had him inviting her in right away. However, she remained silent till the door was shut and she was assured the rest of the dragon family was out for the evening.

"Now tell me why you've left your little hiding hole, Cissy," he teased.

She glared slightly at the nickname before sighing, "I need you to leave Demont, old friend."

Joffrey sputtered in surprise, "What? What ever for?" A look of alarm was quickly spreading across his snout.

"The faeries saw your death," she answered matter-of-factually.

He growled. "Jonah's prophecies leave much to be desired for." Joffrey was shaking his head in disbelief.

"I know you don't believe in them but he does have the gift," Christine rattled off. "A very strong one, I might add," she whispered sadly.

The dragon growled, "So you keep telling me."

"So it has been proven," Christine responded. "However, if it was just Jonah's vision, I might be inclined to disregard it and take appropriate measures to ensure it doesn't come true."

"What do you mean?" he asked, curiosity getting the better of him.

"As you know, the newest member of the group is also a faerie. Her visions come to her in a different manner, so to speak. Jade foresaw your death years ago before she knew it was a vision."

"Fine, what exactly did the boy prophesy this time around?" Dr. Saffron rolled his eyes, not taking Christine's dire warning seriously.

"Something bigger than we imagined is at work here. Something the likes of which we have never seen or could even fathom. It could tear apart the very fabrics of this world if it so chose."

Dr. Saffron stared at her confused. "What are you talking about?"

"You were right old friend! Someone is after the phoenix. I don't know who or why but they'll destroy us all to get at her!"

"Just to get their hands on her?" he asked unbelieving. "They would have to murder us all though!" Christine shook her head. "And this person will if given a chance. This person wants the extermination of us all but first it wants the last of that ancient power."

"What about...?" Joffrey trailed off.

Christine shook her head furiously, "Not here. That is taken care of."

"How do you figure? You're sending all of her protectors away! Who is supposed to protect the phoenix then?"

"I'm not sending them all away. Just the ones that don't stand a chance," Christine said knowingly. "You and the other dragons will be massacred first if you stay," she pleaded.

"What if you just sent her away? Hid her somewhere else far away from here?" Joffrey asked. Maybe the dragons weren't the problem. Maybe if they just got the phoenix away from Demont and the current search for her, everyone would be okay.

Christine shook her head, "I already thought of that and it won't work." She had a confused and somewhat panicked look on her face, "Something is keeping her here."

The dragon rolled his eyes, "Something or someone? That boy will be the death of her!" While Joffrey had enjoyed having Lucas as a student, it was clear to all that he was drifting further away from Lily. The two would never be more than friends unless something changed.

"No, it's not that," Christine frowned. The mage had her own feelings regarding the demon child that was now more like a part of the family. "Something else is keeping her here. I've been trying to break the hold but it's beyond my power. Waylon was the first to alert me to it and even he couldn't see it at first," she revealed.

"Beyond your power?" the dragon asked. Not much was beyond the mage's power, Joffrey's shock at the notion wore off quick at her explanation. "Waylon knows about it?"

"Yes, apparently, Madam Wiley, the second mage on the Council can see magic and she saw the power first. If it was a spell, it was cast long before my birth but I don't think that's it. It reeks of the ancient magic. I think it's related to the original phoenix beings," she reasoned. "The phoenix can't leave for more than a full day before she's forced back."

It was the dragon's turn to be shocked again. "Forced back how exactly?

"I don't know. The faeries tried to take her from Demont several years before I arrived but no one will go into detail about what exactly happened." Christine wrung her hands together in frustration, "Those faeries will be the death of me! They won't share any shred of information unless it benefits them!"

"I should stay here in Demont where I can help!" Joffrey argued.

"It won't work." She shook her head. "They'll come for you first because you know too much," Christine explained. "Even if you were to go underground in the cavern."

The dragon growled, "I have to do something!"

"And get killed?" Christine asked. "Where would that leave her? She would know you died to protect her."

"There won't be any saving her after they get their hands on her. She's too fragile," Joffrey pleaded. He was wringing his paws together as if it would make the situation better.

Christine smiled sadly, "She's a lot stronger than you give her credit for. A lot stronger than even I give her credit for," she added quietly. Christine reached across and patted his shoulder, "All the same, you have to get your family and leave. She'll do a lot better if she isn't worried something will happen to you. Find the council, old friend.
They need to know about this."

Dr. Joffrey Saffron sucked in a breath. The council had originally been set up just after the phoenix wars to prevent that sort of thing from happening again. However, in recent years, the old ones on the council had little to do but hear disputes between different non-human groups. The mages kept the council busy most of the time.

There hadn't been anything serious enough to bring to the council since the discovery of a living phoenix as a small child. Jonah's parents had been the bearers of that news and the initial protectors. The council was right to be fearful someone would come after her. Their time table was just way off. Their time table projected her to be safe until she was out of school and possibly on her own. The council underestimated human nature where power was concerned.

Christine was keeping secrets from the council and for good reason. If they got involved, things would spiral out of control. Neither Christine nor Joffrey would be able to save the phoenix then. Up until now, Christine had been the one demanding they hold off on contacting the council. Could things be so bad that the mage would throw her prior notions out the window?

Christine stood to leave, confident that she'd gotten her point across. "Oh!" she exclaimed. "I almost forgot: He isn't to be trusted!" she growled only loud enough for the dragon to hear. "You and I will be the only ones that know about this!"

Joffrey nodded in understanding. "How much time do I have?"

"A few weeks, at best. You'd do better to leave within the week though," she suggested. Her expression serious, Christine turned and left the dragon to think of all they had discussed. It would not be easy to move his family from Demont without everyone knowing. First thing, he would have to vacate his teaching post and go underground for awhile.

Why did being a guardian to a phoenix have to be so complicated? Phoenixes were powerful beings when they were in their natural state. At least, that's what the few books that survived the centuries indicated. Phoenixes first took human-like forms during the phoenix wars to hide from humans and mages bent on stealing the power within them.

The war hadn't really been a war at all. It was more like a massacre and it was believed to have killed off the entire race of phoenixes. The council now knew that at least some had survived but the amount dwindled until they seemingly disappeared. That was until the orphan Lily was discovered.

Dr. Saffron didn't want to vacate his job and he didn't want to run away from his own unique task of educating the last phoenix; however, he did understand why he was being asked to do so. He did have a few days to make excuses and pack up his family. At least he could say goodbye properly and promise to keep in touch.

It would take some time for him to come up with a convincing lie and he'd have to contact his wife's half-brother in order to fill his place at the school. The only problem would be convincing his brother-in-law without spilling the beans. He wasn't to be trusted.

By the middle of the next week, Zachery Myers was reported missing by his parents. He left school that afternoon and similar to Jade, picked up a snack for the road. Unlike Jade, he didn't have a friend that just happened to be walking home with him. So no one saw the signs and there wasn't a medical mage on standby to save his life.

Three days later, his body was discovered along side the road just outside of Flamewood Forest behind the water tower. Zach, as his friends called him, lived across the street from Jonah and the pair sometimes walked home together but not often enough.

Zach was a shape-shifter, quite familiar with his powers and the means to control them. No one knew what he was including his close friends. He was so masterful at shifting that he would sit in on his classes as plants or seemingly inanimate objects and no one would even notice. His instructors would mark him absent and he would later complain that he was there the entire time, quoting the lectures given and even handing in assignments on time.

Lily suspected he was more than just a shape-shifter but nothing could be proven without asking him or his parents. The boy was bright and should have known better than to grab anything to eat at the school - some people were still in denial. The poison thing could never happen to them, no matter that it was happening all around them.

Even the normal humans were getting sick. Poisoned with Vampire's Curse, a human could spend a week out of school recovering from the lethal poison but the poison wasn't fatal to regular humans.

School officials were talking about closing the school down but children weren't just dying at school. No one could prove where the poison was coming from or if the contaminated food was at the school itself or everywhere in Demont.

The only thing clear was that there was a serial killer on the loose and the authorities had no idea where to even look. Christine and Dr. Saffron thought about telling the police what they knew but they'd have to reveal far more than they could. To save the phoenix, the group had to lay low and find the killer themselves.

Searches for Quaid or someone similar with two-toned red hair proved futile. She was no where to be seen or heard. Her own family that lived in the neighboring town of Yashae had not heard from her since the day before she was fired and forced to leave the city. No one had any idea where she was or what she might be up to. Christine even checked her temporary residence in Demont to see if Mrs. Quaid left any clues to her whereabouts. There was no such luck.

If nothing else, she had motive for wanting to kill the students: drug-induced hallucinations that caused her to go crazy. Hallucinations that had Mrs. Quaid thinking her students were causing all kinds of trouble, stealing from her, kissing her, and even disrupting the entire school in her mind.

It was a wonder that the crazed woman didn't go after the principal for the negligence on his part for not listening to her. Then again, the principal was human and the students she was going after were not.

Christine decided to concentrate her efforts on the school. It was obvious that Quaid was making the school her battle zone. Some way or another she was getting on and off the campus unseen. The question was how?

Lily and Lucas surrendered the key to the old auditorium temporarily pending a thorough investigation and protection spells to keep anyone meaning harm to the non-human students out. Christine wasn't taking any chances this time.

After Jade's near death experience, Lily didn't contradict Christine's orders and only argued a little. Seeing her friend nearly die took some of the fight out of her but not all of it. Lily still refused to return to home schooling.

Dr. Saffron suggested to their parents that they all pull them out and hire a private tutor to teach them all. Of course, he volunteered for the task but then had to abandon the idea when Christine gave him the warning. Not that any of the students would agree to the extreme measures regardless. The whole idea was a matter of huge contention between the teenagers and their parents.

Some parents were even threatening to move from Demont if something wasn't done to protect their children. Since the serial killer started poisoning various foods, six students died and several dozen came down with stomach flu-like symptoms.

In an effort to make themselves look a little better, the authorities tried to downplay the murders by claiming the dead students came down with a particularly deadly strain of flu that mimicked the Vampire's Curse poison. The tactic actually worked for a little while until another student wound up dead viciously attacked outside his own home.

It seemed like a dangerous animal was the culprit behind the attack but Noah Terry couldn't have been killed by a mere animal. Demons were quite capable of defending themselves from animals or people. Their minimal control over fire helped as did the wings that allowed them a chance to escape when necessary.

Somebody knew about all that and was prepared in case he tried to fight back or escape. Whoever killed him attacked him from behind: He never knew what was coming. The culprit threw enough of the Vampire's Curse poison at his exposed skin for his flesh to melt away exposing blood and bones all over the first year student from Demont Secondary.

By the time his parents found him, he was already dead. The authorities added him to the growing list of serial killer victims. Noah was just another name on an ever growing list except that he wasn't. His death revealed that non-human students were no longer safe in their own homes.

With their homes compromised, there was no point in trying to close the schools. All anyone could do was live as normal as possible and pray the serial killer was found soon. Pray that they weren't next.

CHAPTER 7

FIGHT
(TRUE COLORS SHINING THROUGH)

She'd been putting him off for months with different excuses. Mainly, Lily just didn't feel it was the right time to rock the boat with all the murders going on around them. Now, Lily wondered if she had done the right thing. Maybe she should have published the article in their school newspaper but maybe it wouldn't have made a difference. She couldn't keep putting her best friend's article off; it was time.

"Lucas has this great idea to write about the history of Demont!" Lily said enthusiastically. "It would be a great informative piece. What do you think?" Lily asked her co-editor.

"I think Daemione should stick to writing the music-related pieces I assigned him. We're trying to garner sales so we can eventually pay for our own supplies. I'm tired of having to dedicate space for ads just so people in this lousy town will sponsor us," Meagan gripped. "Plus, he barely turns in his articles as is and of course his handwriting is illegible. It takes so long to sort through his writing that I'm better off writing my own article!"

"Don't even!" Lily uttered, her eyes narrowed. "First of all, he turns his articles in to me and I proof it and re-write it prior to you ever getting it. You can read my writing just fine." Her nostrils flared in her anger, "Furthermore, his articles are always on time unlike those deadbeats you wanted on the staff to garner more popularity for yourself!"

Lily was seeing red. You could insult her any day of

the week but insult her family or friends and you had another thing coming. "You have to do all of their work for them and then you just write their names under the article so people will think they actually wrote it." She wasn't finished yet but turned away from her friend and co-editor, "If that wasn't bad enough," she pulled a few slips from her bag, "they brag about how you write their articles for them so everyone already knows they aren't on the newspaper staff. It's just a big joke with them!" Turning around, Lily shoved the slips across the table toward Meagan. "Here! I've been so afraid to hurt your feelings that I've been throwing it all out but see for yourself!"

Meagan was speechless: Lily never stood up to her. She glanced at the slips trying to decide how best to react and spin the sympathy card her way again. The comments on the slips were hurtful and rude. Worst of all they were directed at her personally. Meagan nearly cried in frustration. "Oh yeah?" she countered. "Well, at least I can write! Daemione can't write a decent article to save his own life!"

Lily laughed, "Just because you don't care for what he writes, doesn't mean he can't write a decent article. In fact, his articles alone have garnered enough attention from the musical students to drop at least two sponsors!"

Insulting Lucas wasn't helping Meagan's cause. "Look, I'm trying to keep everything together! It's not like you or anyone else helps out any with any of the extra work. I feel like no one even cares anymore and I just want to quit!"

"Then quit!" Lily shouted. She was fed up with the other girl always griping and complaining. Meagan was always talking about quitting the school newspaper because it was so time consuming but never did. "You know, if any of that tripe you said were true, I might feel sorry for you," she admitted. "Except, that I always help you write the articles that 'your' staff neglects to. So just go ahead and quit like you keep threatening to do and I will gladly keep writing with the rest of 'my' staff," Lily added, crossing her arms in front of her.

"What is that supposed to mean?" she asked confused. "Last I knew, it was 'our' staff! If that ever changes, it won't be 'your' staff it will be 'my' staff." Meagan argued.

Lily nodded, as if agreeing, "You see, that's where

you're wrong. 'My' staff has always and will always be just that because you decided that none of the people I brought in were good enough for the school newspaper. No, they just weren't popular enough for you." Lily turned away to gather her things. "Contrary to what you say about Lucas, Annabeth, and Danah, they all turn in their assignments on time and need very few corrections made to any of their work where as 'your' staff can't be bothered to do anything." She shoved some loose papers violently into her bag, "I take that back," Lily started to correct herself, "They cut class to go to the staff meetings and then show up when we have a print party and celebrate a new issue of our paper. Granted, both of those things usually involve no work and food." Lily rolled her eyes.

"I'm the reason we even have a paper! If I leave, my sponsors will go with me. Try to write a paper without any money!" Meagan threatened.

Lily laughed in amusement, "You forget that my sister owns the pharmacy and I'm pretty sure she could help me get sponsors no problem. Though, it's pretty pathetic on your part to even try that but I'm not kicking you off the newspaper staff." She shoved the last papers in her bag. "But if you don't want to be on the staff anymore, then you shouldn't hang on to it and resenting the rest of us." To think Meagan would even threaten to pull all the sponsors. All Lily could do was shake her head. Calmly, she said, "Look, I told Lucas I thought his article was a great idea and I would run it as soon as I thought the time was right. That we would go from there."

Still feeling hateful, Meagan retorted, "You only told him that because you have a crush on him! Admit it, you think his writing is just as bad as I said it was and the only reason you won't say anything is because you're afraid he will hate you for it." Meagan sneered.

Lily slapped her, shocking both girls. She took a deep breath to get her bearings straight again. "My personal feelings aside, you only hate him because he's not popular and he can't advance your popularity. News flash, Meagan, popularity isn't everything! One of these days you're going to wake up and wish you had cultivated more friendships with people like him and spent less time with your nose stuck up someone's butt!" Lily stormed from the room, slinging her backpack over her shoulder as she went.

"He doesn't even see you!" Meagan yelled after her. "And he never will!"

Lily stopped and half-turned to face Meagan, "No, but at least he has a heart." As she turned, tears pooled in her eyes. Meagan was right about how Lily felt for Lucas but she was dead wrong about his writing. That girl always knew what buttons to push to anger Lily and Lily always let her back in. Call it a weakness or character flaw but Lily was too softhearted for her own good sometimes.

Meagan stood there, starring after Lily. Lily's words hit a little too close to home and she'd reacted purely in anger. This was the first time she'd seen Lily cry and Meagan feared she'd gone too far this time.

Lily was wrong about why Meagan hated Lucas though but there was no way for the other girl to know the true reason. Meagan didn't like sharing. She didn't like sharing toys when she was younger. She didn't like sharing her parents with her older brother. Meagan especially didn't like sharing her friends with other people. To Meagan, Lily was just a commodity of sorts and she did not like sharing with Lucas, Jonah, or any of the other friends that recently entered Lily's life.

Fortunately, everyone was already gone for the day and no one witnessed the argument between the two former friends. Maybe Lily wouldn't remember so well and Meagan could make up her own version and attempt to reconcile the partnership.

Gathering her own things, Meagan made her way out of the newspaper classroom and around the corner to her own locker when she noticed another student.

Vivian Roberts was leaning forward with her head in her locker. She didn't look like she was paying any attention or maybe she was pretending she wasn't. Either way, Meagan had to know what she heard so she could do damage control.

"Vivian, what are you doing here so late?" Meagan asked.

The other girl didn't respond so Meagan stepped closer and cleared her throat.

"Hey, what's going on?" Meagan tried again.

Again Vivian didn't so much as jump at the noise.

Meagan reached out and grabbed Vivian's arm to get her attention but drew her hand back immediately. The girl was cold to the touch.

Without meaning to, Meagan pulled Vivian just enough for the other girl to fall backwards to the ground. Vivian never bent or crumpled in her fall. She didn't ball up or even try to stop the fall. She just fell straight back, her eyes closed as if asleep but the girl never stirred.

Realizing that the other girl was dead, Meagan screamed loud enough to wake the dead and then when know one came, she screamed again.

The next day, rumors flew all over the school about Vivian's death. Meagan wasn't in school. Her parents were advised to pull her out of school for a week and send her to a grief specialist to cope with the shock and loss. It didn't matter that Meagan wasn't close to Vivian. Truthfully, Meagan barely knew her name.

When Meagan missed the deadline, Lily made a decision that would effect everyone on the staff. Instead of postponing the newspaper until the other co-editor was back, Lily called in her own team of writers to help her complete the missing articles.

The paper was on time if only barely and Meagan still did not show up. In fact, Lily didn't hear from the other girl until the middle of the following week when she was called into the guidance councilor's office. Straight away, the councilor introduced herself as a mediator before having Meagan come in.

Mrs. Tindell, the councilor wanted Meagan and Lily to sit down and talk about the newspaper and the problems they were having. She told them that they had to work it out together or the issues would never be resolved.

Lily was shaking, she was absolutely furious with Meagan. It would have been one thing if Lily actually cut the girl from the newspaper staff or even if Lily had spread rumors about the other girl. But all Lily did was fill in since Meagan wasn't there to do her own job.

Granted, Lily also added the first article of many about the history of Demont by Lucas. She'd glossed over the demon aspects to protect her best friend from human prejudices. "I can't believe you'd bring someone else into this!" accused Lily with narrowed eyes.

Meagan was hunched in on herself and was playing the part of the victim. "I didn't have a choice! You cut me out of my own newspaper," she argued.

"No, you weren't here and we had a deadline!" Lily responded, her voice getting a little louder. "Remember those?" she asked. "The newspaper staff and I stepped up to meet that deadline. Where were you?"

"I just found Vivian dead!" Meagan threw out, trying to excuse herself of her own folly. "What was I supposed to do?"

"You could have given us a heads up and told us you weren't going to make the deadline that you set. Or asked that it be postponed till the following week."

"You see?" Meagan turned to the teacher mediator, "This is why I can't talk to her. She's completely unreasonable."

Lily growled, "No, unreasonable is trying to act like you run the newspaper by yourself but really you're just the co-editor just like me. That means I have as much say as you do! Unreasonable is expecting us to put our lives on hold for your pity party!" Lily cringed inwardly but someone had to say something and take a stand.

"Now that was uncalled for, Ms. Nightshade!" Mrs. Tindell interjected.

"I won't apologize," Lily told the instructor firmly before turning back to Meagan. "Did you even know Vivian outside of classes?" she asked but didn't wait for the answer. "Did you know that she was related to Jade? Yeah," she continued, "They just found out they were cousins through Jade's real father. Had just started to really connect." Lily was trying not to tear up, keeping a serious face to hide the utter despair she felt at not being able to console her friend over the loss. "You found her dead but you didn't know her like Jade or any of the rest of us. You make me sick!" she shouted.

Meagan sat still, her skin as pale as chalk. "I found her dead!" she countered madly. "I reached out and touched her," Meagan began before shuddering. She made a disgusted face and ran from the room. The distraught girl dashed into a nearby restroom to wash her hands all over again.

The co-editor of the paper spent the entire week out of school coping with a constant need to wash her hands. Meagan wasn't disturbed by having seen a fellow student dead but rather by having touched the dead body of the other student.

Mrs. Tindell and Lily waited for Meagan in silence before Lily sighed. "Look, it's obvious we're not going to be able to work together after this," she told Mrs. Tindell. "I'm not giving up the newspaper though," Lily said firmly just as Meagan walked back in.

"Neither am I!" countered Meagan, her hands dripping with water.

The mediator looked between the two, trying to figure something out that would work for both groups when an answer came to her. "Maybe neither of you have to."

"What do you mean?" Meagan asked.

"Well, maybe each group can take turns working on the newspaper," Mrs. Tindell tried to explain. She was pulling paper from her desk.

"How is that going to work?" Lily asked, confused. "Even if we only work on the articles we have assigned to each other, we'd still have to come together to print the newspaper."

"Not necessarily. For example, Lily and her writers printed the last paper so why don't you Meagan and your writers print the next one." Mrs. Tindell ignored Lily's snort of amusement and continued, "And then Lily goes again on the next issue. Just take turns."

Meagan nodded, "That could work."

Lily nodded, "I agree to that."

That decided, the mediator sat down with them and worked out a schedule of who would print a paper and when so neither had to deal with the other again. When the schedule was made, the mediator left to make a copy for Meagan, Lily, and an extra just in case.

Lily glanced about the room before looking at her disheveled former friend. Surprisingly, she actually did feel sorry for her former friend. "Look, Meagan. I'll give my team the option to write for both of us that way you have some help."

"No thanks!" Meagan said, her response quick as a whip. "I have a wonderful team of writers on my new staff," she informed cheerily. "We'll let the school judge whose newspaper is the best and then you'll want to quit post-haste!" Meagan declared just before Mrs. Tindell returned.

"Here you are, girls! If you have any problems, don't hesitate to come to me," the mediator told the two before ushering them out of her office. Only time would tell how things were going to work themselves out.

CHAPTER 8

CAPTURED
(THE DASTARDLY DARK MAGE)

Dr. Saffron was returning to his class when he heard voices from the empty classroom next to his. The door was normally locked as the room was used for storage for the science classes; however, now it was slightly ajar. He peaked inside and was surprised to see a student. Dr. Saffron moved to grab the door knob, planning to open the door, when he saw the shadow. He stepped back unsure, just listening to the two.

"I'm not sure, Master," the student admitted.

The shadow was pacing back and forth. "Find me that child!" the shadow demanded.

"I'm trying but someone is killing the students," the student responded. "It's interfering in my search!"

"That problem will be dealt with soon. To think that human could actually hurt me by killing off the children we've narrowed the search too!" The shadow seemed to shake with laughter. "Ha ha ha!" it crowed. The shadow seemed to shrink in on itself. "Amusing as her antics are, I still need that child if my plans are to succeed, mage."

"What do you need with a lousy kid anyhow?" the student asked impertinently.

The shadow seemed to shimmer as a wave of anger rolled through it, "That 'lousy kid' is no ordinary child," it began. "He is the key to everything and I must have him as soon as possible!"

"But what's so special about him?" the student tried again to decipher the secret.

"Do I need to dispose of you like I shall be doing to that Quaid woman?" the shadow threatened.

The student's eyes widened, "No! I'll find him." He started to turn but stopped, "What do I do once I find the special child?"

"You bring him to me." Though the shadow had no features, the space where it's eyes would have been glowed eerily, "And I shall reward you beyond your wildest dreams."

The student smiled before something seemed to dawn on him. "But won't the kid's parents and friends notice him missing?"

The shadow hissed, "By the time they suspect something amiss, you will be long gone and I will have what I want!"

The door slipped open slightly, squealing on its hinges. The shadow disappeared immediately but the student swung around, spotting Dr. Saffron at the door. "Oh no, you don't! You'll spoil everything!" the student gave chase.

Fortunately, the mage knew a few spells designed specifically for dragons. The only downside to the more widely known dragon spells was that they commanded such a great amount of strength from the caster that they rendered the caster all but unconscious.

Spells involving dragons had to be powerful to get through their thick magic resistant scales. Over the years, mages worked on newer spells that didn't drain the caster in order to take down the dragon. One such spell rendered a dragon unconscious using the latent magic lingering on the scales from previous attacks. The spell needed little actual strength from the caster.

Dr. Saffron suspected the shadow was actually looking for the phoenix child but since the shadow knew so little he didn't even know he was actually a she. All the same, he needed to warn Christine and Lily without giving the secret away. He also needed to escape and quick!

If only he'd left a week ago when he originally planned to go! He'd even told the school he'd be leaving to care for his sick mother back home in Aiquad.

The dragon instructor even brought in someone to

replace him: his wife's step-brother Jack, a shape-shifter with a bad attitude. Dr. Saffron was only helping him out for his wife's sake.

Dr. Saffron dodged into his classroom as a spell came flying his way smashing into the wall where it caused plaster to go flying. Dr. Saffron slammed and locked his outer classroom door and hobbled for the secondary exit around the corner and out of sight. He started to head out the door when he heard the door open to his classroom.

There was no one outside and there was no way he would be able to get out of sight in time to hide from the mage. Thinking quickly, he threw the outside door open wide but jumped into the biology classroom around the other corner hoping he'd fool the mage.

Knowing about the adjoining classrooms, the mage went into the biology classroom hoping to catch the instructor unaware. Imagine his joy when Dr. Saffron jumped right in front of him. "Le Uyr Gimli Oltea Uy!" the mage shouted knocking the instructor backwards into the wall.

Dr. Saffron slumped to the floor unconscious. While the spell was designed to kill the dragon victim, no spell was strong enough for that task. The best anyone could hope for was to knock the dragon unconscious and then take him or her out with man-made weapons.

Using another spell that drew off the latent magic, the mage maneuvered Dr. Saffron back through the classroom. He checked the hall to ensure no one was out and about and then moved Dr. Saffron to the storage room. The mage would just have to hide him there until the students and instructors were all gone for the day.

The mage could return to the unconscious dragon tonight when the school was completely clear. In the meantime, the mage had to search out a good place to keep the instructor.

Later in the day, Dr. Saffron's substitute was called in to teach in the missing science instructor's place. Though, the rest of the staff thought it odd that he would disappear so suddenly, no one thought anything of it since he planned on leaving anyway. Surely, his mother must have taken a turn and the dragon had to leave sooner rather than later.

Dr. Saffron's chances got so much worse when a student came into the office bearing a note claiming exactly as everyone thought. The note said that Dr. Saffron's mother was given a very short amount of time to live and the entire family was being called back home.

To make matters worse, the instructor sent his wife and daughter off the week before while he stayed to take care of a few loose ends. His brother-in-law wasn't scheduled to start teaching for another week but not even he was bothered by Dr. Saffron's sudden disappearance. Things were definitely not looking good for the captured dragon.

That night, the mage returned to the school through the science wing door. He'd found the perfect place to stash the dragon until he could complete his mission. There was an old mausoleum just off the school grounds. The building had no windows and only one exit that sealed completely when closed.

Best of all, the building was made of stone and mortar and the dragon wouldn't be able to escape unless he was let loose intentionally. Dragons were said to be weakened when away from their primary elements - sun and water. The mage installed chains himself to hold the dragon and keep him from trying to leave.

Carefully, the mage crept back into the school and unlocked the storage room door. The dragon was still unconscious, wrapped in layers upon layers of spells to keep him that way. It wouldn't do well for him to wake up and escape before the mage could find the child his master needed.

The mage didn't much care for dragons and thought about killing the instructor outright but he didn't want to attract unwanted attention to his mission. A dead dragon would certainly do that. Then again he could just force feed the dragon vampire's blood in the form of the Vampire's Curse poison. However, that might prove problematic with the serial killer on the loose. The mage could not afford to be connected to either the murders or the murderer.

Weaving a spell to lessen the weight of the dragon, the mage dragged Dr. Saffron from the school, using the sidewalk so he wouldn't make tracks in the ground. Making his way to the mausoleum, the mage glanced all about himself suspiciously. He knew he needed to get this done soon so he could contact his master.

After chaining Dr. Saffron up, he locked and sealed the door shut so he could make his call in private. "Master," the mage called through the mirror.

When the shadow appeared, it looked decidedly angry about having been disturbed. "What do you want now, you incompetent, bumbling fool?"

The mage was insulted. No, he hadn't shut the door all the way but he'd taken care of the dragon all on his own without anyone the wiser! "Sir, I've taken care of our eavesdropper. He won't be a problem anymore."

"Did he talk to anyone?" the shadow hissed.

"No, he had no chance before I stunned him with an unconsciousness spell. I've hidden him away in an empty mausoleum for the time being," the mage answered proudly, careful not to disclose the exact location.

"Show me," the shadow commanded.

The mage looked unsure for a moment before he turned the mirror to face away from himself. He pointed the mirror directly at the chained dragon and then quickly flashed it around the empty tomb before turning it back on himself.

The shadow seemed to examine all he was shown before he spoke up again, "Excellent! Perhaps you aren't as incompetent as I thought. I have sent another agent to assist you. He has taken over that meddling dragon's lessons and will help you to pinpoint the child that much sooner."

The mage seemed disturbed by that. He didn't want to share the glory after finding the special kid. "I don't need any help! I can find the blasted child on my own!" he protested loudly.

"That may be so but with two of you on the job, you are sure to find him quicker. I need that child and I need him now! No more slip ups. Get the job done!" the shadow shouted the order before disappearing from the mirror frame.

The mage glared at the mirror. He didn't care if someone was sent to help, he was going to find the child on his own and snatch him before the helper even had a clue! He unsealed the door and nearly stepped out until he caught something moving out of the corner of his eye. He paused, just watching.

A two-toned red-headed woman was dashing toward the school. It had to be the culprit behind the murders! The mage had to let someone know so she could be stopped before she killed the special child.

Waiting until she was out of sight, the mage walked from the mausoleum. Before he left, he performed the same sealing spells as before to keep everyone out of this particular mausoleum. He needed the dragon's disappearance to remain a mystery for now.

The next day, the police were alerted about about the late night activity from the school. School was canceled while officials threw out food and searched the grounds for the two-toned red-haired woman. The rumors flew about Mrs. Quaid coming back to kill all her former students.

That theory didn't hold up for long as not all the children murdered were in her class. The student body was allowed to return shortly before lunch.

Anthony was a mage in his fifth year with one year left at the secondary school. While his grades weren't excellent, they were better than expected given his penchant for not turning in homework or paying attention to lessons. The teen-aged mage just happened to be in theater class too.

Part of the reason he paid so little attention was because he was tasked with the role of finding a special student. He knew that the one they were searching for was not among the current fifth or sixth years which meant that he'd have no choice but to return to the school the next year if he couldn't find that special student soon. He needed more time with the non-human students but the school year would be over soon.

One group of non-humans which was large compared to others was a group formed by a stupid girl named Lily. While the group wasn't really all that big, it wasn't small either. He couldn't just take one person from the group at a time because unless he managed to grab the right one right off the bat then it would alert the others that someone was hunting them. He felt frustrated. Surely there was a way he could get close without revealing what and who he was. As far as he could tell, their group seemed to be possessed of special students though he couldn't fathom what half of them were.

When he arrived to theater class, he discovered that their instructor had taken a personal day. The flake, as he referred to their instructor, neglected to leave any lesson plans which left the students to their own devices semi-supervised by a substitute. Aside from chatting with each other, the class was also going through old costumes.

When Anthony noticed a member of Lily's group being made over like a girl, he saw his opening. He dashed over intent on getting made over too. He would worm his way in, one member at a time until they trusted him and then he would swoop in and steal that which was to be his prize. That was if the special child was in that group.

While Jonah wore a bright sequined purple evening gown that would have been low cut on a female, Anthony wore a dark green glittered gown with a fake white fur wrap. Another student brought out a curly black wig for Jonah to try on. Jonah ended up handing the wig to Anthony who put it on without complaint. Jonah went through the wigs himself and picked out a long blond one.

Lily and Lucas just sat back and laughed at it all. They couldn't imagine it getting any crazier until both Jonah and Anthony sat down and allowed another student to paint their faces over.

"What are they planning?" Lucas asked curiously.

Lily shrugged, "Let me find out." She got up and went over to some of the students helping with the project. After speaking to a number of them, she came back over, a grin plastered on her face. "They're going to see the principal to see if they can prank him."

Lucas raised his eyebrow, "Prank him how?"

"You don't want to know," she answered mysteriously.

Jonah and Anthony who were currently being called Joan and Samantha needed an escort to walk down the hall as the substitute wanted no part in their prank. Lucas volunteered because he wanted to see how this panned out. He agreed on the condition that he could ditch them outside the office in case they got in trouble for their prank.

A fourth student shot from the classroom after them. Marcus wanted to get a picture for the school newspaper. Currently, he was the only staff member still working for both sides. Meagan needed him too much to get rid of him like she'd all but done with the rest of Lily's team.

Marcus always carried a camera around his neck to take pictures at opportune moments. Some of the better pictures ended up in the school newspaper or yearbook much to the chagrin of victims of his pictures.

Fortunately for them, they didn't have to go far before they reached the office as it was right across the hall. Lucas continued down the hall to the secretary's office so he could spy without seeming like he was involved in the whole affair.

"I just need some excuse slips. My parents plan on taking me out of town for about a week," Lucas offered to the secretary.

He heard an exclamation of surprise uttered by the principal before Lucas heard a deep rumbling laughter. He and the secretary both looked up sharply at the door when it flew open to reveal Marcus. Though they heard the principal, they could not see him: "Ms. Juniper, come see what the students have done!" the principal called out merrily.

Ms. Juniper stepped over to the door to see inside. Lucas stepped over just a little and peaked over the short secretary. Mr. Henderson sat in his chair behind his desk. 'Joan' sat in his lap smiling oddly. One of his legs hung down revealing a slit in the evening gown. The hairy leg that was revealed was more than enough to scar Lucas for life in his opinion.

'Samantha' stood behind him, hands thrown across the principal's shoulders as if they were old pals. 'Samantha' was also wearing the principal's hat over his wig. And the principal was just smiling about the whole ordeal, taking the prank in good humor.

Lucas just backed away slowly, not even bothering to grab the forms he'd asked for. He ran from the office and back to class to share what he'd seen.

CHAPTER 9

HEARTACHE
(PLAYING THE PART)

Under normal circumstances, the auditorium had two large closets. One was used to store the props and scenery. The other room was used strictly for the costumes used through years that made up the wardrobe and the makeup equipment for performances.

Without giving the theater class any say or any warning, the principal decided to give their prop room away to a group of students that made signs and other things for different school events. There were signs for the spirit rallies, signs for the student council, signs advertising the school newspaper, and all other manner of school events.

When the students came to take over the prop room, they took everything out and shoved it into the other room without a single care for the costumes or makeup already in it. A large number of the costumes from former productions were ruined in the process when paint splattered over them.

Outraged, the theater instructor confronted the principal about the needless destruction. Mr. Henderson didn't even blink, nor did he apologize. In fact, he made excuses for the whole fiasco and made empty promises to replace everything. Later, he revealed the school budget wouldn't cover the costs of replacing any of the ruined items but the instructor and students didn't know that at the time.

Meanwhile, it was left to volunteers from the theater class to clean out the closet and salvage anything that was worth saving. Lily was the first to volunteer with Lucas and

Jonah volunteering only because Lily asked them to. Annabeth jumped at the opportunity and Danah and Jade agreed to help too. However, when they saw the mess, they weren't so sure they wanted to help.

The clean up effort started out smoothly enough with everything being taken out of the destroyed room. They would eventually have to repaint the walls and shelves. Until the principal followed through on his end of the deal, everything would have to remain the same.

Unfortunately, when Jonah and Lucas were involved, nothing was guaranteed to stay smooth or calm. Without even trying, one would always do something that would annoy or tick off the other. Sometimes it was as simple as the way the other was dressed or in some cases sheer accidents.

"You!" shouted Jonah angrily. He had been sweeping the floor in the wardrobe room when Lucas lifted a giant bag of fake snow that happened to have a hole in the underside. The fake snow spilled out and flew everywhere! It was all just a simple accident but it was enough to set Jonah off.

Lucas took off running and Jonah gave chase. That was until Jonah realized he was holding a broom in his hands still. A wicked idea crossed his mind.

The next thing that anyone knew, Lucas was yelping loudly as he jumped into the air. The broom came flying through the air like a harpoon barely missing Lucas. Lucas came crashing to the ground and off the stage onto a cement floor. The demon stood up and turned to glare at Jonah who was smiling maliciously. "What do you think you're doing?" he demanded.

"Getting even," Jonah replied automatically.

His face taking on a deadly look, Lucas picked up the broom and threw it as hard as he could at Jonah.

Jonah dove behind the curtain as the broom sailed through the air. The broom smacked into the curtain, causing it to rise just slightly before the curtain's heaviness forced the broom to stop altogether. Unfortunately for Jonah, he was behind the wrong curtain, and the broom came crashing down on his back. He yelped loudly eliciting a chuckle from Lucas. Jonah stood up quickly and started to retaliate again.

"Knock it off, you two!" Lily growled, coming from the back of the stage. The group was taking the bigger problems to the back area where they'd be out of everyone's way. The far back curtains and scenery backdrops would hide everything from the audience's view. That way, they'd have their wardrobe room back as it should be.

Most of the old costumes had to be thrown out because the paint was casually tossed into the room and splattered on almost everything. Some costumes were ripped when props with sharp edges were laid up against them.

Based on the paint patterns and manner the costumes were damaged, it seemed like the whole debacle was done purposely. It ticked them off because they worked hard on everything they had.

Every year they had to sew their own costumes whereas other groups were able to order things brand new from shops. Half their props were destroyed now and would need to be replaced by the end of the week because the production was the following week. Of course, they would have to pay out of their own pockets because the theater class fund used up most of their budget on making the props the first time around. The principal claimed it would take months to acquire the funds needed to replace the damages.

As it turned out, the instructor for the theater class had students from other classes come in and work on props and costumes to improve their grades in her other classes. Meanwhile, the cast and crew from the play worked overtime during the week and after school to rebuild props and sew new costumes for the production. And the instructor paid out of pocket to rent from a local costume store to replace the more difficult to make costumes.

Everyone sacrificed time and effort but none more so than Lily's group of friends. Most of them with the exception of Jonah only had the props and costumes to speak for their talents and wanted their efforts to speak entirely for themselves.

As for Jonah, being cast as lead, he made every effort to ensure the show would go on if only so he'd get the chance to perform. This was the first big role he ever landed. If he was only playing another minor character or cast behind the scenes again, he might not have even bothered.

By the night of the performance, the class ended up a few performers short due to students developing stage fright or canceling outright at the last minute. Right away, Anthony stepped up to help. He joined the class too late to audition for a part but asked to be an understudy.

No one was prepared for Marcus, a minor actor, not to be there. The instructor quickly threw both minor male parts to Anthony. The boy would be playing a waiter and the priest for which Marcus originally was cast.

That left one part without a performer and there was only one understudy left that could possibly play the part: Lily. Lily rehearsed the part on several occasions with Jonah; however, she was still hesitant to accept the role.

Lily loved acting because it meant she could pretend to be normal. She could pretend to be anything but what she was. This part required more from her. Jonah was the male lead and Lily would share the spotlight as female lead with two other girls. That didn't bother the phoenix girl.

Lily was hesitant because she would have to share a kiss with Jonah which to anyone else wouldn't seem like a big deal. To anyone else, it probably wasn't. For Lily, sharing a kiss was huge. Never once in her short life had Lily kissed anyone or been kissed by anyone. She didn't want her first real kiss to be the result of a performance.

Lucas thought his best friend looked nervous before the play started. Truthfully, he couldn't remember ever seeing her look this type of nervous. She was flustered and wouldn't look anyone in the eyes. She wouldn't even talk to anyone. Surely, she would be able to act her part. Her first big role, he thought he remember her saying. Lucas wanted to talk to her but there was no time left. The demon boy had to leave for the light and sound booth.

With everyone seated, the instructor walked out to present the show. She seemed to ramble on about how proud she was of the students because of the 'mishap' the week before. Finally, Ms. Maecott stepped off to the side and told everyone to enjoy the show. The instructor walked off stage and then the curtains opened to reveal what looked like a sitting room.

Jonah was sitting on the couch, his legs propped up on the small table in front of him. He looked relaxed when the actress playing his mother walked in. She berated him for not being settled down with a wife and children. After all, she wasn't getting any younger.

Immediately, Jonah responded that she wasn't getting any older either as being a vampire meant she lived forever. The actress railed at him that she wanted grandchildren so he needed to get a move on. He brushed her off but confided that he'd just not found the right person. The actress told him she'd found the perfect someone for him and that he was going on a blind date that very night.

The curtains closed briefly and then reopened on a courtyard. A porch swing sat center stage with potted plants and flowers everywhere. Jonah's character entered from the right with the first date. He brought her to the swing where they both sat down. The couple talked for a short time before Jonah's character got so frustrated with her better-than-you attitude that he leaned forward to bite her.

When the girl slumped to the floor seemingly lifeless, his mother stepped back into the scene. She was disappointed in him but said she had anticipated this. His matchmaking mother already had a second blind date set up for him for the next evening.

The curtains closed again. When they reopened, the stage was decorated for a lovely meal between a couple complete with a booth and table. Jonah's character walked in with his second blind date. Jonah moved to pull out her chair but she sat in his chair instead. Anthony came over to serve them and left after taking their order. His date ordered for him.

When the food came, she kept taking food off Jonah's plate instead of eating her own. She even snatched the bill when it came before Jonah could so much as reach for it. Scoffing at the bill, she pulled out the necessary cash and then asked for a to-go bag for her own food since she'd only eaten Jonah's. Jonah looked disgusted.

He scooted closer to her and the pair looked about to share a kiss before Jonah's character bit his date on the neck. When she slumped down on the table as if asleep, the mother came in and chewed him out. She proceeded to tell him that she was willing to overlook his past dates. She had another date in mind and he'd better not mess it up.

The curtain closed again and opened to a sandy scene. The lights were dim and it appeared to be the beach at night. Jonah was walking hand-in-hand with Lily. They looked like love birds just walking along and chatting about everything and nothing at all.

Lucas looked on with envy remembering that Jonah would get to share a kiss with her for this scene. His mind screamed at him that the faerie knew Lily longer than he did too. Lucas had no idea that Lily was dreading this scene as much as he dreaded watching it.

As they neared the edge of the stage, they turned, their backs to the audience staring at a life-like full moon painted on canvas. Then the couple turned to each other, holding each others hands. They leaned in to kiss and suddenly the curtain closed without warning.

Surprised, the students rushed to prepare for the next scene. Lily and Jonah changed into wedding attire as the crew members changed the scenery. The rest of the cast were already dressed and joined them on stage to play wedding guests, complete with the actress playing the mother crying loudly.

The curtain opened to Lily and Jonah's characters so close that it looked as if they were kissing though neither actually was. When they broke apart, the wedding guests cheered and the couple walked off stage like they were going on a honeymoon. The curtains closed again for the second to last time. The audience clapped loudly complete with a few cat calls and whistles.

Lucas silently seethed. He knew that was what the characters would do but seeing it actually happen was another matter altogether. Then again, Lily wasn't supposed to play that part. She was just supposed to be the understudy. Just like that, Lucas hated Jonah more than he had before.

The next time they opened the curtain, the whole

cast, including the first and second date stood in a row and bowed before the audience that continued applauding. They bowed in their line a few times before being called forward separately. As each student was called forward, they bowed again to cheers for how well they'd acted.

Finally, the instructor called the rest of the class that helped behind the scenes including the light and sound crew. She didn't call them up separately like she had the acting students but it was better than nothing. Afterward, the curtains closed for the last time leaving the instructor to thank everyone for coming. The crowd murmured amongst themselves as they were dismissed.

Meanwhile, behind the stage and in the wardrobe room, the students were getting into their regular clothes. "Thanks," Lily whispered to Anthony appreciatively.

He smiled back, "You're welcome." Anthony was investigating this group in case the special child his master wanted was in it. Granted, the mage had to pretend that he actually liked them which wasn't easy. In the end, Anthony knew his efforts would be worth it especially after he presented the brat to his master and got his reward. The mage already planned on being long gone by the time anyone learned of his treachery.

Anthony wondered briefly if his tactics would work and the group would confide in him like he needed in order to find out which one of them was the special child his master required. What disturbed him most was that his master had not specified what was so special about this person. Instead, Anthony was assured that he'd know when he came across him.

There were three males in this group: Lucas, Jonah, Marcus, and on occasion Lucas's friend Daniel. Of the four, he thought Jonah seemed the most likely given that he was just plain weird but liked showing off. Every day, Jonah would change his appearance somehow. Usually he added some form of coloring to his hair and then changed it to a different color the following day.

To Anthony, Jonah acted like he was starved for attention but he needed more information first to see if Jonah was the person he was looking for. Then again, the special child could be any of the four or none of them at all.

Daniel thumped Lucas on his ear after the show was over. "Nice job on the lights and sounds!"

Lucas grabbed his ear. "Thanks, I think," he grumbled. "What did you think of the last minute cast changes?" he asked suddenly.

"They were alright, I guess," Daniel responded. "Then again, Lily has always been a great actress. It's just these temporary instructors don't know how to cast worth a flip!"

Lucas blinked, "Wait, how do you know Lily?" Lucas was putting up a few of the light cue sheets but stopped to wait for Daniel's answer.

Daniel laughed nervously, "We dated a couple years back. No big deal."

"What happened?" Lucas blurted without thinking. "I mean, if you don't mind me asking," he added. It was stupid to think that Lily might not have ex-boyfriends in her past. She was friendly toward everyone.

"We were just too different," Daniel said, shrugging. The look on Daniel's face told another story altogether though. It was clear the other boy still very much liked Lily.

Lucas's gut twisted in pain. There was no way he could pursue a relationship with Lily now that he knew about Daniel and Lily. He almost kicked himself for even inviting Daniel to come see him in action tonight. If he would have left things alone, he would have just continued working up his courage without a shred of guilt. Now, everything was different.

Thinking about it more, Lucas realized things changed before now. The demon boy was keeping his distance every since Lily revealed that she was the last phoenix. It didn't help matters, that he was always so busy and that his father hated her.

Daniel was watching Lucas for a few minutes before he realized the other boy was waiting on a response. "Oh, that's too bad," he muttered, trying to sound sympathetic.

Daniel just shrugged again, trying to make it seem like exactly like he'd said. "Let's get out of here and go celebrate your first light and sound gig," Daniel suggested, wanting to put distance between himself and his old flame.

Lucas nodded, "Sounds like a plan. I just have to put this stuff up and we can go." Daniel helped him so they could get out of the auditorium quicker. The two friends finished quicker than it took the rest of the cast to finish changing back into their regular clothes and then left quietly.

The demon boy didn't even stop to say goodbye to Lily because he felt guilty about liking her. Lucas didn't want to hurt his good friend Daniel now that he knew how the other boy felt about Lily.

Lucas wanted to know why he had to be the honorable one when no one would do the same for him. A little voice in his head answered that someone had to do it and Lucas frowned all the more.

CHAPTER 10

MISSING
(GETTING HER STORY)

Lily's part in the school play was talked about for weeks. It was the first time she was allowed to shine as an actress and the student body was impressed.

Unfortunately, it was Meagan's turn to put out a school newspaper with a review of the play. The vengeful girl could have left matters alone and refused to comment on the play. She could have run an article that told of the hardships the class faced in order to make the performance.

Instead, Meagan wrote a scathing review in an attempt to embarrass Lily and the rest of her staff. Of course, that backfired on Meagan and caused such an uproar that she was forced to print a retraction in her next edition.

Lily's newspaper was now more popular than Meagan's and her hatred for Lily grew substantially. Meagan lied when she told Lily that she had a new staff ready to write for her own newspaper. The other girl had no one and was doing her issue all alone.

The truth was that Meagan wanted to be popular but she was far from being popular. She wasn't super smart, pretty, athletic, or even charismatic. The only thing Meagan had, in her own mind, was her ability to manage everything.

Meagan managed her friendships by telling her friends what other people said about them or rather what she claimed people said about them. Then she reminded them over and over what the other person said about them. It was her way of isolating them from other people so she didn't have to share their attention. The tactic worked well enough but then she followed it up with something else.

She wasn't kind to her friends. She teased them mercilessly and could be downright cruel in her dealings with them. Then Meagan actually expected them to just forgive her and stick with her. It was a wonder her friendship with Lily lasted as long as it did. Then again, Lily tended to ignore the bad and only saw the innate good in people.

Essentially, Meagan was a bully to her friends but she only treated her friends like that. She was a completely different person to acquaintances or even to the popular students that she envied. Meagan treated them like kings and queens, practically drooling over every word they spoke.

It took too long for Lily to see Meagan clearly. Meagan blamed Lucas, and to a lesser extent Danah, for turning Lily against her. It didn't matter that Meagan treated Lily badly or that none of Lily's other friends had anything to do with the friendship between the two.

Meagan only saw red where Lily was concerned anymore. Meagan would teach her! She would teach her former friend a lesson she'd never forget for choosing Lucas over her. To think all these years wasted being friends with Lily when she could have just found other friends.

That wasn't entirely true. Her friendship with the flame-headed girl had meant a lot to Meagan. Lily never saw anyone but a normal girl where Meagan was concerned. Lily treated her the same as she did anyone else. Better even then she deserved.

Maybe that was why Meagan was trying so hard to make her school newspaper look better than Lily's school newspaper. She wanted Lily to see what she was capable of. Meagan wanted Lily to forgive her and be her friend again.

Investigative reporting was something Meagan was looking forward to studying after she graduated from secondary school. There was a nice trade school in Xitar that Meagan applied for. She was just waiting to see if she was accepted or rejected. Though most students waited a little while longer to apply to trade schools, Meagan wanted to get a jump on her future.

Her older brother Melvin would graduate this year and planned on joining the military in the capital Jodacai. While Demont was on the northern end of the island nation, Jodacai was on the southern end. Melvin was set to move so far away that he wouldn't be able to come home very often given the rigorous training and work schedule the military set out for their recruits.

Meagan was looking forward to him leaving since she would more or less have her parents to herself for a whole year. Even after she went to college, she'd be able to spend more time with her parents than her brother since Xitar was only half the distance compared to Jodacai. So much closer that her parents would have to stop by and visit her first before going to see her brother. They might even have to stop after seeing him as well.

Eventually, Meagan would be able to travel the entire nation once she landed her dream job as an investigative reporter. Coincidentally, that was the original reason she petitioned to get the school newspaper started back up. She needed the newspaper to help her get into Xanibar University in Xitar.

Meagan never shared that with Lily though. There were a lot of things Meagan never shared. Though she was considered a bully by her friends, Meagan wasn't always this way. She used to be all smiles and laughter. Meagan used to not have any secrets but everyone gets hurt. No one is safe from the pain life sometimes deals them.

Meagan learned that lesson the hard way. She was still paying the price for being too trusting and unguarded. The entire right side of her body was a mass of burns she suffered the night of the Great Fire.

That day was just like any other except Meagan saw something that she shouldn't have and then she told a friend. It wasn't long before the story spread and Meagan was dragged along to something she wanted no part of. Some time in the night, the little Meagan managed to run away but not before she'd been severely burned in the fire that raged the city that night.

Meagan knew the truth about Lucas and his family

but she knew better than to tell anyone ever again. She knew humans were responsible for the Great Fire and the countless deaths that night. When the investigators came to figure out how the fire started, the then eight-year-old Meagan feigned ignorance. She was even interviewed about her burns but she wouldn't talk.

In a way, that's what introduced Meagan to the world of investigative reporting and gave her a bigger source than you'd expect a secondary school student to have. The police officer that investigated her burns kept in touch with her over the years and often revealed interesting tidbits of information under the right circumstances. Sometimes, all the teen had to do was sit in the department long enough and she'd hear a juicy detail about a recent case.

A scarred teen, Meagan knew she wouldn't be accepted or welcomed in society again so long as she bore the scars that the world gave her. As a reporter, she would be famous for her articles and not for the horrifying scarred up face she'd been living with since she was eight.

Meagan was in the middle of writing an investigative piece on Mrs. Quaid, who was believed to be the serial killer. She'd already published an article about the crazed former instructor in her previous issue of the school newspaper but she needed some kind of proof to go with the new article for the front cover.

If she was correct in her investigation, Mrs. Quaid was hiding out somewhere around the school. Meagan staked out on top of the school a couple days a week watching for some kind of clue. Fortunately, she saw Mrs. Quaid running away from the school the day before Lily starred in the school play.

The former instructor ran into the old city cemetery right down the road from the school. Meagan thought it was a great place to hide. No one was buried in it anymore and people tended to steer clear of it because they thought it was haunted by the ghosts of the Great Fire.

Meagan didn't have the same qualms. If anything was haunted, it was Flamewood Forest where most of the people involved in the fire perished that night. Now that place was something to stay away from.

Meagan crept into the cemetery through one of the many open spots where the brick wall was coming down. She quickly ducked behind a large headstone so she wouldn't be seen by Mrs. Quaid or anyone else. If the former instructor wanted to stay out of sight, she would have to be staying in one of the buildings on the cemetery grounds. Otherwise, someone would have spotted her by now.

There were eight separate mausoleums and two storage buildings in the immediate area. Meagan eliminated the two storage buildings right away because groundskeepers would need to access them on a regular basis to keep the cemetery clean. All the same, she checked both buildings first before eliminating them as viable choices.

She was careful as she moved through the cemetery, stopping to watch for movement before ducking behind another tall headstone. The most likely mausoleum for Mrs. Quaid to stay in would have to be one of the small buildings near the entrance to the cemetery. They would make for the easiest places to duck into to get out of sight quick.

The mausoleums on the opposite end of the cemetery were too far away from the school and too open as was the lone mausoleum in the center of the cemetery. Meagan didn't bother with any of the three but she was still careful to stay out of sight of all three just in case. Today she was investigating the five by the entrance.

Just as she was about to step out from behind a headstone, she caught a glimpse of movement. She ducked back down and peaked around to see what or who it was.

Twigs were stuck out in her tangled hair and her teeth shined a yellowish-red from months of living without a shelter in the cemetery. It was a wonder the woman had eluded capture so long. Someone should have seen Mrs. Quaid coming or going at some point based on her appearance alone. Then again, people tended to ignore undesirable things.

Crouching down even lower, Meagan watched as her former instructor left the cemetery. When she was sure the elder woman was out of sight, Meagan dashed to the mausoleum that Mrs. Quaid visited a moment before.

Suddenly, she was glad she had her camera. One quick picture of where the crazed serial killer was staying and then she could get out of there.

Briefly, the teen debated publishing the story in the school newspaper before telling the police. Wouldn't that be a grand way to show up Lily and the rest of her team? Meagan almost laughed to herself as she pushed the door open just enough to get inside.

Right away, Meagan reeled when the smell hit her senses. It was clear the former instructor was living in the mausoleum. Her filth and waste littered the small stone building. The teen looked around, searching for some sign that would prove Mrs. Quaid was the killer when she spotted something clear and shiny under a newspaper.

It wasn't just any newspaper but one of her own school newspapers complete with an article about Mrs. Quaid printed across the front. She remembered writing that article about the former instructor going crazy while still teaching and then being escorted from the school and city.

Meagan snapped a shot of the paper before moving it out of the way to see what was under it. She jumped back in shock. Underneath the papers was a seemingly human hand grasping an empty vial. The hand was half eaten away probably by the poison.

She turned and vomited. After recovering, she turned back around to snap a photo. Meagan could leave after that because it was proof enough. The only thing she lacked was a picture of Mrs. Quaid to further her claim.

There was no way Meagan would be able to keep a lid on this until her issue of the school newspaper came out but maybe she could sell her story to the city newspaper. That would still make Lily and the rest of her staff look bad because they hadn't bothered to investigate like Meagan.

She almost laughed to herself but the severed hand in front of her was still too much. She spun around to leave and came face to face with Mrs. Quaid. Meagan jumped backwards in surprise right onto the hand. Feeling the hand beneath her feet and hearing the sound of the bones cracking was too much and Meagan yelled out in horrified disgust. She wanted to run but Mrs. Quaid was blocking her path.

"Do you know the wonderful thing about this poison?" Mrs. Quaid asked her as she held up a vial of the Vampire's Curse poison. She was smiling, her expression that of a psychopath with one too many screws loose.

Meagan shook her head. The only things she knew about Vampire's Curse was that the poison was called that because it had vampire's blood in it. Well, she did know that it killed non-human students when ingested and apparently burned away their flesh when applied topically.

That meant Meagan was safe from the poison and her former instructor would have to find another way to kill her unless Meagan could escape. It shouldn't be hard to get past the crazed woman since the teen was in better shape.

The former instructor's smile widened until the woman was laughing at her own private joke.

Seeing this as her opening, Meagan made a beeline for the door. She almost made it out too when liquid splashed across her right side over the scar tissue. And then Meagan screamed as the liquid burned on her skin, setting her very flesh on fire all over again.

The laughter was gone but the smile was not. "You see the wonderful thing about the Vampire's Curse is that your victim will always burn no matter if they're human or not. In fact, humans actually suffer more for this poison because they aren't paralyzed like the non-humans are."

Meagan started to black out from the pain when she heard what she was sure was meant to be reassuring.

"Don't worry, Meagan," Mrs. Quaid soothed, "You won't be troubled by those scars ever again."

And she wasn't. Meagan's entire right side was eaten away by the poison.

The remains of Meagan's body were found outside an abandoned house on the way to the hospital. It was far enough from the cemetery to not draw any attention there and close enough to the school that it could be said the girl was on her way home.

Her camera was just about destroyed but thanks to Marcus's expertise with cameras, they were able to salvage the last pictures taken. Or at least, someone was able to. Neither the police nor Lily's group learned about the last pictures Meagan took. Instead, someone else intercepted the knowledge.

When Meagan and Lily first started the school newspaper, Lily was given the task of writing memorials for the students killed. Even after the two parted ways with the newspaper, Meagan left the memorials for Lily to write.

Regretting how their friendship ended, Lily did what she hadn't for any of the other victims and interviewed Meagan's parents. She dug into her former friend's history before writing a moving two-page piece on Meagan memorializing the teenager that only wanted to be loved by all.

Within a few weeks of Meagan's gruesome murder, a display case was cleared out to be used as a memorial of the students killed. Someone put a framed copy of the article in the case with her picture. No one would forget who Meagan Tiller was ever again. If they did, there would always be something to remind them.

When all was said and done, Lily mourned her former friend like a best friend would.

Chapter 11

Attack
(Running Out of Time)

Practice makes perfect or so they say. Lucas sighed in frustration. Everyone else was already gone but he stayed behind to practice for the last concert of the year. He was assigned a solo and didn't want to mess up in front of everyone! To think, Lucas, a demon, was playing a solo for the sixth year graduation!

Unfortunately, that meant he needed more practice so he either had to skip hanging out with his friends on days that he stayed late or just meet them later if there was time. Lucas almost wished he hadn't agreed to take on the solo for the sake of nerves alone. It was a lot of responsibility and if he made one little mistake, everyone would know. At least the demon boy wasn't going to be on stage acting like Lily and Jonah had a month back.

Lucas would die of embarrassment if he had to get on the stage and act a part out. In a way he envied Jonah and even Lily their ability to get in front of a crowd and be able to act or talk. Jonah was cast as lead in the play this year and originally Lily was only cast as understudy before being thrust into the lead at the last minute.

Don't get him wrong, Lucas was capable of getting in front of scores of people and playing various music ensembles. To him, playing music and acting were two completely different things though. It was like so much of his concentration went into playing the instrument and concentrating on it alone that he didn't even pay attention to the audience watching him. He enjoyed playing music more so than he did pulling pranks.

Then too, he wasn't playing a solo part but rather one instrument in a larger group of different instruments. He wasn't even the only one playing his chosen instrument! So missing a note was nothing compared to freezing up on stage, forgetting a line, or even a wardrobe malfunction. At least that was the argument he used as to why he never tried out for a part in a school play with Lily, Jonah, or even Annabeth on occasion. His little half-sister was even braver than he was where acting was concerned!

That was the argument Lucas had used before now. Assigned a solo, his thoughts shifted greatly. Lucas was too nervous to even voice his fear to his parents.

Today, Lucas was all alone. Usually, some of the others in their group stayed after waiting on him to finish up. The group had other engagements.

Danah and Jade took off to the faerie's house immediately after school. Danah was helping her friend babysit her little brothers.

Annabeth was supposed to meet his mom so the pair could try to find Jenny the fox. After his mom and sister nursed the baby fox for a few weeks, it was ready to be set free again. Of course, they checked on Jenny from time to time and today was to be one of those days.

Lily and Jonah stuck around a little bit working on the school newspaper but they both left at least an hour before. Or at least, they told him they were leaving an hour before. He had no way to really know if either actually did leave since both were known for surprising him.

Whatever the case, Lucas was alone now. The city had been warning everyone to stay in pairs in case the serial killer struck again. They released new information claiming the murderer was a red-headed female but that wasn't news to Lucas or anyone in their group. They already knew that and more from Christine's contacts.

Figures Lucas would be the odd one out today of all days. He felt like just going home and not stopping by the cavern as he normally did. Between the newspaper, his musical endeavors, and his family research, Lucas had been spreading himself too thin in his opinion. He was just so exhausted.

The demon wasn't even paying any attention to where he was going as he left the school through the main office doors. He rarely if ever used those doors because it always made the trip home or to the cavern that much longer. Not to mention, the creepy cemetery that he had not been in since he'd walked it with Lily the day Mrs. Quaid was fired.

Briefly, Lucas entertained the idea of going to check out his ancestor's graves again to see what names he recognized now that Lucas was researching his family history. The thought was short lived when he caught a glint of red hair from the corner of his eye.

Wondering if Lily hadn't gone home like she told him she was, he turned in that direction to see if it was her. There she was, running toward him and Lucas smiled until he realized she was yelling something. His best friend almost seemed frantic but he couldn't make out what she was screaming.

Lucas caught movement out of the corner of his eye again, this time something flew at him from behind and splashed all over his folded wings. "Ugh!" he said before the painful burn of the acidic poison started burning threw the leathery-like flesh, bone, and sinew of his wings. He screamed and fell to his knees.

"Lucas!" screamed Lily, still a little distance away but he could hear her now.

Lucas was on his side, facing away from her but he saw his attacker. It was Mrs. Quaid like they thought. His former history instructor was the serial killer and now she'd dealt a lethal blow to him. The two-toned red haired woman heard Lily and like a coward turned tail and ran away. Probably back to where she came from. Lucas tried to keep his eyes open through the pain so he could at least tell Lily where the woman went to.

Nothing short of a miracle could save him from the Vampire's Curse poison especially since they hadn't planned for this scenario. The poison when used topically incapacitated the victim rendering them immobile until the poison finished eating through their flesh and bone. It was a horrifying way to die.

Any moment now, Lily would run up and see his mangled wings. Would the poison jump to his body and eat at the rest of him? He was supposed to be watching Mrs. Quaid but his mind was taking him elsewhere.

Lily skidded to a stop behind him. She was careful not to touch the damaged wings or the poison. The phoenix girl moved around so he could see her. "Stay with me, Lucas!" she cried, tears streaming down her face. She ripped a necklace from her neck: the poison cure Vitroli hung from a small vial attached to the chain.

Lucas thought Lily shouldn't look so sad and wanted to tell her that. His mouth wouldn't move to form the words. He involuntarily winced on the inside but the outside remained the same as the searing pain entered his back. It wouldn't be long now.

Shaky hands pulled the cork from the vial and then Lily brought the vial to Lucas's mouth. She didn't have enough hands to do as they'd done in the cavern with Jade.

There was no way she'd be able to save him. She really shouldn't be crying. Lucas would have laughed if he could, his thoughts were so out of sync. It must be the poison. The pain spread to his shoulders and he wanted to scream.

Lily was laying down parallel on the ground to him now. Lucas would have blinked. When did that happen? Just as the pain became unbearable, he heard his best friend apologizing. He thought she must have been apologizing for not getting there in time or not staying with him till he was ready to go home.

Lucas regretted that Lily was here to see this but he didn't regret her getting there in time to stop Mrs. Quaid before she threw more poison on him. Maybe then his family would have most of his body left to bury.

On the plus side, at least Lily wouldn't suffer like him. The phoenix would live to fight another day.

Lily threw one arm around his body to hold him in one place. What was going on? Then, she followed that up by throwing one leg around his legs. Lily must have been trying to immobilize him all by herself.

Lucas wanted to tell her to stop. He wanted to warn her that she would touch the poison but Lucas's mouth remained immobile.

He was shocked then when she flipped him on his back, the wings completely gone now. She was sitting on top of him now and the tears still fell from her eyes. Now they fell on Lucas's face calming him and seemingly halting some measure of the poison.

He wondered if the tears might entirely heal him and then remembered the discussion about Vitroli. The poison antidote used phoenix tears taken while Lily was in her phoenix form. The tears in Lily's human form were only good for healing minor things.

Lucas just regained the use of his mouth again when Lily did something that took him completely by surprise. Using her free hand, she put the vial of Vitroli to her mouth and emptied the contents. Lily didn't swallow the antidote though. Instead the phoenix girl leaned down, put her mouth against his own, and forced the liquid into his mouth. At the same time, she pinched his nose with a free hand and forced his own body to swallow the antidote.

His body immediately tried to reject the antidote but Lily held her lips firmly in place to stop him from spitting it back out. Her hand still stayed glued to his nose to keep him from ejecting the antidote that way. She held him in place - one arm wrapped around the right side of him and his left arm flailed every which way. Lily had her feet wrapped underneath his legs to keep them from moving too much.

Lucas was sure by the expression on her face that he was hurting her but until the Vitroli worked through his system, he had no control of his actions. Just as the pain from the poison stopped, a new pain started as the antidote worked to reverse the effects of the poison. The pain was intense and reminded him of the time Jonah poured pure phoenix tears on his wings as a child.

When Lucas blacked out, Lily wasn't entirely sure if Vitroli was working on her best friend and he was still thrashing about on the sidewalk. If she let him go, Lucas might do more damage to himself than if she held on to him. There was no choice in her mind. She would do almost anything to spare him pain.

The sky was getting darker when Lucas opened his eyes again. Lily was still crying over him, not sure if she'd got to him in time. The phoenix girl was also still sitting on him. He cleared his throat to get her attention.

Lily sat back up. The phoenix girl would have rolled off of Lucas except that his wings were flayed out around them. She caught herself before she reached out to caress the underside of one.

"Thanks," Lucas said, his voice full of sincerity. "You shouldn't have risked your own life to save mine but thank you."

Lily shook her head, "My life wouldn't be the same without you. So there was really no choice." If only Lucas valued his life as much as Lily did. She tried to stand but ended up falling since her limbs were still mixed up with his. She fell backwards away from Lucas.

"You okay?" he asked.

Lily laughed, "You're the one that almost died. I'm supposed to be asking you that."

The demon shrugged from his spot on the sidewalk. "How did you know I would need the antidote?" he questioned.

"Good ol' friend, the faerie," she responded, getting to her feet. She reached a hand out to help Lucas stand. "Let's get home so Cissy can make sure the poison's all out of your system."

"Please tell me that the reason you were alone is because everyone else went after Mrs. Quaid, right?" Lucas asked, accepting her hand.

Lily shook her head sadly, "There was no time. We were just outside the forest when he got the vision and I had to race all the way back just to get here in time." The pair was headed toward the cavern. "Jonah ran straight to the cavern to get help but he already knew no one would make it in time."

Lily and Lucas walked the rest of the way in silence, both looking a little worse for the wear but otherwise fine.

When they arrived, Christine was pacing nervously in front of her lab while Jonah sat twiddling his thumbs comfortably. Danah was back early from her babysitting experiment. The only ones missing were Jade who still had to babysit her brothers and Annabeth who was off with his mother somewhere.

Thinking of his mother, Lucas remembered he needed to get home to babysit Julie. "I just remembered, I have to go watch my little sister!"

"Not so fast!" Danah smiled, fangs and all. "Julie is in my room taking a nap. Your mom asked me to watch her when you didn't come home with Annabeth."

Lucas smiled in gratitude before turning to Jonah. "Faerie."

"Oh joy!" Jonah exclaimed sarcastically. "You saved him!"

Lucas glared, "Thank you Jonah for getting her there in time."

Jonah blinked owlishly, completely surprised by the gratitude. "Don't thank me!" he tried. "I would have let you die but she leaves little choice in the matter." The faerie rolled his eyes. "You didn't find me running to your aide," he added, smiling maliciously.

"Only because you didn't want to watch," Danah retorted smugly.

Lily blushed but didn't respond to the banter. "I'm just gonna go lay down."

"Oh, no you don't!" Lucas crowed and grabbed her arm before she could escape. "I want Cissy to look you over first and make sure there's no poison in you now because of what you did."

Lily sighed, "Fine but then I really am going to bed." She almost lost him today. There was no question as to how Lily felt about her best friend. She would do just about anything for the demon boy. Lily always would.

After everything that happened today, Lily knew Lucas couldn't or wouldn't see what was right in front of his eyes. It was just like Meagan said when they argued about the newspaper: Lucas didn't see her and he never would.

Christine checked out the demon first to make sure the poison was out of his system before she checked Lily who seemed fine. When the results showed traces of the poison, Christine pulled her little sister to the lab.

"You touched the poison didn't you?" Christine asked quietly when she had Lily in the lab alone.

"No," Lily denied before yawning.

Christine shook her head, "Then how did it get into your system?"

Lily blushed bright red before yawning again. "Don't know." The flame-headed girl must have poisoned herself when she was keeping Lucas from spitting the antidote back out. She knew the method was risky but what else could she have done with so little time? It seemed the only option at the time.

The mage narrowed her eyes, "What did you do?"

"Nothing!" the phoenix girl argued. Really, Lily should never have left Lucas at the school alone. They knew someone was on the loose killing non-human students. Christine warned them all to stick together as a safety precaution. There was safety in numbers.

"Somehow I just don't buy it. In any case, we would just be wasting the antidote if we gave it to you," Christine explained. "You only have one option left, Lily."

Lily glared, "I'd rather die!"

"Well, you just might if you don't force it!" Christine argued.

"Besides, you don't even know for sure if that will flush the poison from my system. I'd just be going through all that pain for no reason. At least, with the poison, I can die peacefully," Lily tried to argue but it even sounded lame to her ears.

"Fine!" Christine declared. "Lucas!" she shouted so the demon in the other room would hear her.

Lucas came a moment later, "What's up?"

Christine smiled cruelly at Lily, "Lily has ingested some of the poison and the only way to flush it out of her system, so to speak, is for her to force a burning. However, she's being stubborn."

"Traitor!" Lily uttered under her breath at Christine who just continued to smile sadistically at her.

"Lil?" Lucas asked using the nickname she loved so much. "What's she talking about?"

Lily sighed, "There's Vampire's Curse in my system but the antidote doesn't work on me. Nothing from me can help me."

"What can we do then?" he asked, feeling powerless all of a sudden. "You can't die, Lil. We can't lose you!" he said, terrified his best friend would die for trying to save him.

"Fine!" Without further argument, Lily exploded in a burst of flame. It was probably the heart wrenching look on Lucas's face that did the trick. She couldn't stand to see him hurt and Christine knew that. Her sister took advantage of that to force the issue.

Lily could have controlled the explosion but in her anger, she wanted Christine to feel the heat from the magical fire. A forced burning would probably work just as Christine suggested it would and burn away the poison and prevent it from killing her as it would a normal non-human.

While phoenix tears and potions involving phoenix ingredients didn't work on Lily, a forced burning was her own defense mechanism against poisons and other fatal dealings. The downside was that forced burnings hurt a lot. They hurt more than a lot and the pain lasted the entire time she was in her phoenix form and she was stuck in that form for at least a week if not longer.

Christine shrugged as if Lily did this every day, "For that little stunt, you're staying with him until you're back to normal!"

CHAPTER 12

CAUGHT
(THE MASTER SOLUTION)

It was a full week before Lily transformed back into her human form. As it turned out, Christine wasn't serious about Lily staying with Lucas while she was stuck in her other form.

No, Lily's tears were too useful in new potions like Vitroli. If they could stockpile enough of the antidote, maybe they could do some good with it. Christine did have Lucas help collect the tears though which was a bit embarrassing in Lily's mind.

Lily missed other obligations while she was out for the week. Fortunately, she had Danah to finish putting the newspaper together and printing it for the end of the week issue. Lucas and Jonah helped too when they weren't fighting with each other. The demon and faerie pair really enjoyed fighting with each other.

Her absence didn't go unnoticed but it was still too soon for anyone to put the pieces together.

With Meagan's death, Mrs. Quaid was forced to lay low so the police didn't catch her in her own little game. The crazed woman was about to start her killing spree again with the worst offender among her former students.

Quaid was surprised to learn that the demon boy was seemingly unharmed after her attack on him. It was time that Mrs. Quaid set her sights on another target. She wanted her former boss to suffer more than she did the students. The former instructor wanted him to suffer the same humiliation and rejection that she did upon losing her job.

Barely escaping a local mage's keen investigating skills, Mrs. Quaid knew she would have to eliminate the potion-making mage if she intended on moving forward with her plans. There were still so many more non-human students left to poison. Maybe she could implicate the mage in the murders and then carry on while the mage was dealing with the aftermath?

Mrs. Quaid knew from her findings that Dr. Saffron took the vial of Revealer Potion to the mage to inspect after Mrs. Quaid pretended to find it. All she needed was to leave a small vial of the Vampire's Curse poison at the pharmacy with a list of victims and some random students she had no intention of killing. She could make this work if she could pull off contacting the authorities without getting caught.

Some one would have to see the evidence before the mage could get rid of it all. Breaking into the store seemed the only possibility since Mrs. Quaid had been unsuccessful in following her home. A week later, she was prepared to break in when she came face-to-face with her former employer outside of her hiding place in the mausoleum.

Though Mrs. Quaid was in over her head, she'd been mentally preparing herself for this confrontation. She wanted her former employer 'the master' to know that she wasn't going to stop till every last non-human child was dead. He would never find the special child he was looking for in time to prevent the massacre.

She had not expected to be seeing him quite so soon and was a little afraid of what he might do. "What do you want?" she sneered when a shadowed form of a man entered the room.

He was dressed in a thick black cloak that covered every bit of skin from head to toe. The heaviness of the cloak prevented even a small portion of his face from showing. "You bumbling fool!" he screeched at Mrs. Quaid. "Now they have been forewarned!"

Mrs. Quaid looked at him perplexed. "What are you talking about?" she asked, her curiosity piqued.

The shadowed man growled, "The phoenix child's

keepers!" He paced the room, "The only reason I brought you, Madam Quaid, into this search was to find the child undetected. I figured even a human couldn't mess that up," he revealed, throwing his hands into the air. "I was clearly wrong," the man added.

"A phoenix child?" Mrs. Quaid questioned, skeptical of the claim. "That race is dead," she spat at him.

He shook his head, "No, there is but one left. One way or another, I will have that phoenix and its power!"

"And I thought I was crazy," she ridiculed.

The shadowed man stopped pacing, his hood raising slightly but not uncovering him, "Oh, but you are. You've murdered five innocent researchers with no clear reason why," he smiled sadistically.

Quaid looked confused, "No, I didn't." The former teacher was shaking her head in denial.

"You see, Madam Quaid, you've been bumbling since you came into town," he informed as he clasped his clawed hands in front of him. "I didn't expect that of you since I'd been told you were a highly intelligent human."

A chill went down her back and she fought to stay calm, "What are you talking about?"

"Don't you get it yet? Your incompetence very nearly killed the child I was looking for! You alerted the handlers that I'm here and the authorities are wise to a murderer on the loose. Not just any murderer but a serial killer!" he shouted at her.

She took a step backwards but refused to show fear. "So what if I did? You ruined my career and expected me to just sit back and let you get away with it?" Mrs. Quaid asked, anger replacing the fear.

"No, you ruined your own career when you chose to use methods outside your expertise to try and find the child," he countered. "You could have found the child without resorting to a potion with vampire's blood in it but you made your choice." The shadowed man took a step forward toward Mrs. Quaid, "And now it's time for me to make mine."

"What are you going to do to me?" she asked, taking another step back only to discover her back against the wall.

The shadowed man paused, surprised, "You really don't get it, do you?"

Mrs. Quaid shook her head vehemently.

"Think about it," he ordered, venom dripping from his voice. "The police have a case to close and I have loose ends to tie up if I want to undo any of the damage you've caused me."

"You can't do anything to me!" she yelled, her eyes wide. Maybe if she screamed loud enough, she could prevent the repercussions to her semester-long murder spree.

"Oh please, Madam Quaid, you and I both know that is a lie," the shadowed man said, advancing on the shorter woman. "But let's prove that, shall we?"

Mrs. Quaid ran as fast and as far as she could but it wasn't fast or far enough to escape her fate and the shadowed mage.

Waylon Radcliffe didn't like having to follow up on things that should have been shared with him but sometimes, the old mage had no other choice. About two and a half months before, Waylon stopped receiving updates on the phoenix child.

After an inquiry, the council leader learned the regional guardian left the area with his family. It only took a week to find out that Dr. Saffron did not go with his family nor did the dragon contact his family after they left.

The only thing left for Waylon to do was visit the primary guardian for the phoenix child and find out what exactly was going on. "Christine!" he called, coming into the mage's pharmacy.

A dark haired teenager stood behind the counter, she gave him an appraising look before stepping out and into a hall. Waylon could only imagine she must be getting Christine or else some other supervisor.

Moments later, he heard footsteps and Christine stepped out. The dark-haired girl was gone. "Waylon?" she asked, surprised by his appearance.

Waylon nodded, "We need to talk."

Christine started to tell him to go ahead but was interrupted.

"Privately."

An hour or so later, Waylon was in the cavern where he saw the dark haired girl again. She was with a red haired girl. The old mage wondered if one might be the phoenix but didn't contemplate that long before Christine was ushering him into her lab.

"You didn't need to come check on me!" she accused. "I stopped experimenting. My charges mean too much to me to risk them or their safety."

Waylon shook his head, "It's not that, Christine. There are other problems brewing at the moment."

"What problems?" she asked.

Sighing, the old mage ran his hand through his hair, "Saffron hasn't checked in with me in over two months."

Christine looked guilty for a moment. "I had to send him away," she admitted uneasily, staring at the not-so-smooth table surface.

"Oh?" he asked. "So, you're hiding him from his own family now?"

Christine looked up sharply, "What are you talking about? Joffrey left with his family!" While Christine was aware of the dragon instructor's plan, she wasn't entirely sure it had gone smoothly. Truthfully, the mage hadn't been able to reach the dragon in about the same amount of time. "Didn't he?" she asked uneasily.

Waylon shook his head. "His wife said they left ahead of him and Saffron was supposed to join them a week later. The old dragon never made it and he hasn't contacted them since. What is going on up here?"

Closing her eyes, Christine took a deep breath. It was time to come clean. "There was a nut case on the loose killing the non-human children with the Vampire's Curse poison. It's been take care of, really!" Christine defended. "I asked Joffrey to leave as a precaution. One of the faeries saw him dying during all of this and we just wanted to save the phoenix the heartache from it. He's one of her favorite instructors after all."

"Are you sure about all of that?" Waylon asked suspiciously.

She nodded, "Positive." She opened a drawer and

brought out a newspaper. She slid the paper across the table. "The police are saying she killed herself by applying the Vampire's Curse topically to herself."

The newspaper article told all about how Norma Quaid, former history instructor at Demont Secondary School, was found in the same area as the first five victims. A note was found next to her body detailing the first few deaths and how she must have pulled them off. Only Jonah, Lily, and Christine knew the truth about those deaths.

Paraphrasing the letter, the newspaper stated that Mrs. Quaid only started killing the students because in her mind, they were responsible for the end of her teaching career. She couldn't let them get away with it but she didn't count on the guilt. Mrs. Quaid felt so eaten up by remorse that taking her own life was the only way out.

According to the letter, she killed herself in the same manner that she'd killed all of her victims: the Vampire's Curse poison.

So with a letter and evidence detailing her crimes, the police didn't look any further. Not that it would have mattered because Mrs. Quaid did die of the poison; albeit, not in the same way most of her victims did. Her body was half-eaten away by the topical application of Vampire's Curse. A painful but silent way to die, there was no real way to contradict the letter.

"And what was the point in her killing spree? The actual point?" he clarified.
Christine paused, trying to figure out what to say and how to say it. On the one hand, Quaid was killing students for exactly the reason that was in the newspaper. On the other hand, the crazed woman was not responsible for the first five murders. And now a good friend and regional guardian was missing.

"The truth, Ms. Nightshade," Waylon said sternly.

"I don't know everything," Christine tried. "That crazed woman was killing the students because she used a highly dangerous potion to identify which students were human and which were not. Are you familiar with the properties of vampire's blood when mixed with the Revealer Potion?"

Waylon shook his head, "Enlighten me."

"Well, when the blood is added to that particular potion, it's usually in such a low amount that you can't tell it is in there. However, the person using the potion would eventually know. My best guess is that she used it as a cleaner to get the best results. The vampire's blood was released into the air when it was initially sprayed on the surfaces. Then the blood entered her nasal cavity and shot up into her brain. It killed some pretty pertinent brain cells and caused her to start hallucinating among other things."

"Why was she using a highly illegal potion though?"

"I don't know," Christine said truthfully. "My best guess is that she didn't like non-humans. I mean, I have other theories but that's all they are. There is no conclusive proof to support any of them."

"Why didn't you use a spell to find her?" he asked suspiciously. "Better yet, why didn't you come to me?"

Christine shrugged. "None of the spells worked. Don't you think I would have tried them all if it meant protecting them? To be honest, I didn't think we needed help at first," she admitted. "Then, the murders just kept escalating. I actually told Joffrey to report back to you. He must have been abducted before he got the chance."

Waylon nodded his head. The old mage let out a breath and ran his hands through his hair. "We can't afford to share the secret with anyone else," Waylon told Christine.

"I know."

"All the same, I'm going to send another dragon up here," Waylon informed. "Temporarily, of course!" he hurriedly added when Christine looked like she was going to protest. "He'll be apprised of the situation but not anything to do with the phoenix."

"So when are we to meet him?" Christine asked.

"You probably won't. I'm putting him in charge of protecting the children - human and non-human alike. We can't have another incident like this. Thirteen victims!" Waylon shook his head in disbelief.

"Actually, it was only ten," Christine winced.

Waylon blinked, "The paper said thirteen."

"Yes, but the first five murders weren't committed by her," she responded.

"And that brings it down to eight victims. How do you get ten?" the old mage asked, skeptical.

This was where things got a little sticky. "You see, two victims were never reported because we kind of used a potion I created to heal them before the poison fully killed them." Christine laughed nervously. "They're friends of the phoenix," she added as if that would make a difference.

Waylon nodded, not at all happy at the situation. His frown seemed to change as a thoughtful and skeptical look all at once took over his features. "You have a cure for the Vampire's Curse poison?" he asked, mildly disbelieving.

Christine smiled slightly, "Yes?"

"That's the greatest news I've heard to come out of this mess," Waylon admitted. "When can you bring it before the council for approval?" The younger mage winced again which caused Waylon to correctly interpret that there was something in the antidote that wasn't easy to acquire, "What did you use?"

"I may have used a small amount of phoenix tears," she admitted.

Waylon nodded. "So let me get this straight. You've been experimenting again and now you're involving your charges in it?"

Christine looked outraged. "I'm not just 'experimenting' as you put it! Not that it really matters because you warned me against experimenting with my magic not with making new potions. There's a reason for that: making new potions is not against the law!" she argued. "As to my charges being involved, we decided we needed a cure for the Vampire's Curse just in case. As it turned out, that was a good thing. We were able to save a faerie child and a demon who have been made junior guardians by the phoenix child's hand," Christine continued.

"This secret isn't child's play!" Waylon ground out. "How could you let her make such a stupid mistake?" he accused.

Christine shook her head, "You don't understand.

Lucas, the demon, is her best friend and Jade, the faerie, is a battered child in need of what the phoenix child alone can offer. Both will play a part in her future - that much, the faeries will admit to."

"Hmm," Waylon murmured, thinking over all the new information. "I don't like this. None of this looks good, Christine. I don't even begin to know how to explain any of this to the rest of the council."

"Then don't," Christine responded. The younger mage shook her head and held up a hand when Waylon began to protest. "No, listen!: She is stubborn and headstrong but she's thriving now. The phoenix child has friends and considers us her family. She thinks of you as her uncle, Waylon. How can we take that away from her without turning her against us?"

Waylon turned the situation around in his head, "For now, the situation is under control but I want you personally to update me. No more messengers and I want to know everything that is going on no matter how insignificant it may seem."

Christine nodded."Thank you, Waylon. You won't regret this!"

Waylon gave her a stern look before turning and leaving. He rarely saw the phoenix child and he never called her by name. He and Christine worked out a system that minimized his contact with her in case he was ever compromised - an extreme safety measure but nothing was infallible.

The aging mage found himself loving the child he was partially responsible for keeping safe. Waylon even sent her and the vampire girl gifts each year on their recognized birthdays since neither actually knew when theirs was.

Really, it was no wonder the girl might see him as family. With a mixed up family like the one she lived with, it wasn't surprising she'd call him her uncle. Still, Waylon had crossed the line. Somehow or another, the old mage got too close and now there was no going back.

His first priority should be her safety, not her happiness. Now, Waylon wasn't so sure. Didn't the last phoenix alive deserve happiness too? Why couldn't she be left to live like every other non-human child?

Waylon was already gone from the cavern when the name of the demon child registered to him. Wasn't Lucas the name of a fellow council member's son? A council member that would rather see the phoenix dead than deal with the consequences of her being alive.

INDEX

JODACAI
(THE WORLD AS WE KNOW IT)

Earth was once a great populace planet with land and water to spare. The great oceans surrounded such majestic land masses with all of natures wonders. As the years rolled by, the Earth became an uninhabitable wasteland. The land, once so rich in natural resources, was dying of poisons in the form of radiation and pollution. Having been warned of the damage, the Earth's governments were prepared and started mass evacuations into the outer recesses of space. Suitable planets had been found throughout the Milky Way galaxy to house the once over-crowded human and animal populations. However, once the human refugees settled on the new planets, communication between the different groups ceased.

In contrast, not much is known about early Gaeshar history except what has been preserved in ancient texts. Most of those texts were scattered among the different types of beings on the planet. Prior to the mass migration of humans, history was passed along orally from generation to generation. Most of the beings lived in a controlled harmony brought about by an understanding of each other and truces passed during different periods of trial and conflict.

During the century that followed the mass migrations, the different worlds advanced or regressed according to resources available on the new planets and compatibles of new and old life forms. The humans of Earth hoped to fix the mistakes of their past so that history wouldn't repeat itself. At least, that is what the humans told themselves. Putting that into practice was another story altogether.

A large group of humans settled on a planet called Gaeshar that was eerily similar to the old Earth. So similar, that when refugees landed, they didn't take notice of the lifeforms already on the planet. Studies of Gaeshar never picked up other lifeforms and the refugees didn't ask questions. At first, the human refugees assumed the beings were just other refugees sent ahead to make way for their arrival. However, as time moved forward, the refugees came to realize that the other lifeforms weren't human and they had never come from Earth.

Some of the native inhabitants of Gaeshar had wings or scales while some had special powers. The refugees came to love, hate, and fear the native inhabitants. Most of the natives began hiding their powers and their differences from humans. As the natives were feared and hated on their own planet, history seemed to be repeating itself. Decades passed and natives began hiding their true selves away like creatures in darkness. Extra limbs like wings were either hidden under cloaks imbued with spells of concealment or the natives lived in secret communities away from humans altogether. In instances where natives didn't hide, humans rose up and devastated the native population with disease or outright murder.

Some of the native inhabitants had migrated to a large island continent called Jodacai where they intended to be free of the normal humans. The island nation was separated from the rest of the planet by hundreds of miles of oceans which made it ideal for the natives. They could live without fear of disease or death; however, their intentions were for naught as humans soon followed in their own migration. Jodacai came to be just like the rest of Gaeshar with the native inhabitants being the minority. The population of natives dwindled from the once populous world it had once been. Outnumbered by the humans, the natives struggled to survive on the world that had been their home long before the refugees came to Gaeshar.

The earliest recorded being on Jodacai was so dissimilar from humans, the phoenixes were referred to as magical birds and not actual beings. At the time, phoenixes were only magical birds as they had never needed another form. After learning about the power associated with phoenixes, hunt parties were organized to capture and kill the magical birds. The phoenixes took on human appearances to better hide from the human hunters. It was believed that most, if not all of the phoenixes came to be extinct during this time known as the Phoenix Wars.

APPENDIX I

PEOPLE
(HUMANS AND NON-HUMANS)

Council of Seven
Faeries:
*Clarane Milkweed is a very compassionate woman with small iridescent wings.
*Howard Bobbet is the youngest member on the council. He's rather hard to miss since his blond hair practically glows in the dark.
*Zelos Dupre is a pessimist with anger issues. His voice is cold and he does not like getting involved in the lives of other people. He's very good friends with Lucien Daemione.
Demon:
*Lucien Daemione is known for swift judgment calls involving the harshest punishments possible and is always arguing with Bettye the vampire.
Vampire:
*Bettye Dysnoski is the oldest member on the council and quite possibly the oldest person on Gaeshar. The vampire wears a veil over her face and has extremely long hair. She's known for arguing with Lucien the demon.
Dragons:
*Sephone Sliver once lived in a small town in the Yende Desert about thirty miles from Gyent. Like other water dragons, her scales are blue green in color.
*Felton Noveen was born in the mountains of the Furiete Mountain Range. His scales are a dull red color like other mountain dragons.
Shape-Shifters:
*Jeron Ryback is quiet and prefers only to speak when necessary. He tries to listen to the entire issue before making judgment.
*Debora Mythra is quite enthusiastic about life. Her emotions are always too the extreme in that she's never just happy, rather she's ecstatic, or just mad, rather she's furious.

Mages:

*Waylon Radcliffe is the head of the Council of Seven. At nearly four hundred years old, he holds the award for second place in age. In his younger days, the mage researched the phoenix beings and searched for survivors.

*Regina Wiley can see and feel magic more clearly than any other mage that Waylon's come into contact with. For that reason alone, Waylon has counted Regina as an integral part of the council. She's half Waylon's age.

*Leland Neveah is the newest member to be appointed to the council. He doesn't yet understand the way the council works and is quite impatient to get things done.

Daemione Family

*Lucien Daemione – Patriarch of the family. Only demon on the Council of Seven. Acquires rare items for people for a living.

*Anne Daemione – Matriarch of the demon family. Sometimes helps her husband with his work but otherwise stays home and takes care of their children.

*Lucas Daemione- eldest child of the family.

*Julie Daemione – youngest child of the family. In Primary School.

Decatur Family

*Genevieve Decatur - Annabeth's mother. Genevieve grew up with Anne and dated Lucien before the two were forced apart by an arranged marriage. Genevieve is a shape-shifter that specializes in animal transformations. She studied to be an animal doctor.

*Annabeth Decatur – child of Lucien Daemione and Genevieve Decatur. Her mother was a shape-shifter making her both a shape-shifter and a demon.

Nightshade Family

*Christine Nightshade – Eldest sister and matriarch of the family. Christine is a mage that is known all over Jodacai for her advanced potions and knowledge. Her powers are quite reputable as well.

*Lily Nightshade – Middle sister. Lily was discovered as a phoenix by the faeries when she was seven. Christine took over her care when she was around nine years old.

*Danah Nightshade – Youngest sister and a vampire. Danah was orphaned at a young age and lived on the streets. Christine found her when she was about five years old and took her in.

Williams Family

*Jonah Williams – faerie with a particularly strong gift for visions.

Brooks Family
*Heath Brooks - Demon patriarch of the family. Works on commission to build and design things for every day and not so every day use.
*Marlena Brooks - Shape-shifter, mother of Daniel.
*Daniel Brooks – half shape-shifter and half demon, dated Lily and then later Jade. Childhood friend of Lucas. Good at sports and music. In a band.

Nightingale Family
*Serena – Jade's mother.
*Jade – Danah's best friend. Dating Daniel Brooks
*Johnny – Twin brother of Jeremy; younger brother to Jade.
*Jeremy – Twin brother of Johnny, younger brother to Jade.
*Albert Jr. - Jade's youngest brother;
*Trevor (deceased) – Jade's birth father, murdered before Jade was born.
*Albert Daviane – Jade's step-father, incapable of holding a job and often forces Jade's mother to support the family.

Appendix II

Places

(Cities and Landmarks)

Gaeshar - a planet similar to Earth that was inhabited by Demons, Vampires, Dragons, Faeries, Mages, Shape-Shifters, and Phoenix beings prior to a mass migration by humans to the planet.

Jodacai - Jodacai was pieced together by a series of cities and towns founded by different native groups. Demont, the oldest city on the island, was founded by demons. Likewise, Troale was founded by faeries. The cities were all connected by technology brought over from Earth by humans: a rail way and trains. While humans had brought disease and prejudice to Gaeshar, they'd also brought some of their old technologies that had improved upon the lives of some of the natives. The inhabitants came together under a single flag in 2709.

Aiquad - founded by forest dragons in 2714. Dr. Saffron's family is from this city. Located on the southern bank on the Kaimout River.

Daraigone - founded by the desert dragons in 2708. Located in the middle of the Pequine Desert.

Demont - the oldest city on Jodacai is located at the northern tip of the island. Founded by demons in 2698.
Bordered on the west by north and south Deibose forest. bordered on the east by Flamewood forest and the Joria mountain range. Demont sits at the edge of Jodacai Nation, bordered by a range of mountains to the east and a foreboding forest to the west. North of Demont was an ocean and south was just the flat lying plains of the territory. The city was infamous for it's cold wet winters and hot dry summers.

Erath - founded by human refugees in 2730. located just south of the Sinai mountains

Fenix – founded by the phoenix beings in 2738 but then completely destroyed in 2739. Located on the northwestern edge of the Sinai Mountains. After it was destroyed, it was sealed off from the rest of the nation and served as a reminder of the atrocious nightmare being committed against the native inhabitants.

Furiete – founded by mountain dragons around 2711. Located in the middle of the Teria Mountain Range bordering the west branch of the Kaimont River

Gyent – Founded by water dragons in 2704. Gyent is on the south western shore of Jodacai in the Yende Desert.

Haidye – second city to be founded by demons. Founded on the bank of Lake Jokai in 2720

Jodacai City – the capital of the Jodacai Nation which is located at the southern tip of the island. City renamed in 2709 to reflect it being the capital. The Sievere Jungle is just to the north east.

Konhue – Founded around 2727 at the northern shore of the Kaimont River just north of the Kaimont Island Oasis.

Naite – Founded 2796 just east of the Sievere Jungle

Sievere – Founded 2756 on the western edge of the Sievere Jungle

Troale – founded by faeries in 2700. The Daemione family resided here for roughly eight years after the Great Fire. Troale is bordered on the south and east by the Kaimont River

Vaylom – Founded by vampires in 2702 at the southern edge of the Joria Mountain Range

Xitar – Founded by shape-shifters in 2715. Xitar is a trade school town located just outside of Fenix Forest. It's the largest city on Jodacai.

Yashae – founded by vampires in 2718. Yashae is located just south west of Demont in South Deibose Forest

Driftwood Forest - located just south of Fenix forest and Xitar. driftwood forest is actually shaped like a giant tree branch

Fenix Forest - located north of driftwood and west of Xitar. Fenix forest is shaped and named after the majestic phoenix beings

Flamewood Forest - located east of Demont and west of the Joria mountain range. partially destroyed during the great fire but the destroyed part of the forest grew back quicker and stronger than it was before. the citizens of Demont believed it to be haunted.

Fort Baethyl - located on Demont's north western edge on the northern coast of Jodacai. military base in the north Deibose forest
Joria Mountain Range - mountain range that runs halfway down Jodacai's north eastern edge.

Kaimont River - a river that runs through the eastern side of the island nation and branches out in two separate places forming large lakes. (West Kaimont River forms Lake Jokai and South Kaimont River forms into Lake Dipius)

Lake Dipius - formed from the southern Kaimont River branch

Lake Furie - the largest lake on all of Jodacai located in the very center of the island. Kaimont River feeds into it and branches out on the southern end into the western and southern Kaimout Rivers

Lake Jokai - formed from the western Kaimont River branch. Bordered by the Teria Mountain range

Mt. Furie - tallest mountain on Jodacai located in the Teria mountain range

North Deibose Forest - Deibose forest was divided into two by the railroad association. located on the northern end of Jodacai, west of Demont.

Pequine Desert - the northern most desert on all of Jodacai is dotted with rolling sand dunes. Daraigone is located in the center of the desert which is located north of the Teria Mountain range and west of Lake Furie.

Sievere Jungle – a large jungle located around two stray mountains just north east of Jodacai City in the south of the island nation. The jungle continues over the southern branch of Kaimont River.

Sinai Mountains- the smallest mountain range on Jodacai forms at border between Erath and Fenix on the south eastern coast.

South Deibose Forest – Deibose Forest was separated into north and south by the railroad association.

Teria Mountains- Second largest mountain range in Jodacai with the tallest mountain of Mt. Furie. Lake Jokai sits at the base of this range.

Yende Desert – Located on the south western edge of Jodacai, the desert is considered a large beach though it is almost as big as Pequine Desert. The city of Gyent is half-way down the coast of this desert.

APPENDIX III

THINGS
(EVENTS, SPELLS, POTIONS)

EVENTS

*Phoenix Wars – A dark time in the history of Gaeshar in which humans (and some non-humans) hunted and killed the phoenix beings to near extinction. Took place over a four year period between 2736 and 2740.

*Great Fire – A magnificent fire that took place in 2999 in Demont's city history that killed enough of the population and burned much of the city to have left a lasting impression on the residents.

*Fenix Massacre – After the phoenix beings were discovered in having taken human forms, the city of Fenix founded by those phoenix beings was completely leveled with the entire population being massacred by a wartime general named Horatio Daemione.

SPELLS

Le Uyr Gimli Oltea Uy - Spell that uses the lingering magical residue in the air around you and on your being to kill or knock out a person.

Fales Cotlr – the title given to demons before humans came to Gaeshar. The title was replaced with demon.

Zer Vin - Spell freezes the intended target in place

Pesot – Separates a potion/object/etc into its original parts/ ingredients; can cause an explosion

POTIONS

*Nightmare Reliever Potion: A temporary potion that allows the mind to work through issues causing nightmares without being addictive. Ingredients: Pheonix tears (for mind healing), Chamomile (for anxiety brought on by the nightmares), Valerian (for restful sleep), Honey (for Taste).

*Daiglow: A temporary potion that allows a vampire to walk about during the day without having to worry about damage from natural light sources that would normally cause burns that develop into fatal open sores. Ingredients: Phoenix tears (to heal the skin), Dragon scale (ground up, to protect the skin from the light), Phoenix ash (to allow the skin to reform after its burned)

*Headache Remedy; Simple liquid potion used to alleviate head pains.

*Vampire's Curse: a powerful poison used for killing all non-humans excluding vampires. Primary ingredient: Vampire blood (causes illness in all people but lethal to other non-humans)

*Revealer Potion: When subject(s) comes into contact with, causes a red rash on the skin that lasts for an hour but is only visible to someone who knows how to look; topical use only-causes sickness when ingested; Primary ingredient: ground vampire fang (causes blood to rise partially to an outer layer of skin); faerie plume (causes the victim to not see the rash); citrus (for smell); vinegar

*Modified Revealer Potion: Powdered vampire fang, Shredded faerie plume, Citrus, Vinegar, Vampire blood

Continue the adventure

with the next installment in

The Phoenix Chronicles:

Demon's Flame!

Available online December 2016.

When the new dragon, sent by Waylon, starts asking questions about the Great Fire, Christine gets worried that someone will find out about the phoenix hiding in plain sight. The bigger question is, what really did happen all those years ago when a fire destroyed so much of the ancient city and killed so many people? Does Waylon and the council suspect that the phoenix was involved?

Meanwhile, a new girl at Demont Secondary catches Lucas's eye and she isn't want she seems! She puts a wedge between the best friends and unknowingly opens the door for someone more sinister to step into their lives. Daniel, Jonah, Lily, and Lucas only have a year left at Demont Secondary and maybe in Demont. What awaits the friends this year?

The dark mage is closing in on the phoenix. It's only a matter of time before Anthony and the shape-shifting substitute figure out who the real phoenix is. With kidnapping already on their list, what other lengths will they go to in order to find her?

THE PHOENIX CHRONICLES

DEMON'S
FLAME

AMANDA COLEMAN